HOW TO ROCK BRACES AND GLASSES

HOW TO ROCK BRACES AND GLASSES

A NOVEL BY MEG HASTON

poppy

LITTLE, BROWN AND COMPANY
New York   Boston

Poppy

Hachette Book Group
237 Park Avenue, New York, NY 10017
For more of your favorite series and novels,
visit our website at www.pickapoppy.com

Poppy is an imprint of Little, Brown and Company.
The Poppy name and logo are trademarks of Hachette Book Group, Inc.

The publisher is not responsible for websites (or their content) that are not owned by the
publisher.

First Paperback Edition: September 2012
First published in hardcover in October 2011 by Little, Brown and Company

alloyentertainment

Produced by Alloy Entertainment
151 West 26th Street, New York, NY 10001

Excerpt from "Guys and Dolls" by Jo Swerling, Abe Burrows, and Frank Loesser. Copyright
1951 by Jo Loesser, Jo Swerling, Jr., and Peter Swerling (renewed in 1979). All rights reserved.

"I've Never Been in Love Before" by Frank Loesser (Frank Music Corp.).
All rights reserved.

"Go Your Own Way" by Lindsey Buckingham (New Sounds Music).
All rights reserved.

Book design by Liz Dresner
Hand-lettering by Carolyn Sewell
Map design by Leah B. Mantini

Library of Congress Cataloging-in-Publication Data

Haston, Meg.
How to rock braces and glasses / Meg Haston. — 1st ed.   p. cm.
Summary: When popular middle schooler Kacey Simon gets braces and glasses
and is rejected by her crowd, she befriends a boy who is in a punk rock band
and discovers some things about friendship, relationships, and herself.

ISBN 978-0-316-06825-3 (hc) / ISBN 978-0-316-06824-6 (pb)

[1. Popularity—Fiction. 2. Rock groups—Fiction. 3. Bands (Music)—Fiction.
4. Interpersonal Relationships—Fiction. 5. Middle schools—Fiction. 6. Schools—Fiction.]
I. Title.   PZ7.H28145Ho 2011   [Fic]—dc22   2011009384

10 9 8 7 6 5 4 3 2 1

RRD-C

Printed in the United States of America

For my family, who has loved me through everything
(even braces and glasses)

LIGHTS, CAMERA . . . ADVICE!
Thursday, 7:42 A.M.

Real journalists are born with a sixth sense. It's our most reliable source, an inner voice that tips us off when there's more to a story than meets the eye. My sixth sense has never been wrong, which is probably why I'm the first broadcast journalist in the history of the Marquette Middle School TV station to have her own weekly segment. Most people think my success has something to do with my hard-hitting interview style, which once reduced a corrupt student body V.P. to on-air tears. Live.

But I'm pretty sure it's my sixth sense.

Take this morning before homeroom, when my best friend, Molly Knight, sailed into the Channel M news studio between my vocal warm-ups and wardrobe check. Her petite frame was bundled in a quilted ivory puffy coat and she'd accessorized with a white mohair scarf and earmuffs. It looked like that purebred from the fancy cat food commercial had her in a headlock.

Instantly, a familiar shiver shimmied from my right pinky toe to my left earlobe. *Enter sixth sense.* Molly's icy blue eyes were shining with breaking news.

"I'm Kacey Simon, and this is *Simon Says.*" I cleared my throat and leveled my eyes at one of the four cameras arced around my mahogany anchor desk. Not even secretive best friends interrupted my preshow mojo. "I'm Kacey *Simon. I'm—*"

"Please. Like everybody at Marquette doesn't know Kacey Simon." At the back of the studio, the double doors whooshed to a close. Molly leaned dramatically against the silver patch of wall next to my framed headshot and blew a few long platinum flyaways out of her eyes. The sixth grader holding a boom mic over my head whipped around to check her out. Typical.

"Ninety seconds to air, people!" Carlos, my sassy bite-sized student producer, was the only guy in the studio who wasn't drooling over my best friend. He hustled across the crowded set, cradling his rundown clipboard like it was the Olympic torch and he was about to take the gold in the speed-sashay finals. "Can I get wardrobe on set, please?"

"So what's up, Mols?" I spun my cushy desk chair around a few rotations, the Chicago skyline backdrop melting into glittery swirls of silver and gray. Three rotations and my long auburn waves whispered *effortlessly tousled*. Any more than six and they'd have screamed *ROLLER COASTER–SEXY! BUT SEMI-UNPROFESSIONAL!* "Why aren't you in homeroom?" I came to a stop and eyed the red digital countdown clock on the back wall. Almost show time.

"No reason." With a coy smile, Molly strolled past the four camera guys and into my spotlight, the fake diamond snowflakes in her ears practically blinding me. I rubbed my brand-new violet-tinted contacts into place. She had until my segment was over to notice them. And to spill her secret.

"Eighty seconds!" Carlos plopped into the director's chair behind the row of cameras, then adjusted his wireless headset.

"And I still need wardrobe!" I yelled. The black patterned tights beneath my lavender mesh mini were starting to itch, but I didn't care. You know what they say: no pain, no network TV gig.

"Coming, Kacey!" Liv Parrillo, the third member of my foursome, who moonlighted as my stylist for the show, shouted off set.

"Sooo . . ." Molly rasped, leaning over my desk with a grin. Her voice always sounded like she'd just rolled out of bed with a mild case of laryngitis. Middle school guys thought it was even hotter than her long blonde mane. Only I knew the hair didn't count, since it was fake. She'd spent six months' allowance on extensions after she'd burned off her real hair with this Japanese straightening treatment she found on Craigslist.

"Sooo . . ." I widened my eyes and triple-blinked. Still nothing. "What's up?"

"Just stopped by to watch the b-cast, obv." Molly's high cheekbones and the tip of her button nose were flushed, meaning she was either lying or humiliated.

Sixth sense said . . . *lying.*

"Whatever you say." I shuffled the script on my desk three times, then set it aside. Scripts were like understudies. I never actually planned on using mine, but it was nice to know it was there. "Now *move.*" I gave her scarf a playful yank. "You and your dead cat are in my light."

She shrank away from the desk and pouted, pretending to be hurt. "But Tatyana says I look like a total pro."

Tatyana was Molly's Russian ice-skating instructor. Every year, Molly picked a new extracurricular, and every year, she got really excited about the outfits and then quit when she realized she wasn't Olympics-bound. Last semester it was gymnastics, which meant tight ponytails and glitter hairspray. In sixth, it was horseback riding, which meant multiple pairs of riding boots. "I'd tell you that you looked like a pro if you paid me fifty bucks an hour, too."

"Please." She straightened up and strode past the slack-jawed camera guys, taking a seat next to Carlos. When she crossed her legs, a pair of cream lace-up boots made their debut. "No, you wouldn't."

"No, I wouldn't. Because real friends don't lie." I made a mental note to snag the boots for next Thursday's broadcast. Say what you wanted about Molly's extracurricular outfits; at least she had the guts to take a fashion risk. It was the thing that had drawn me to her last year, at the start of middle school. Marquette forced all incoming sixth graders to attend a weekend camping trip-slash-orientation before the start of the semester, which sounded lame but turned out to be the perfect place to scout a few new BFFs for my transition into middle school. And you had to love a girl who showed up to a team-building hike in a camouflage tank dress, matching olive-green eyeliner, and hiking boots with a slight wedge heel. I'd told her she looked like Appalachian Barbie. And she'd stuck by my side ever since.

The double doors in the back parted again, bringing me back to the bustling studio.

"HEYYY, PEOPLE!" Abra Laing, the fast-talking, gum-chomping sixth-grade anchor of the Marquette Minute, which aired after my segment, made a beeline for the green screen to the left of my anchor desk. Abra got the job because she shouted EVERY WORD AT THE CAMERA LIKE IT WAS THE MOST IMPORTANT NEWS IN THE HISTORY OF THE WORLD, EVER. Also, she was the only talker fast enough to fit the morning announcements into a sixty-second spot.

"Thirty seconds to air!" Carlos announced while Abra tore off her coat and tossed it behind the screen. "WARDROBE?"

"Chill, man. I'm right here." Liv hurried into the spotlight, twisting her inky, shoulder-length curls into a messy knot at the nape of her neck. She was wearing a fitted white tank top and her shriveled Italian grandpa's slouchy charcoal overcoat, which she'd belted at the waist with a vintage tuxedo cummerbund. Only Liv would think to accentuate her curves with old man hand-me-downs. And only Liv could make it work.

"Girl, you're gonna love this piece." Liv produced the sticker-covered flute case she used for her start-up accessories line, LīVthreads, and lowered it onto my desk. "I used one of my dad's old shirts and a tutu." She popped the silver latches on the case and rummaged through a musty-smelling heap of glinting costume jewelry, fabric swatches, and feathered headbands. A few seconds later, she held up a flower pin made of plaid flannel and frayed purple tulle that matched my skirt exactly.

"Liv! Love it." I inspected the perfectly jagged edges of the petals. "You'll sell out before lunch." I never went on the air without one of Liv's custom designs. They were my good luck charm. And judging from LīVthreads's sales this year, *Simon Says* was hers.

"Hope so." Liv's wide jade eyes shone with gratitude as she leaned forward to pin the flower to my black silk top. She smelled like rose oil and her grandpa's pipe tobacco.

My right eye twitched involuntarily.

"Contacts!" Liv lunged across the desk. "Violet?" She cupped my face in her warm hands. "This shade is gonna POP on camera." Her olive skin glistened under the studio lights. Secretly, I'd always been jealous of Liv's year-round Italian tan. My skin only had two shades: translucent and, when I wasn't careful in the summertime, lobster.

"And it matches the pin! AND it brings out your red highlights!" Liv continued.

"I KNOW!" I shrieked. Ducking to the side, I rolled my eyes at Molly. At least *some* people noticed the important details in life.

Mols pretended to be too busy dusting the snow off her boots to notice.

"Ten seconds!" Carlos wiggled his tiny designer-denimed tush in his chair. "Do your thing, Miss Simon."

Liv lifted a peace sign, then hopped off the stage and took a seat next to Molly. "Hey, Michelin man. Love your tires."

"You wish you could pull it off." Molly's nose flushed again. *Humiliated.*

The studio lights brightened over me, and my pulse slowed instantly. You'd think doing a live broadcast in front of the whole school every Thursday morning would make me nervous. But you'd be wrong. I never felt more relaxed than I did on air.

The studio was instantly still, silent except for the low buzzing of the lights and my voice as I hummed the new intro I'd written for the show. In a matter of seconds, I would enlighten an entire school and help someone desperate for guidance. Helping people was my calling. I wondered if Mother Teresa found hers before eighth.

"In three, two—" Carlos popped his collar, then signaled me with a single index finger.

I raised my eyes to camera two, ignoring the sudden burning sensation beneath my violet lenses. "Morning, Marquette. And welcome to this week's edition of *Simon Says.* I'm Kacey Simon."

Over to the clock to check for time. The red digits blurred, and I blinked until the lines were sharp again. *Three seconds in. Focus.*

"Today's letter comes to us from Psycho-Stalked in Social Studies." I paused and smiled the trademark Simon Smile I inherited from my journalist mom: wide, confident, and just a teensy bit secretive.

"Stalked writes: 'Dear Kacey, love your show. You're the best.'" I did have three Marquette M-my Awards that seemed to agree. "'I'm hoping you can help. So this same guy has been sitting next to me in social studies since sixth grade, and I'm in eighth now. He's a total geek, and he won't stop asking me if I need a study buddy. I've tried everything: glaring, Facebook defriending, even going over to his house to get help in U.S. history, and then telling him I'd date one of our founding fathers before him. But he's not getting the point. What do I do?'"

I looked directly into the camera. "Dear Stalked, I'm gonna let you in on a little secret. I just got new contacts. Which means I'm seeing sharper than ever now. Which *means* I can see exactly what's going on here."

Molly leaned forward, her mouth slightly open. Liv cocked her head. The dimples in her cheeks deepened in anticipation.

"To defriend your stalker on Facebook means you had

to friend him in the first place. Mixed message. Going over there to do homework before you break his heart? Mixed message. And if your, and I quote, 'glare' looks anything like this?" I shot the camera my best flirty smirk, which Molly taught me at her last sleepover. "Mixed. Message." I clasped my hands on the desk and stared Stalked down. "I hate to break it to you, but you're totally into being psycho-stalked. Simon Says: Accept the date before he finds a new study buddy."

One of the camera guys (I think it was Camera Guy Three) burst out laughing. Mols and Liv air high-fived.

Nailed it. I pursed my lips in a knowing smile. "This has been Kacey Simon, reminding you that when you do what Simon Says, you win. AccessoriesdesignedbyLivParrillo, preorderatwwwdotfacebookdotcomslashlīvthreads."

Liv raised her right hand in a peace sign.

"Now to Abra Laing with the Marquette Minute. Abra?" I swiveled a quarter turn to my left, averting my eyes from the pouffy pink scrunchies holding Abra's pigtails captive.

"TH-THANKS, KACEY!" Abra stuttered. She'd been super awkward around me ever since I told her that with a voice like hers, she had an excellent future in used car commercials. She hadn't even thanked me for clarifying her career path. "I'M ABRA LAING, AND THIS IS MAR-QUETTE! IN A MINUTE!"

I pushed back my swivel chair and reached for my Channel 5 messenger bag under the desk. By the time I resurfaced, Mols and Liv were already sitting cross-legged on the desk.

"Awesome b-cast," Molly whispered hurriedly, braiding, unbraiding, and rebraiding her "hair." "Um, so I've got news."

"Called it." Casually, I slung the messenger bag over my shoulder and stood up. If Molly's news was actually *newsworthy*, I'd have already broadcast it. Right?

"My parents caved last night." For the record, Molly still hadn't noticed my contacts. "My birthday party's gonna be girl-boy!"

"What?" I gasped. "But the party's in two days!"

Liv wrinkled her nose. "But what about The Drake?" Molly's mom worked in public relations for The Drake Hotel downtown, and she'd arranged for us to have a spa day on Saturday, followed by a sleepover in the penthouse suite. We'd been planning our spa treatments and mini-bar raid for months. "What about my organic seaweed wrap?"

"Boys don't do seaweed wraps," Molly hissed. Her eyes flitted to mine. "Right?"

I pretended not to hear. "Why didn't you text last night?" I demanded.

Molly bit her bottom lip, trying to hide her smile. Did she think I couldn't tell she was psyched to beat me to a girl-boy party? Please. I was a *journalist*.

"A REMINDER THAT THE SPRING MUSICAL! *GUYS AND DOLLS*! STARRING KACEY SIMON AS SARAH BROWN! AND QUINN WILDER AS SKY MASTERSON! GOES UP IN TWO WEEKS!" Abra yelled.

Molly's smile wavered at the mention of the show. Understandable, since she was my understudy. And Quinn Wilder, resident seventh-grade hottie, was my onstage smooch partner. Not even a boy-girl party could beat Quinn and his winterfresh lip-locks.

"So Kace. I need your help, like, ASAP," Molly admitted, her voice dropping even lower. "I need new party ideas. Ideas boys will like."

In the back, the clock flipped to 7:55 A.M. "Homeroom, girls," I said crisply.

"But what are we gonna *do*?" Molly whined.

"Home. Room." Not that I didn't know how to throw a party. But how was I supposed to know what boys liked, when the only boy in my house had moved out four years ago? Molly had a dad. Couldn't she ask him? "We'll figure it out at rehearsal."

"But you're in every scene!" Molly whined. "We won't have time!"

I swallowed a sigh. Sometimes I wished Molly would just write in to *Simon Says*. That way I could just give her the straight story. She deserved the truth, just like everybody else.

Dear Kacey,

I'm having problems. No, it's not that I can't even see purple contacts when they're staring me in the face. My problem is my best friend. It's just that I'm always coming in second. For example, she got the lead role in the spring musical, and I have to be her understudy. To make matters worse, I'm incapable of making a move without asking her advice. Just once, I want to be first at something, like throwing a boy-girl birthday party. But deep down, I know I can't do it without her.

Will I ever get to be in the spotlight on my own, or am I doomed to a life in the wings?

Signed,
Second Best in Seventh

Dear Second Best,

Thanks for your letter. It must be really hard to admit you're jealous. (Who wouldn't be? Your BFF sounds amazing.) Here's the thing: In life, there's the star of the show, and then there's the supporting cast. It sounds like you fall into the supporting cast category. But don't be sad, Second Best. Simon Says: Supporting characters are still kind of important. Think about it. Without a supporting cast, who would vamp while the lead's changing costumes?

Signed,
Kacey Simon (The Lead. On air, and in life.)

TRUE LOVE IS BLIND (OR GETTING THAT WAY)
Thursday, 2:42 P.M.

By the time the final bell rang that afternoon, I was still floating on a post-show high. Maybe it was the high fives I'd gotten in homeroom after the broadcast, or the rumor that Psycho-Stalked spent study hall Facebook flirting with her stalker. The success was almost enough to make me forget that Molly had killed my dream of a penthouse sleepover. And the fact that my new contacts were launching a deadly assault on my eyeballs.

As I hurried to my locker, the seventh-grade hall (also known as Hemingway Hall) was starting to fill. Marquette was made up of four long hallways connected in the shape of a square. Sixth, seventh, and eighth had their own halls (Joliet, Addams, and Hemingway), plus a fourth for the cafeteria, auditorium, television studio, and administrative offices (Silverstein). Each hall was named after a famous, dead Chicagoan. And every few years, the students had to repaint their hallway to commemorate their dead Midwestern celeb. Something about team building. This summer, the girls and I had painted all the seventh-grade lockers silver, then stamped them with quotes from Hemingway novels.

By the time I reached my locker, Molly and Liv were already waiting for me.

"You'll never guess what I just did in study hall," Liv announced proudly.

"Sold out of those flower pin things?"

"Yeah. Thanks, by the way. But that's not what I'm talking about." Liv scratched at a quote about fishing from *The Old Man and the Sea* on the locker next to mine. It peeled instantly under her thumbnail.

"Ummm . . . I give up." I twirled the dial on my padlock, the spinning digits blurring out of focus. I rubbed my eyes until the numbers were clear again, then tugged at the padlock and flung open the rickety metal door.

"So you know how the skirt on your *Guys and Dolls* costume used to go below your knees?" Liv's voice was muffled. Beneath the door, Molly's boots shuffled impatiently.

"Yeah." I tossed my backpack onto a pile of textbooks

and checked my reflection in the mirror. The violet color around my pupils looked cooler than ever, but the whites of my eyes looked . . . pink.

"Well, your friendly neighborhood costume designer got a little creative."

I slammed the door and we were nose to nose. "You didn't."

"Mid-thigh is way more flattering." Liv batted her dark lashes. "Quinn's gonna love it."

"LIV!" I lifted my hand for a high five.

Molly jumped in and slapped my palm. "Wanna know what *I* did during study hall? Tried to come up with a hot boy-girl party idea." She yanked up the sleeves of her thin white cardigan and planted her hands on her hips. The puffy coat had disappeared after the broadcast. Good girl.

"I told you, go with Paris." Vanessa Beckett, the fourth in our group, strode toward us. In her fitted bomber, skinny jeans, and super-short pixie cut, she actually looked kind of French. I would have mentioned it, had the subject of the pixie not been, how do you say, *le sore subject*?

When Nessa got to my locker, she pocketed the stack of neon flashcards she was always carrying around for one test or another, then air-kissed me on both cheeks. The air kiss had been the routine ever since she got back from Paris last week, where her shrink mom had attended an international psychiatry conference, and Nessa had tested the language barrier with a scissor-happy French hairstylist.

"Cute boys and pastries!" I pressed my winter-ravaged lips together and air-kissed her back. Molly read my mind and slapped a worn tube of strawberry Burt's Bees into my grip.

"Sounds like a party, *n'est-ce pas?*" Nessa flicked a clump of dark bangs away from her eyes. "Ugh. I can't wait for my hair to grow out."

I didn't know why she was so self-conscious about the cut. With her exotic, almond-shaped eyes, mocha skin, and wide, even smile, she could have rocked a bald cap.

"I *told* you, the pixie looks amazing." I slathered a waxy layer of Burt's over my pout. It was the closest I was allowed to get to lip gloss before high school. "Fact: Yes, long hair softened your jaw line a little."

Nessa's delicate fingers flew to her jaw.

"And fact: Hair this short draws attention to your ears. But fact: Going this short takes serious confidence. I don't know another girl at this school who would do that."

"*Pardon?*" Nessa's eyes narrowed. "Who said anything about my ears?"

"Can we *please* get back on topic?" Molly piped up. "My party?"

"Later. Time for rehearsal." I spun on the heels of my

worn glitter Converse sneakers and snaked through the crowded hallway. The kids obstructing our path seemed to step aside as I led the girls down the hall.

"Two days," Molly reminded me over hallway chatter and the ding of neglected cell phones. "The party's in Two. Days."

"Got it," I sighed.

At the corner of Hemingway and Silverstein, I glanced through the door that led to The Square, the heated courtyard in the center of Marquette's four halls. Colorful drawings, quotes, and a four-square court were chalked onto the slate tiles. The stone bench in the center, where the girls and I ate lunch, was the one unchalked piece of real estate. People knew better.

We rounded the corner onto Silverstein. The first set of double doors was just steps away. Which meant that Quinn Wilder was just steps away.

My heart vibrated in my chest at the thought of Quinn, possibly coating *his* lips with Burt's *at this very second* in anticipation of my arrival. Every girl in the entire school had a crush on Quinn Wilder, but I hadn't really noticed him until earlier this month, when we'd both auditioned for *Guys and Dolls*.

Correction: when he'd heard I was a shoo-in for the role of Sarah Brown, the good-girl romantic lead, and then he just *happened* to show up to audition for the role of Sky Masterson, the smooth-talking gambler who wins Sarah's trust. And her heart.

Coincidence? *Pas du tout.* Especially since being in the musical meant Quinn had to give up his position as captain of the guys' basketball team this season. Now *that* was true lo—

"Kacey!" Out of nowhere, a suitcase-wheeling band geek in full uniform came barreling toward me, blocking my path to Quinn. "Kacey Simon?" She came to a stop just inches from my face.

"That's what they call me." The girls and I took a collective step back, and I cringed. There was so much metal in this girl's mouth, I could practically check my reflection in her incisors.

"Oh . . . mygod. It's you." Out of breath, Band Geek pawed through the front pocket of her suitcase and ripped out a pen and a smudged piece of paper that smelled like expired Cheez Whiz. "I'm . . . your biggest . . . fan. Will you sign my journalism syllabus?"

"Seriously?" Nessa rolled her eyes and reached into the inside pocket of her bomber jacket, producing a small yellow notepad and pen. As student director of *Guys and Dolls*, she used the pad to note when actors screwed up. Lately, she'd started noting when anyone outside of our group screwed up, in life. Without taking her eyes off Band Geek, she flipped to a fresh page and scribbled a quick note.

"No problem." I bit my lip to keep from laughing and pressed the crinkled paper against my thigh. "Simon Says: Try smiling with your mouth closed. It will totally accentuate your pouty lips, instead of your metal mouth." I thrust the syllabus back into her hands. "There you go."

Band Geek's lips trembled as she stretched them over her teeth. They didn't quite touch.

"Better." I nodded encouragingly. "It'll take practice."

"Mmmm mmmmmmmmmm." She nodded, her cracked lips turning white with effort. Then she turned and scurried down the hall.

"Nice work, sister." Liv squeezed my shoulder. "Another soul saved."

"What can I say?" I led the girls to the auditorium doors and whipped them open. "I'm a giver."

Marquette's auditorium was built to look like an old-time theater, with creaky plush seats and gold-plated numbers on the armrests. A gold-flecked carpet lined the center aisle from the doors to the orchestra pit. Heavy velvet curtains with thick tassels hung from the high ceilings. And a trio of spotlights cast the stage in a golden glow.

Center stage. It was where I was meant to be, at least when I was off the air.

Straight ahead, the cast of *Guys and Dolls* was standing in a circle onstage, holding hands and doing vocal exercises over the sound of the band warming up in the orchestra pit.

"Just finishing warm-ups, girls," called Sean, first-year U.S. government teacher by day/drama advisor by afternoon. He'd insisted we call him Sean since day one, because he thought it made him look cool. Which was probably the same reason he wore designer jeans to rehearsal. Ew.

"Sooo sorry we're late, Sean." I hustled down the aisle, and my crew followed. "Crazed fans, you know?" We hurried up the steps to the stage. I took a spot directly across from Quinn, so I could watch him toss his sandy blond bangs out of his eyes like he was just getting out of the swimming pool. Molly, Liv, and Nessa took the spots to my right, bumping Jilly "It's *Jillian* ever since I got accepted to Northwestern's theater camp" Lindstrom out of the way.

"One more exercise before we get started," Sean said. "I'd like you all to close your eyes."

While Sean and Jilly pretended to be trees blowing carelessly in the wind, Quinn refereed a heated thumb war between his two basketball buddies, Jake Fields and Aaron Peterman. I squinted, trying to zoom in on Quinn's lanky, athletic frame. But I couldn't get a clear picture. His bangs blurred against his face, making his head look like a khaki blob floating over a gray henley and jeans.

"You okay?" Molly's hot breath on my ear made me jump.

Yeah, I mouthed.

"'Cause your eyes look kind of red."

"Probably just the lighting," I hissed.

"You sure? Because you can't miss my boy-girl party."

"Okay." Sean clapped his hands together and opened his eyes. "Good work. Now let's get started. Liv, take the sixth graders backstage and get them fitted for their dancing dice costumes."

"Right on." Liv exited stage left, followed by a herd of extras.

"Where's my student director?" Sean hopped offstage and took his seat third row center.

"Here!" Nessa waved her notebook authoritatively. Student director was the perfect role for her. She got to boss people around and beef up her transcript at the same time.

"As long as we have the band, why don't we rehearse a few musical numbers?" Sean suggested. Now that he was far away, I could see the individual strands in his over-gelled goatee. But Quinn, who had meandered closer to me, looked like a reflection in a hazy funhouse mirror.

What was going on?

"Or, we could practice the 'wedding scene.'" Nessa put air quotes around the words *wedding scene*, since everybody knew that was code for *Kacey and Quinn's Onstage Smoochfest*. "I'm feeling like that scene could use some work."

I was feeling like Nessa was a genius. I mentally crossed my fingers.

But Sean ignored the suggestion. "We'll start with 'I've Never Been in Love Before.' Let me have Kacey and Quinn downstage center, please! The rest of you, don't go far."

"So . . . hey." The hovering blob in front of me smelled like winterfresh gum.

I rubbed my eyes. Hard. But this time when I opened, the view was still a yummy-smelling gray and blond Monet.

"Hey," I murmured back, smiling like I could absolutely see him.

"You going to Sugar Daddy after rehearsal?" Then came a whiff of almond extract that must have meant a hair toss.

I shivered as the scent washed over me. "Yeah." It was obviously just a way for Quinn to keep talking to me, since we always went to Sugar Daddy after rehearsal. And things were heating up between us. Two weeks ago, I custom-ordered a butterscotch cupcake with dark chocolate frosting and mini-marshmallows. And last week? He ordered the same cupcake. It was only a matter of time before we split one. Which was basically the same as kissing.

"So," I said, searching for his aqua eyes through the haze. "Are you going to Molly's party Saturday?"

"Yeah." And then he said: "Cool contacts."

Quinn!

Wilder!

Liked! My contacts!

My legs shook. It wasn't nerves. It felt more like . . . love shivers. Combined with fate. Combined with the teensiest bit of fear that I might be going blind.

The band launched into the intro. I let Quinn grab my hands and lead me around the stage as he sang his solo, a ballad about how his "character" had never felt this way about "any other girl." The strength in Quinn's voice, and the way he squeezed my hands super tight, showed me he meant it. Nobody was that good an actor.

When he finished, I opened my mouth to belt out

my opening line. "I've neeeeeever been in looove befoooooore—"

"Hold it!" Sean bellowed, silencing the band. And me.

"CUT!" Nessa yelled unnecessarily.

I squinted into the spotlight and dropped Quinn's hands. "What?"

"Kacey, is everything all right?" Sean's forehead collapsed into four distinct waves. "Do we need to go over your blocking again?"

"No." My eyeballs were starting to feel like they had rug burn.

"Because you were looking over Quinn's shoulder instead of looking lovingly into his eyes," Nessa clarified. "Like the script says."

"I think something's wrong with her eyes," Molly volunteered from the second row. "Maybe I should take her pl—"

I whipped downstage left. "Nothing's wrong with my eyes, thankyouverymuch." I crossed my arms over my chest to keep from clawing out my contacts.

"Maybe we should take a break," Sean suggested.

"No!" I screeched. "No break." While the rest of us were just trying to get through rehearsal, Molly was vying for her big break. And I knew her well enough to know how the scene played out in her head.

MOLLY

Kacey, what's wrong? You look
terrible.

SEAN

Maybe you should sit this one out,
Kacey. Maybe Molly should sub in for
the rest of rehearsal.

MOLLY

(looking shocked) Gasp! I never
thought of that! Okay! I mean, if
Kacey doesn't care.

KACEY

Wait! No! *(Faints in horror and has
to be carried offstage by the tech
crew.)*

Molly sprints to the stage and rehearses
song with Quinn.

Enter BROADWAY TALENT SCOUT.

BROADWAY TALENT SCOUT

You're amazing! Ever thought of a
career on the stage?

MOLLY

(looking shocked) Gasp! I never
thought of that! Okay! I mean, if
Kacey doesn't care.

Molly goes on to win record number of Tony
Awards for Best Performance by a Middle-
Schooler.

Over. My. Dead (and blind). Body.

"Let's just take five, everybody," Sean said. "I think we could all use a break."

"Later, Simon." Quinn's Altoid essence faded into the wings.

I lowered myself to the stage in a huff. I needed a butterscotch cupcake with chocolate frosting and mini-marshmallows delivered downstage center. Stat.

After a few seconds, the smell of strawberry Burt's Bees drifted by.

"Kace? Want us to take you to the bathroom?" Molly's fake hair grazed my shoulder.

She sounded sincere, at least. And since I needed a fresh coat of Burt's before Quinn and I stage-kissed . . .

"Okay." I nodded. I felt the pressure of Nessa's grip on my left forearm, then Molly's on my right. I jumped to standing.

"Your solo sounded really good," Molly offered as we shuffled down the aisle.

"Dead on," Nessa agreed.

"Totally. Wicked pipes," offered the boy blob blocking the double doors.

I stopped in my tracks. So did Molly and Nessa.

"Huh?" The most I could make out was a paintbrush

stroke of electric blue at the top of Mystery Boy's head, a white T-shirt, and jeans that . . .

I scanned again, for confirmation.

. . . *tapered* at the ankle.

"I said, wicked pipes," the kid repeated. "You have a really good voice."

"Oh. I know." Newsflash: skinny jeans? Unacceptable boy attire.

"Mind if I hang out and listen?" Pretty gutsy for a boy in girl jeans. Who was this kid? I knew everyone at Marquette worth knowing, and I'd never seen him before.

"Actually? This is a closed rehearsal," I informed him.

"Cool jeans," Molly cooed, flicking her high pony flirtatiously.

I swallowed. *Was she going blind, too?*

Skinny Jeans raked one hand through the blue streak in his hair. "I just heard the music and thought you guys sounded pretty good, so—"

"So buy a ticket," I snapped.

"Three dollars in advance, five at the door," Molly rasped, her voice sounding ten times more hoarse than normal. "We're selling them at Sugar Daddy later."

Skinny Jeans didn't seem to hear her. "Fine. I see

how it is." His laugh was slow, relaxed. "Break a leg." He turned and pushed through the doors.

"She will, with these new contacts," Molly said. Her voice dropped to a whisper once the doors swished shut. *"Who was that?"*

She was obviously asking me, since I was the first to know everything around Marquette. The student body made it official last year when I got voted *Most Likely to Know All Your Secrets, and Then Televise Them.* Molly got voted *Shiniest Hair.* Too bad she burned it all off.

"New kid from Seattle. I heard he's in a band," Nessa put in.

"I'm so into bands," Molly breathed.

I fell into a seat in the back row, my head suddenly swimming. Which was worse: Nessa knowing about Skinny Jeans from Seattle before I did, or Molly publicly falling for a boy in tapered pants? "Wait. How did I not know about this kid?"

"Maybs you don't know everything around heeere," Molly sing-songed.

I raised my left eyebrow. "Ex*cuse* me?"

"I'm def inviting him to my party." Molly tugged her ponytail holder from her hair and did a shampoo-commercial hair toss, sending a gust of wind my way.

"You might want to rethink a date with blue hair," I

offered with a tight smile. "That streak would wash you out. Oh, and P.S.? A little blush would do wonders for your skin tone right now."

Molly inhaled sharply. Nessa coughed.

"Break's over, folks!" Sean announced onstage. "Let's get back to it."

I grabbed Molly's wrist before she could take off down the aisle. "I'm just saying. You deserve somebody way cooler. Somebody with normal hair."

But instead of thanking me, she pulled away and stormed toward the stage.

My jaw dropped. I wanted to remind her that I'd just saved her from public humiliation. That I could have stood by and watched while she crushed on a blue-haired auditorium lurker. But instead, I'd taken the high road and told her the truth. Because friends don't let friends date punk.

FEEL THE BURN
Friday, 7:02 A.M.

Moving out of the room I used to share with my little sister, Ella, and having the third floor to myself was necessary for several reasons. For one thing, no self-respecting seventh grader should have to wake up to the sight of Cookie Monster underpants.

Secondly, the attic was practically custom-designed for me. Mom used to produce her own news segments up here, so there was a flatscreen on the wall across from my bed, right above my pink Lucite desk. The floating aluminum shelves that used to hold Mom's demo DVDs now showcased my legendary sneaker collection. We even converted the sound booth in the corner to a photo booth with a teal velvet curtain. One wall and the floor were painted in light green chalkboard paint. Liv had sketched her entire fall line over my bed. The rest of the walls were covered in bulletin board material.

But the most perfect thing about having the third floor to myself? Mom and Ella might not hear my tortured moans as my contacts seared violet-colored craters into my corneas.

"Kacey?" Mom's bare feet sounded on the polished wood stairs.

I flopped on my unmade bed and buried my face in the cool satin pillowcase, wishing my pink-and-black-plaid duvet would swallow me whole.

"Your breakfast is getting—" The footsteps stopped in the doorway. "Kacey? Are you sick?"

The mattress dipped as my mom sat on the edge of the bed. She placed the back of her hand on my forehead. It had to be her left hand, since it was ringless. On her right she wore two thin silver bands: one with my name and birthday engraved on the inside, and one with Ella's.

"Just resting my eyes," I lied into my pillow. I couldn't admit defeat now, since Mom hadn't wanted me to get the contacts in the first place. I'd have to wait until it seemed like my idea. Then I could calmly, casually inform her that I WAS GOING TO GO BLIND IF I DIDN'T REMOVE THESE FIRE-SOAKED EYE COASTERS OF DEATH RIGHT. NOW.

A clattering sound erupted from the kitchen two floors below, followed by a loud crash.

"*Moooooooooooooooom!*" Ella screeched. "*'Scuuuuuuuuuuze meeeeee!*"

I snorted into my pillow. Ever since Ella figured out that if she said "please," "excuse me," and "thank you," she didn't get into trouble, she'd used them as get-out-of-jail-free cards. Interchangeably.

"What am I going to do with you girls?" The bed creaked as Mom stood. "You coming?"

"In a sec." I rolled onto my side and stared at the wall. Tacked next to Molly's birthday wish list was an 8-by-11 black-and-white candid of the girls and me huddled around a campfire, the first night of the orientation weekend before the start of sixth grade. We were wearing Marquette hoodies and holding s'mores skewers with flaming marshmallows on the ends. We'd been assigned to the same scavenger hunt team. When we won, Liv had said that was The Universe's way of telling us we were meant to be best friends. Nessa didn't believe in The Universe, but told us we were way smarter and cooler than her elementary school friends, which was enough of a sign for her.

I slipped out of bed and unpinned the photo, running my fingers over its slightly curled edges. I gasped when I saw the picture underneath.

It was an old shot of me and Dad, the last picture we'd taken together before he moved to L.A. We were on the Ferris wheel at Navy Pier; my eyes were screwed shut and I was gripping a giant fluff of pink cotton candy. He'd bought it for me right before he told me he was leaving. The smell of cotton candy still made my stomach turn.

I stabbed the pin back into the board, obscuring Dad's face. Then I gathered my hair into a tousled chignon, secured it with one of Liv's antique brooch clips, and ducked in front of the full-length mirror on the back of my closet door.

I squinted at my reflection, then backed up a few steps so I could actually see. I may have been going blind, but that didn't mean everybody else was. I wore ripped skinny jeans, a fitted black cap-sleeve top, and a silk emerald slip dress that used to hit at the knee and belong to Liv's oldest sister. Until Liv ran it through the dryer. Now it fell to mid-thigh. And belonged to me.

"KACEY!" Mom shouted.

"Coming!" I tightened the laces on my black Converse and hurried downstairs.

"Hey, you." Standing behind the island in the center of the kitchen, Mom was spooning something out of takeout Chinese containers. Salty traces of egg drop soup and Tater Tots hovered over the threshold.

"Dinner for breakfast!" I grinned, the pain in my eyes instantly dulling.

Last year when I mentioned that Nessa's family sometimes had breakfast for dinner as a treat, Mom decided that we could do the Simon family version: dinner for breakfast, since Mom's job as Channel 5's solo evening anchor meant she wasn't usually around for dinner.

Humming my part of the duet with Quinn, I dumped my Channel 5 messenger bag on the floor by the stainless steel dishwasher and sat down at the table in the breakfast nook. I ran my fingers over the fuzzy etchings in the dark wood. I'd carved everybody's name at their place when I was a kid, in case anybody forgot where to sit.

Across from me, a pair of glittery white fairy wings peeked out above the table, rising and falling in slow rhythm.

I turned around in my seat and rolled my burning eyes at Mom. "WHERE'S ELLA, MOM?"

Loud breathing sounded from the window seat. The fairy wings shook with silent laughter, snowing silver glitter over the Tater Tots on Ella's plastic Disney princesses plate.

"Don't know, baby." Mom's auburn curls danced around her shoulders as she hurried around the counter and deposited a plate of Chinese takeout next to the fruit bowl in front of me. "Guess we'd better start looking."

"READY OR NOT, HERE I COME!" Ella yelled, jumping up on the window seat and laughing hysterically. Her red corkscrew curls bounced around her flushed cheeks.

I gasped, pretending to be scared. The terror wasn't exactly an act when I saw her outfit. Ella had strapped the fairy wings over the giant Channel 5 T-shirt I used to sleep in, which she'd tucked into a hot-pink tutu. Her red-and-white-striped tights were faded and had an unidentifiable purple stain on the left knee. All of this would have been semi-acceptable for a girl her age—if my old purple training bra hadn't been doubling as her headband.

"Mom!" I shrieked.

"Down, please." Mom took Ella's hand and gently tugged her to seated. "Eat your Tots."

Ella shoved a Tater Tot in her mouth and reached for her spoon, holding it like a microphone. "Kacey. What are you having for breakfast?" She waved the spoon-mic in my face.

"Sesame chicken," I said over a cold mouthful.

"Yuck," Ella decided, snatching back the mic. "Back to you, Mom."

"Thanks, Ella." Mom turned toward me.

I tried to squint her black warm-up suit into focus. Useless.

"Are you sure you're okay?" Mom's voice was laced with worry. "What's wrong with your eyes?"

"They're red," Ella reported into her spoon.

"Everything okay with your contacts?" Mom asked.

"Yup." I dumped sugar into my hot chocolate and took a gulp.

Oops.

"Salt." I coughed, doubling over my plate as my eyes teared up. I grabbed Ella's orange juice and swished to get rid of the taste.

"Kacey." Mom said firmly. "What's. Going on. With your contacts?"

"Nothing, Mom." I swiped a banana from the fruit bowl and shoved back my chair. "I have to get to school."

"That's a wax banana."

"Fine! They buuuurn!" I moaned, clamping my eyes shut. Oh, sweet relief. I wondered how long I could go without opening my eyes. Maybe I could get one of those cute Seeing Eye dogs. I'd always wanted a black Lab, but Mom said the townhouse was too small. She could hardly refuse if a puppy was a medical necessity.

"That's it." I heard the click of Mom's nails on her BlackBerry. "I'm making an emergency appointment with Dr. Marco after school."

"But I have rehearsal!" I protested.

"Not today, you don't." She hadn't used that tone since her hard-hitting interview with the city commissioner. And all of Chicago had seen what happened when he tried to argue.

"Kisses!" Ella disappeared under the table and reappeared on my side.

I leaned down to kiss her on the cheek. "Bye, Mom." I grabbed my messenger bag and ducked out of the kitchen and into the foyer before Mom could force me to take out my contacts on the spot.

"Dr. Marco! Don't forget!" Mom yelled after me.

I yanked my coat and scarf off the brass rack by the door and hurried outside.

The front steps were icy, so I gripped the wrought-iron railing and took each step slowly, squinting into the sunlight. I probably looked like Mrs. Weitzman, our next-door neighbor, who had cataracts and smelled like tuna fish and Vaseline.

Heading down Clark Street, I wondered how to play it with Mols once I got to the Armitage stop. She hadn't texted at all last night, which probably meant she was still mad from rehearsal. But I wasn't going to fake being sorry for giving her good advice. She should be the one apologizing to me, for making a scene in front of my future first boyfriend.

"Ow!" With zero warning, a tall, bony lamppost rammed into me and squealed. Only we didn't have any lampposts on my block, bony, squealing, or otherwise. "Kacey?"

I backed up a few steps. "Paige?" The lamppost was Paige Greene, my other next-door neighbor, seventh-grade class president, and my ex-BFF from Joliet Elementary. "Or should I say, Grim Reaper?"

"I'm in mourning," she said, looking down at her black coat, leggings, and boots. She smoothed her dark jaw-length bob importantly. I fought the urge to ask her if she'd cut her bangs herself.

"For your political career?" Everyone knew Paige was going to lose the eighth-grade election to Imran Bhatt, since Imran's dad managed a Six Flags and offered to get the entire grade free passes. When Paige lost, it would be like the fifth-grade election all over again. Only this time, it would only be embarrassing for one of us.

"I'm in mourning for the *environment*." Paige adjusted her Tina Fey glasses on her long nose.

Until two years ago, Paige and I had been best friends. We'd planned to go to college together and pinky-swore we'd live together when we graduated. We'd even picked the perfect place: an amazing condo with a balcony directly across from the Millennium Park skating rink, where my dad used to take us every Tuesday in the winter.

When I was a kid, I'd always thought we'd be friends forever, but then I grew up and realized that people move on. People leave, and you can't get worked up about it. Nothing lasts forever. That's just life.

I hurried blindly in the direction of the El, and Paige matched my stride. "I have a student council meeting," she informed me as if I'd asked. "We're voting on replacing all the candy vending machines with organic snacks."

Silently, I groaned. Did Paige not get that we weren't friends? If the friendship obituary I wrote in fifth grade hadn't done it, she could have gotten the message from the past two and a half years of silent treatment.

"It's just that my platforms this year are so important. And I think I have a good shot at getting reelected, since I ran last year on a commitment to make a change, and I've done that, right? Remember my slogan? *Time to Turn a New Paige?*"

"Paige!" I yelled over the roar of a bus churning by. It sprayed a fine mist of dirty snow over the sidewalk, drenching my Converse. "Hate to break it to you, but presidents have no real power. Especially in middle school. Do you seriously think anybody's voting yes on whole wheat crackers for the vending machines?"

Paige's eyebrows disappeared beneath her crooked bangs. "Honestly? Yes. Fifty-six percent of girls aged ten to eleven have a moderate to strong interest in cutting trans fats from their diet."

In other news, one hundred percent of Kacey Simons, aged thirteen, had no idea why they'd been friends with Paige Greene in the first place.

A DATE WITH DOCTOR EVIL
Friday, 3:37 P.M.

"Kacey Simon. Didn't expect to see you back here so soon." When Dr. Marco leaned over the exam chair with his mini flashlight, his spicy cologne burrowed up my nostrils into my brain, making my stress migraine a million times worse. I forgave him because he rolled his r's, which would be cute if he weren't solely responsible for making me miss rehearsal.

"Mom forced me."

"I see. And have you been using the drops I gave you twice a day?"

Drops? I squeezed my eyes shut to block out the tiny light daggers screwing into my pupils. "Weren't those optional?"

"More like mandatory." And then he did it. The *tsk*.

The *tsk* was the universal sound all doctors made when you were in serious trouble. My dentist, Marvin Haussmann, D.D.S., was a major *tsk*er. Specifically when I swore I'd been flossing and then his assistant, Darleen, whose claim to fame was an honorable mention in a Jessica Simpson lookalike contest, snitched that she just excavated half a chocolate cupcake from my upper molars.

"I'm concerned she's having an allergic reaction," Mom butted in from her seat by the door. "Her eyes have gotten worse since she left for school this morning."

"Waaay worse." Ella snapped the elastic on the black eye patch she'd found in the waiting room. "Ow."

Tsk. "Looks like you have a minor infection, Miss Kacey."

"But this pair is probably just defective, right?" I hooked my nails into the leather chair. I'd already chosen my outfit for Molly's party: a gray off-the-shoulder sweater dress with over-the-knee boots and one of Liv's birdcage veil hairpins. AND VIOLET CONTACT LENSES, for a pop of color. "You just have to give me another pair? And then I'll be fine?"

With every second Dr. Marco didn't answer, my heart rate was tripling, thrumming to the beat of Quinn's voice. *Cool contacts. Cool contacts. Cool contacts.* What if Molly kissed Skinny Jeans from Seattle before I offstage-kissed

Quinn? Was there no end to the lengths she'd go just to beat me at something?

"RIGHT?" My throat was starting to feel tight. I was probably having an allergic reaction to the idea of Molly beating me at anything. It wouldn't be natural.

Dr. Marco pushed back his rolling stool and headed for the door. Once he came into focus, I noticed that his curly black hair was still over-gelled, even though I'd told him last time: When they said *dime-sized amount*, they were serious. "Take your contacts out for me. I'll be right back," he said.

"Kacey Elisabeth," Mom said as the door clicked closed. The dreaded double name. And in the dark, which made it even freakier than usual. "What was our agreement?"

"Hold on." I hunched over in my chair and pretended that taking out my contacts required live coverage–level focus. The second they landed on my fingertip, the wildfires in my eyes smoldered to contained brush fires.

"Kacey! Did you know crickets hear through their knees?" For once I was glad Ella had no concept of when to be quiet.

"Liar," I said, crossing my fingers for a tantrum.

"Miss Deirdre *said*!" Ella stomped her foot right on cue. "Their ears are in their *kneeees*!"

But Mom didn't skip a beat. "Kacey? Our agreement?"

"ThatIcouldgetthemaslongasItookcareofthem." It was the same agreement we'd had when I got a ferret in fifth grade. That agreement didn't last long, either. But only because Ella made the ferret a mini theme park complete with a Gravitron, which was just a fancy name for a run through the spin cycle. *Rest in peace, Oprah Winfurry.*

"That's right. And do you think you've shown that you can be responsible enough to take care of them?"

I don't answer leading questions so I kept my mouth shut.

Dr. Marco reappeared in the doorway and flipped the overhead light on.

"Ahhhh!" I pressed the heels of my palms over my eyes. "Dr. Maaaarco!"

"POLO!" Ella shrieked gleefully.

"Sorry." Dr. Marco chuckled, adjusting the dimmer to the candlelight setting. "So here's the deal. It's going to take a couple weeks for that infection to heal."

"I'll do the drops every day this time. Twice. Swear," I promised.

"Twice a day," Mom repeated.

Dr. Marco opened his fake lab coat and fished around in one of the inside pockets, probably looking for a pamphlet on juvenile glaucoma.

I cracked my neck on both sides and closed my eyes.

"You should make these into massage chairs. Then people probably wouldn't hate coming to see you so much."

"Kacey." Even without looking, I could tell Mom was massaging her temples.

"I'll keep that in mind." Dr. Marco's voice came close to my ear, and I felt something cold and weighty settling onto my nose. "Try these for me."

"What?" My eyes snapped open. Those crunchy black curls were six inches closer and about six zillion times more defined than they had been a minute ago. It was suddenly painfully obvious that someone was in desperate need of a pore strip.

My hands flew to my face and collided with chunky plastic. "What's going on?" I gulped, bolting upright. "What are these?" My toes curled in my Converse.

Dr. Marco lifted a handheld mirror in front of me, revealing a pair of thick-lensed tortoiseshell glasses that took up at least seventy-five percent of my face. Then he threw his head back and let out an evil cackle, the overhead light illuminating his every wrinkle as he hissed, "*Any last words?*"

Okay, fine. What he actually said was: "*Your new glasses.*"

I ripped off the frames. "Is this your idea of a joke?" My voice cracked, making me sound uncertain. But I'd never been more sure of anything in my life. Glasses meant immediate social death. And now was not my time. I would *not* be one of those girls who peaked in middle school.

Dr. Marco's lips were moving, but no sound was coming out of them. All I could hear was this loud static buzzing in my ears. It was like dead air—the same sound I'd be hearing once all my friends ditched me, Quinn Wilder moved to Canada to get away from me, and *Simon Says* was cancelled on account of an unacceptably ugly host. If the show went down the drain, then my entire broadcast career was finished. And if my career was finished, what did I have?

Nothing. Except for a giant hunk of brownish-orange tortoiseshell perched on my worthless face.

". . . just for a little while, while your eyes heal," Dr. Marco was saying.

"You don't understand." *Coolcontacts.Coolcontacts.Coolcontacts.* "I *can't* wear these."

"Why not?" Dr. Marco's forehead crinkled.

I racked my brain for excuses, apart from the obvious. What would my friends say if they were in my place? Molly would somehow find a way to make glasses seem . . . sexy secretary, but Liv would—

"They're tortoiseshell. And that's inhumane to all

the . . . endangered . . . turtles." My stomach lurched, and I didn't even try to stop it. It would serve him right if I threw up all over his non-massage chair. "I'm calling PETA."

"Kacey Elisabeth." *Again* with the double name.

"Have you guys *seen* me in these?"

Dr. Marco patted my shoulder. "It won't take long, Kacey," he said gently. "Just a couple weeks. When your infection heals, you can go back to contacts."

I tilted my head back and blinked at the ceiling, scanning a mental list of upcoming personal appearances. *Molly's party. Classes. Rehearsal. OPENING NIGHT. The cast party, where I was supposed to have my first offstage kiss with Quinn Wilder.*

I rubbed my eyes, surrendering to the tears spilling down my cheeks. I didn't even care anymore if Dr. Marco saw me cry. He'd already seen the worst.

He'd seen me in glasses.

"I think you look smart," Dr. Marco tried, holding up the mirror again. He lifted the frames and nudged them gently onto my nose, but they kept sliding off.

I snuck another glance into the mirror. Puffy green eyes, red nose, and splotchy cheeks. I looked like someone else. A girl who huddled in the corner, trying not to be noticed. A girl whose school pictures haunted her for the rest of her life. A girl who was completely alone. A girl who was a . . . loser.

"That's it." I ripped off the frames again and lunged out of the chair, yanking my messenger bag over my shoulder. "I'm outta here."

I think Mom called my name, but all I could hear was the sound of my own pathetic sobs and Quinn's voice saying, *Coolcontacts.Coolcontacts.Coolcontacts.*

My phone buzzed in my bag as I stalked through the waiting room and headed for the elevators. "What?" I choked.

"Change of plaaaans," Molly chirped annoyingly. "Instead of The Drake? We're going someplace way better. I can't tell you where, but here's a hint—"

I couldn't. Not now.

"I have a bad—" I reached into my coat pocket and found a discarded gum wrapper. Then I crinkled the foil into the receiver. "—can't hear—tunnel—"

I hung up. It was unbelievable how shallow some people could be. Who cared about birthday parties when horrific, tragic things were happening in this world? Unspeakable disasters, wreaking havoc on millions of helpless victims across the globe? Hurricanes. Floods. Earthquakes.

Glasses.

GIRLS JUST WANT TO HAVE FUN
(PREFERABLY AT THE DRAKE)
Saturday, 7:45 P.M.

After Dr. Marco's stunt on Friday afternoon, I was very over surprises. So my patience was stretched thin by Saturday night, when Mom and Ella dropped me off in front of Molly's mystery party location on the south side of Chicago.

I'd stashed my glasses in the backseat pocket of the car, and it took a second for my vision to adjust to the building: a vinyl siding–encased warehouse on an otherwise abandoned block. I closed my eyes. *Stay calm.* Maybe it was a hallucination, an undesirable side effect of the drops. But when I opened my eyes, there it was again.

What had Molly done? Nobody in their right mind would show up to a party at this dump, much less host one voluntarily. I squinted through my birdcage veil at the blinking neon R CK 'N OLL sign hanging crooked over the automatic glass doors. Was this a . . . *roller rink?*

The second I stepped through the doors, Nessa and Liv rolled toward me. "WHERE HAVE YOU BEEN?" they yelled in unison.

"Traffic." The lie tasted sour on my tongue. I was supposed to be the girl who told it like it was, not the girl who almost didn't show and then lied about it. My fingers flew to the bridge of my nose. Even though I'd taken my glasses off, I could still *feel* them lurking on my face.

"Can you believe this?" Liv did a shaky figure eight through a pile of stale yellow popcorn. The frayed ends of a vintage headwrap fluttered behind her like the windsocks on Mrs. Weitzman's back porch. "So retro chic."

I blinked at her in disbelief.

"You won't believe Molly's outfit," Nessa warned me, straightening her oversized black sweater. In the musty heat of the rink, her forehead was starting to glisten more than the delicate jeweled headband crowning her pixie. "It's like she's got multiple personalities." With a shrink mom and a dad who taught African-American studies at Northwestern, Nessa considered herself an expert on three things: mental illness, test taking, and getting into a good college. "Only these days, we call it *dissociative identity disor—*"

I tuned her out and squinted at the roller rink, which was encased with (bulletproof?) Plexiglas. The floor was painted black to look like a record and was spinning slowly around a tiny red stage, where somebody had abandoned a drum set and a keyboard. There were a few fuzzy white-haired figures bobbing around, but with four minutes until Molly's party was supposed to start, I didn't see anybody from seventh, middle school, or even this century. Including Quinn Wilder.

"Ohmygod." My hand found its way to my open mouth. Had Molly taken a fall during her last skating lesson? It would explain her crush on the new kid from Seattle the other day. And . . . this.

"Oh, come on." Liv pressed the rubber stopper on her skates into the carpet, then hiked up her chunky purple leg warmers. "It's . . . kitschy."

"Please. Kitschy's just a fancy way of saying tacky *and* outdated." I eyed the leg warmers warily. "On the bright side, those leg warmers totally match the vibe. Nice work."

Liv's jaw clenched. "They're Rosemary's," she said defensively. Liv's parents were hippies who had named all three girls after something nature-related. There were Rosemary and Autumn, and then there was Liv. She told everyone, Nessa and Mols included, that Liv was short for Olivia. I was the only one who knew the truth.

"That's no excuse, *Willow*." Or should I say: *Living Willow Parrillo*. No joke.

"Huh?" Now Nessa looked sweaty *and* confused.

Willow Parrillo tripped backward, colliding with the skate counter. "What is *with* you this week, Kace?"

"Oh, I don't know." I coughed on a lungful of stale nachos and mildewed carpet. "I was hoping to be in the middle of a salt scrub by now, but picking the gum off my new boots is just as fun, right?"

Nessa cleared her throat uncomfortably. "So, um, Mols won't tell us what we're doing here. It's supposed to be a surprise." She raked her hand through her cropped cut and nodded at the picnic table on the other side of the rink, where Molly was admiring her reflection in a giant silver birthday balloon.

I flicked my flawless flatironing job over my shoulder and stalked around the rink, kicking old candy bar wrappers out of my path. This was the worst party ever. Quinn probably wasn't even coming.

"Heeeeeey!" Molly let her makeshift mirror float to the ceiling when she saw me. A chunk of her face-framing layers was dyed hot pink, and she'd ditched her winter-white accessories in favor of black skinny jeans, a black tank top, and metal dog tags. "So? What do you think?" she said expectantly, doing a twirl. "Are you totes surprised?"

"Avril?" I blinked. "Is that you?"

"Identity crisis," Nessa diagnosed under her breath.

Molly was too busy stroking the hot pink highlight over her left eye to hear.

"Test. Test." A heavy thumping sound echoed over the speakers, followed by an acoustic guitar riff. "Test."

I recognized that voice. Slowly, I turned around to face the rink. It was all one hazy, dilapidated watercolor, but I could still make out a bright blue hair streak bobbing onstage.

"Skinny Jeans?" Now my scalp was starting to sweat. "You moved the party and dyed your hair to look like cotton candy for SKINNY JEANS?"

"FYI, his *name* is Zander Jarvis, *not* Skinny Jeans," Molly corrected me, handing over a stinky pair of skates. "And his band plays here every Saturday night. His old band in Seattle, Hard Rock Life, was amazing. They won a Sammy, aka the Seattle version of a Grammy, for best new artist."

"Hard Rock Life?" I echoed. "Lame."

"Test, test." Skinny Jeans's voice echoed through the room. "I'm Zander Jarvis, on bass we have Kevin Cho, Nelson Lund on keyboard, and on drums, The Beat. We're Gravity and we'll be holding it down till close."

Molly squealed like a squeak toy.

"Senior skate hour is wrapping up for the night, so we're gonna send you all out with our take on a classic Sinatra jam."

Molly hooked her thumbs over the metal-studded belt slung low around her hips and swayed to the opening cords of "My Kind of Town."

"Okay!" I yelled over the music. I couldn't even look at her anymore, so I just started pacing. "We'll tell people you're sick and you have to reschedule. Some place way better than this." You only turn thirteen once and I wasn't about to let my formerly sane best friend do it here.

"Too late." Nessa said dryly, her eyes cutting to the door. "It's time."

"Hey, Simon." A crisp wave of ocean-scented bodywash drowned out the heavy scent of denture cream and social suicide. The tiny hairs on the back of my neck stood in salute.

"Wilder." I whipped around, coming nose to nose with Quinn. Jake Fields and Aaron Peterman stood behind him, but I barely noticed. The way Quinn and I called each other by our last names made me feel like we were starring in our own private crime drama rated M for mature.

"Hey." Quinn nodded at Molly. Hair toss. "Happy birthday, or whatever."

Molly blinked. "Thanks, Wilder." When she last-named him, it sounded like they were on the same football team.

"And, uh . . . you did really good in rehearsal yesterday."

My stomach lurched. I'd completely forgotten that my date with Dr. Marco meant Molly had finally taken my place onstage.

"It just felt, like, totally natch, you know?" Molly flicked her pink streak at the exact same time Quinn hair tossed.

While Quinn, Aaron, and Jake dumped their presents on the nearest picnic table and a fresh herd of kids from seventh shuffled toward us, I revised the game plan. Too late to take the party someplace cool. Time for damage control. I lunged for Molly, gripping the wrist without the metal-spiked bracelet.

"Hey!" She writhed under my grip. "Kacey!"

"Come on." I yanked her around the perimeter of the rink, stumbling blindly. Liv and Nessa rolled close behind. When we got to the bench by the front doors, I plopped down. Prime real estate.

"What are you doing?" Molly huffed, rubbing her wrist.

"Giving your party the Heimlich." I kicked off my party boots and took a nauseated breath. Then I did the unthinkable and stuffed my feet inside the skates. They were warm. And moist. But I did it for her. *Ewewewewew*. "Consider this the V.I.P. area," I instructed, lacing them up tight enough to make my toes tingle. "Let everybody else come to us."

Molly nodded slowly. "Bril."

"Nessa, seriously, unless you take off some of those layers, you're gonna get shinier than the Clearasil *Before* girl," I advised, pulling my hair into a high ponytail. My eyesight was fuzzy, sure, but some things were impossible to miss. "And Liv?" I wrinkled my nose at the leg warmers.

"Hilar," Molly giggled.

"And if *you* want any guy to realize you're more than just a gorgeous head of"—I cringed and lifted my fingers in air quotes—"'hair,' try using complete sentences."

Molly's eyes widened. Liv tugged off the warmers begrudgingly while Nessa tore off her sweater, revealing a shimmery gray tank underneath.

"There. You guys look awesome. Now one of you get the guy behind the rental counter to dim the lights. The less we have to see of this dump, the better. I'll take care of the music." I stood up quickly, feeling slightly light-headed. But in a good way, like I'd had one too many cupcakes. "Ready? Break."

It was only a few filthy feet to the rink. Slowly, I slid my skates back and forth like I was on Mom's elliptical machine, keeping my arms outstretched in front of me. When I reached the edge, I gripped the clammy, paint-chipped railing and hopped on. I made it to the stage just as Skinny Jeans was wrapping up the Sinatra tune.

"Hey!" I yelled over the crash of cymbals. "Skinny Jeans!"

"Hey. Guys and Dolls!" Skinny Jeans's voice boomed over the mic. I felt myself being pulled onto the stage as the entire rink went silent. "Got a request?"

"Oh, I dunno," I said casually. "Something from this century, maybe? Or is that too much to ask for Molly Knight's thirteenth birthday?"

"Molly's birthday, huh?" Then the blue streak swam away from me, toward the rest of the band. "Hear that, guys?"

"FIVE, SIX, SEVEN, EIGHT!" The Beat yelled, and the band launched into a hard rock version of "Happy Birthday."

"Yeaaaaaaahhhhhhhhhhh!" the crowd hooted at the exact same moment the lights dimmed and the disco ball hanging from the ceiling lit up, sending glittery silver stars cascading over the rink. Some of the guys herded onto the rink with a football. And standing right at the foot of the stage was Quinn Wilder, flashing a smile that totally outdazzled the disco ball.

"Come on!" Wilder grabbed my hand and pulled me into the rink.

"Quinn!" I had to steady myself against his boy-chest. Fine by me.

"So you skate really good," he offered, still holding my hand.

Well. You skate really well. But I didn't say it out loud. "Thanks!" I yelled.

"We should have a skate-off." His breath smelled extra minty, which made sense. I learned in science class that when you start to go blind, your other senses turn super-human. "Girls versus guys."

"What is this, *High School Musical*?" I shot back.

"Scared?" His lips were no more than three inches from my ear.

I didn't know if it was the drum vibrations thumping through the floor, the flashing disco ball, or the proximity to Quinn Wilder's mouth, but I was suddenly positive that a girls-guys skate-off was the

Best.

Idea.

Ever.

"I'm gonna go get a cupcake!" I yelled, a sudden wave

of nerves washing through my body. With any luck, what Quinn saw next was me gliding effortlessly into the darkness, instead of me clomping blindly through the rapidly filling rink toward the Plexiglas.

Molly threw her arms around me the second I reached the V.I.P. bench. "Aaron Peterman just told me my party's, like, ten times better than his party last year!" Her gaze fell on the stage, and her lips parted slightly. "Is Zander not the most amazing?"

"I hope that's a rhetorical question." I straightened up, swiped two cupcakes from an open Sugar Daddy box, and handed one to Liv. "So Wilder and I are organizing a guys versus girls skate. You game?"

"How very after-school special," Nessa teased, taking a swig of Diet Coke.

"So I had this dream last night." Liv scooted over, and I wiggled into the seat next to her. "You and Quinn, like, started dating at the cast party!" She rolled her skates back and forth on the carpet.

"Liv. You're not psychic." A gaggle of girls I semi-recognized from homeroom skated slowly by our bench, looking desperate to stop. "Your dream was just common sense."

"Or was it . . ." Liv narrowed her eyes mysteriously, ". . . The Gift?"

"I'm sensing . . ." Nessa closed her eyes. ". . . total crap."

I burst out laughing, silvery disco stars washing over me. The stress of Dr. Marco's office and all the arguing with Mom over the stupid glasses was finally starting to dissolve.

"We're gonna take a quick break," Skinny Jeans murmured into the mic. "But we'll be back in a few, so stick around."

"I'm asking Zander if he wants to skate." Molly popped onto her feet.

"Wait. Skinny Jeans? *Now?*" I swallowed a sticky clump of icing. She could *not* start dating Skinny Jeans before I started dating Quinn. "No. Don't."

"Why not?"

"Because." I sighed. "'I just turned this party around. I need to relax before the boy-girl skate-off."

"So don't come." Molly shrugged, slathering on some Burt's Bees.

"Fine. I'll come," I huffed. "But only 'cause it's your birthday."

When we got back to the stage, Skinny Jeans didn't even look up.

"Back already, Guys and Dolls?" He strummed a chord.

"By force," I clarified to the blue streak. "Which is

probably the only way you made it into those jeans. Here's a hint: Maybe try the men's department."

The entire band went silent. Apparently, the alterna-geeks were missing the humor gene.

"Hey." Molly elbowed past me. "I'm Molly."

"Yeah, I remember. Happy birthday." Another chord.

"Thanks. Your band's amazing. I'm so glad you guys could play for my party. You're like this wicked cross between Weezer and Radiohead."

Wicked? Radiohead? Weezer?!

"Anyways, I was thinking maybe the rest of the band could take over for a few songs. We're having a skate-off in a few and you should join."

"Yeah. I'm kind of working." Skinny Jeans shrugged.

"So take a break." Molly cocked her head to the side.

"We kind of just did. Sorry."

Silence.

"Wait. *'Sorry'?*" Molly sounded confused. Apparently nobody had informed the new kid that you didn't say no to Molly Knight. Unless you were me.

I reached for the mic. "Simon Says hit the rink," I announced to the sparkly, spinning abyss in front of me, saving Molly for the millionth time. I nodded to the band, and they launched into a new song. "Girls versus guys."

"I can't believe he blew you off," I said as I hopped off

the stage. "Those jeans must be cutting off blood flow to his brain." But when I squinted at her face, all I saw was an enormous smile.

"He's so committed to his art," she breathed. "Hot."

"You're delusional," I muttered, dragging her to the circle forming at the edge of the rink. Quinn was break dancing at the center.

"Wild-er! Wild-er! Wild-er!" the guys hooted while Quinn spun on his head.

Quinn whipped his body to standing while the circle erupted in screams and cheers. Then he did a victory lap around the circle.

Until he got to me.

"Come on, Simon!" he yelled, grabbing my wrist. "Let's go!"

"Quinn!" I shrieked, pawing blindly at the air.

"Si-mon! Si-mon! Si-mon!" The guys switched chants as Quinn whisked me to the center of the action and spun me around. Without even trying, I was skating backward on pure adrenaline, floating through the pulsing, starry air to the screams of everyone at Marquette. It was an out-of-body experience. Some would call it nirvana. Others would call it heaven. I called it Saturday night, starring Kacey Simon and Quinn Wilder.

Quinn Wilder. Somehow I'd lost sight of him in the sea

of fuzzy, chanting faces. I whirled around in search of my costar. But before I could find him, I slammed into something. *Someone?* And then my brain switched to slow-mo. Suddenly my skates were in the air, hovering over my head. *Wait. I don't know how to do a back flip.* This was definitely not part of the Kacey-Quinn romance montage. *Stop! Do-over! Rewind!* Somewhere far away, somebody screamed my name. *Molly?*

Overhead, a giant, spinning disco ball. And then my movie cut to black.

PARTY FOUL FALLOUT
Saturday, 9:39 P.M.

In breaking news situations, a responsible journalist gathers as many facts as possible to avoid jumping to conclusions and subsequently freaking out. Those of us in the business call it gathering the five W's: Who, What, Where, When, and Why.

Allow me.

Who: Me.

What: A warm white light pouring over me. Head throbbing. Mom, murmuring my name from far away.

Where: Last time I checked, a busted warehouse.

When: Sometime after Molly's lame-turned-amazing birthday party.

Why: Isn't it obvious? A warm white light? I'M. DEAD.

"Kacey. Kacey." Now it was a man's voice, deep and

gravelly. My eyelids fluttered open and I stared directly into the light.

"*God?*" I whispered.

Only it came out sounding more like this: *Mraaaaaw?* Because there was something thick and dry and fluffy stuffed in my cheeks, which were numb. And my jaw was throbbing more painfully than the time I did sixty-five minutes of live coverage on last semester's Lunch Lady Mutiny.

I tried to lift my hand to massage my jaw, but it was as heavy as lead.

"Kacey." A hand pressed down on my shoulder, and I squirmed beneath it, jerking away from the light. It wasn't my time! I hadn't gotten to do all the things I wanted to do before I graduated from middle school. Like revolutionize broadcast television! Off-stage smooch Quinn Wilder! Finish the entire Big Daddy cupcake at Sugar Daddy to get my name on the chalkboard over the register!

"Here she is." Mom's warm breath tickled my ear, and the white light dimmed. Then I felt the heavy plastic frames settling onto the bridge of my nose. I tried to scream, but nothing came out.

"Welcome back, kiddo." A dark shadow leaned between me and the light, and tiny gold fireworks exploded in front of my pupils as my eyes adjusted. The sharp, skinny red and white stripes came into focus first. Then came the navy cursive embroidery that read MARVIN HAUSSMAN, D.D.S.

Not God. Just my too-nerdy-to-live dentist, who said things like "kiddo" (and once, "okie dokie, artichokie," which should be grounds for a malpractice suit).

"What's going on?" I murmured groggily, which sounded more like *Mraaaaaw mraaaaaw mraw mraw?*

Luckily Mom read my mind. "You fell at Molly's party," she said gently, her fingertips grazing my throbbing cheek. It reminded me of when I was a little kid, and home sick from school. "Looks like you chipped a molar. Dr. Haussman was nice enough to meet us at his office to take a look."

"My pleasure, Sterling." Dr. Haussman slid on his wire-rimmed glasses and leaned over the exam chair. "All righty, little lady, let's get those cotton balls out of your mouth. Then we can talk about our options." As Marvin Haussman, D.D.S., leaned over and pulled out the cotton balls, his silk sleeve grazed my cheek. This must have triggered some sort of PTSD flashback, because suddenly, the entire night came screaming back at warp speed, with sound and everything. And I saw the Sunday morning headline in cold, hard black and white: WORLD'S YOUNGEST BLIND JOURNALIST TRIPS OVER SHAGGY-HAIRED HOTTIE DURING

STEAMY PRE-KISS DANCE-OFF; HELD HOSTAGE BY DORKY DENTIST IN
SILK JAMMIES.

I screamed and bolted upright, slamming my head into
the overhead exam light.

"Kacey!" Mom gasped. "Careful!"

"Owwwwwwwwwww!" I bellowed, collapsing back
into the chair. But the pain in my head and mouth was
nothing compared to the pain of knowing that Quinn
Wilder had seen the fall. Was he having second thoughts
about me? About us?

"Easy, kiddo." Dr. Haussman's potbelly shook when he
chuckled.

Oh, is this funny to you? I wanted to scream. *Is my
public humiliation amusing?*

"Now let's get you upright so we can chat." The exam
chair hummed beneath me.

I raked my hands through my hair. How could he be so
calm at a time like this? He had no idea what it felt like
for a public figure to hit rock bottom.

"Believe it or not, it's a good thing you fell when you
did." Dr. Haussman cleared his throat. The middle button
on his pajama top shimmied dangerously, threatening to
free itself from the buttonhole. "Forced me to take a look
at your wisdom teeth, which are coming in very tight.
They're altering the alignment of your entire mouth."

The exam light was starting to make me sweat. "Is there a point to this?"

"Kacey, let Dr. Haussman finish." The sympathetic cushion to Mom's voice was starting to deflate.

"The point is that you're going to need orthodontic work to address these concerns, or I'm afraid you'll see a fairly severe maxillary prognathism in the next few years."

"Translation?" I jerked my head toward Mom. I hated it when adults used big words. It was like when some people were just trying to help certain geometry teachers by politely mentioning that short-sleeved shirts with dancing patriotic teddy bears on them should be reserved for pediatric nurses and insane cat ladies. And then certain geometry teachers sent a note home threatening *disciplinary remediation*. Which was PSAT for *detention*.

Mom pressed her lips together like she was blotting her lipstick. "You need braces, or you'll end up with an overbite," she said gently, interlacing her fingers with mine and squeezing.

My entire body went tingly, then completely numb, as if Dr. Haussman had just injected me with a giant shot of Novocain.

"Due to the placement of your wisdom teeth, Invisalign isn't an option," Dr. Haussman said from somewhere far away. "You'll need braces, plus a night retainer and headgear."

Dazed, I stared at the reflection of the bug-eyed tortoise-shell frames in Mom's eyes. They invaded my face. That girl wasn't me. Her cheeks were puffy, her eyes glazed over. Her hair was matted to her head. She was . . . ugly. I bit the inside of my cheek. Hard.

"Mom," I managed, squeezing her hand. "No. Please." She had to understand. If I ever showed up at school looking like this, everyone would abandon me. Just like Dad abandoned her. Us.

"I'm sorry, Kacey. This is just something we're going to have to do."

"But . . . I can't." Hot anger churned in my gut. *Stop him, Mom. Please.*

"Kacey," Mom said gently. "It's just braces, sweetheart."

But I knew she was lying. It was never *just braces.* First you got braces. Then you lost your television show because the camera guy was blinded by your braces, which was an occupational hazard. Then Quinn Wilder decided not to like you anymore, because who wanted to stage-kiss a girl with metal welded to her teeth? Then the rest of the school decided not to like you, because Quinn Wilder's hair tosses were very persuasive. Fast-forward a few years, and you were reading the lotto numbers on basic cable somewhere in one of the Dakotas because no one else would even look at you, let alone hire you as a journalist.

Clearly, Dr. Haussman didn't understand this unavoidable chain of events, either. Or else he wouldn't have snapped on his little paper mask and said the two most torturous words in the English language:

"Open wide."

H IS FOR HOMESCHOOL
Monday, 6:45 A.M.

On Monday morning, the only thing vibrating louder than my Channel 5 ringtone alarm was my jaw. I kept my eyes screwed shut and slapped at my nightstand until my phone hit the floor and skittered to a silent halt.

"You up, sweetheart?" Mom called from the bottom of the stairs.

"Aaaarrrghhh," I moaned. I was never getting up again. Not after taking a face dive in front of my ex-future-boy-friend-hyphen-costar.

"Kacey?" A soft finger poked my arm.

I lifted my head a few inches off my drool-soaked pillow to see Ella's blurred, juice-stained mouth hovering just inches from my cheek. A gleaming roll of tinfoil was wrapped around her face like—like—

Headgear.

I slapped at my pulsing cheeks. Or I would have, if there hadn't been a barbed wire fence strapped around my head and protruding at least six inches in front of my lips. When my fingers hit the headgear, it felt like a jellyfish had taken up residence on my face.

Frantic, I ran my tongue along my teeth. But my smooth, pearly Simon Smile was gone. Vanished. Replaced with a junkyard of jagged metal parts that were wound tighter than Nessa during midterms.

"Ahhhhhhhhhhhhhhhhhhhhhhh!" I screamed, kicking off my duvet.

Ella fell backward, an old pair of mom's reading glasses slipping off her small nose onto the floor.

"Owwwwwww!"

Ignoring her, I scrambled off the bed and ran for my closet, kicking a pair of inside-out skinny jeans out of my path. I gripped the edges of the full-length mirror on the door and leaned toward the glass.

"Girls?" Mom's footsteps pounded up the stairs. She rushed into my room, ducking under the slanted ceiling. "What's going on?"

Staring at the reflection of myself encased in metal, I pinched my upper thigh. But instead of waking up, I left two crescent-shaped dents above my bruised knee. This wasn't a nightmare. This was real.

"Kacey pushed me!" Ella wailed through a mouthful of tinfoil.

"Kacey?" Mom perched on the side of the bed and pulled Ella into her lap. "Is that true?"

Ordinarily, the sharp edge in her hard-hitting-question voice would make me squirm. But every cell in my body was already in pain.

"Kacey?" Mom prompted me again. Gentler this time.

I wanted to scream. Yell. Hit something. Things like braces and glasses weren't supposed to happen to *me*. They happened to chess club historians, and math club founders. Student government junkies. The Paige Greenes of the world. The Band Geeks. Not the Kacey Simons.

I whirled away from the mirror and pawed at the velvet curtain to my photo booth. Then I took a deep breath and collapsed onto the bench inside. The photo booth never lied.

"Sweetie," Mom tried again. "Calm down."

Ignoring her, I slammed the glowing green button inside with my fist. Most people wouldn't be able to look at themselves in this state. But I needed the cold, hard truth. Even if it killed me.

The flashbulb inside popped four times.

"Honey. You've got to take a breath." Mom's voice barely rose above my heartbeat and the churning photo booth. How could she have let this happen? I was never speaking to her again.

Ella drew the curtain and climbed into my lap, clutching the dreaded photo strip. She smiled, apparently over her tantrum. "I think it looks pretty. Sparkly! Like your teeth have earrings!"

I groaned, swiping the photo. I stared down at the gritty black-and-white image. Swollen, pursed lips and puffy cheeks stared back at me, along with a deepening bruise on my cheekbone, and a thick wire orbiting my head.

"You know, Kacey, it doesn't matter what you look like with braces." Mom pulled the curtain back all the way.

Right. Next she was going to tell me that it was what was inside that counted. You know who wrote that line? People with braces and glasses.

"Maybe you'll even start a trend. Remember the time you broke your arm in fifth grade? What happened when you showed up to school in a cast?"

Fine. So maybe a few kids came to school the next week with fake, Sharpie- and glitter-decorated casts of their own. Maybe the principal even caught that one girl about to take a dive off the jungle gym so she could break a bone for real. But this was different. Nobody in their right mind was going to fake braces and glasses.

"Your classmates *love* you," Mom said earnestly. "You're Kacey Simon. And what's the Simon women's most important accessory, on the air and off?"

"Oooh! Oooh!" Ella leapt out of my lap and waved her hand in the air. "Confidence!"

I bit my cracked bottom lip and swallowed the lump in my throat.

"I remember the first time I knew you were going to be a reporter." Mom pulled me out of the booth and into a hug. Her bathrobe smelled like soap. It made me want to cry. "You were six years old, and—"

"Like me!" Ella threw her arms around both of us.

"Just like you," Mom said, humoring her. "I was covering that student protest at Loyola, and I couldn't get a sitter, so I brought you with me."

I half smiled, half grimaced.

"You were interviewing the student body president and using your Elmo spoon as a microphone. I'll never forget how excited you looked, being right there in the middle of all the action." Mom squeezed my shoulder. "You're still Kacey Simon. And you still have a job to do."

As much as I hated to admit it, she was right. I had a responsibility to my public. If I let braces and glasses take me off the air and off the map, who would help everyone at school? So I'd have to memorize my scripts since

I couldn't read the teleprompter. Doable. So I'd have to learn ventriloquism so I never had to open my mouth on air. Okay. I'd pay for lessons with the settlement money I'd win after suing the roller rink for having hazardous party conditions.

"Let me hear you say it." Mom nudged me. "Who are you?"

I rolled my eyes. "I'm Kaythee Thimon."

My stomach catapulted into my throat. *Wait. That was wrong.* Okay, I just had to enuuuunciate, just like Sean was always saying at rehearsal. *Take two.*

"I'm Kaythee Thimon," I repeated, louder this time. My blood ran colder than leftover sesame chicken. No. Not possible.

"Kaythee! Thimon! Kaythee! Thimon!" Ella squealed.

My jaw lolled open, weighed down with metal and doom. No. *Nonononononono.*

I ripped my off my headgear, tensing at the pain. "KAYTHEE. THIMON." The room swam before my eyes, spinning out of control. I gripped Mom's arm for support. "DO I HAVE A LITHP?"

Mom averted her eyes, pretending to pluck a piece of lint from her bathroom. "I'm sure it will go away when you adjust to the braces. You probably just have to get used to speaking again. But it may take a while," she said gently.

A while? I didn't *have* a while. Homeroom was in less than an hour. Plan B.

"I think I'm thiiick," I moaned, stumbling toward my bed.

"Oh, sweetheart." Mom shook her head. "I heated up some soup and made smoothies, so you won't have to chew." She was acting like she hadn't even heard me. Like she didn't even care. "Be downstairs in ten. Ella and I will drive you if you get a move on." I heard her quick steps down the stairs, followed by the slow thud of Ella's.

We interrupt this broadcast with a special announcement:

Kaythee Thimon Ith Thuper Thcrewed.

THEEN AND NOT HEARD
Monday, 8:04 A.M.

Before I dragged myself across the threshold to Sean's homeroom, I tucked my glasses away in my bag, bent over, and gave my waves a shake. A girl could only hope that volumized hair and a chunky metallic gold infinity scarf would cover her chapped lips and chipmunk cheeks. And if enough blood rushed to my brain maybe I'd pass out, break something, and get to go home for the rest of the semester.

My sweaty palm slipped against the door handle. I wiped my hands on my chocolate-brown leather leggings and tried again. The door opened and I stepped into the back of the classroom.

"OPENING NIGHT TICKETS FOR *GUYS AND DOLLS*! ON SALE! NOW!" Abra screeched from the flatscreen mounted in the front corner when I tiptoed inside. Sean stood with his back to the class, using a yardstick to turn down the volume on the television. Everyone else had already plugged their ears with iPod buds.

In our usual back row seats, the shadowy outlines of Molly and Liv shifted toward me. Molly's pink streak tilted in curiosity, and Liv's dark curls bobbed with concern. In the row ahead of them, Nessa's highlighter-yellow flashcards stopped their shuffle.

Up in the front row, Paige Greene sat with the other dorks, including half the string section of the school band and Imran Bhatt. Even with my 20/500 vision, Paige's bob looked asymmetrical.

"Kacey. I thought you were *dead* or something!" the pink streak whispered when I stepped over a pile of backpacks and took my usual seat between the pink streak and Liv's hand-crocheted knit cap. In the next row, Nessa's neon flashcards started flying again.

"Mmmmm," I nodded, staring straight ahead at the television like I wouldn't even think of missing Abra's segment.

Molly planted a new black glitter day planner in front of her mouth and leaned toward me. "Wait. That's not Burt's. Are you . . . wearing *gloss*?"

I managed a pinched smile. I'd lacquered my mouth

shut with two coats of Mom's super sticky peach gloss. Desperate measures.

"I'M ABRA LAING, AND THAT'S MARQUETTE! IN A MINUTE!" Abra bellowed. "NOW OVER TO RYAN BURKE FROM SIXTH! FOR THE WEEK'S LUNCH MENU!"

"Did you get the healing energy I was sending from my room?" Liv whispered on my right. "I spent all day Sunday generating good vibes."

"Mmmm," I said again, staring at the back of Nessa's neck, amazed that she could treat this morning like any other Monday. Like my entire world hadn't flipped upside down, and then blacked out in the middle of the skating rink. I pursed my lips tighter together and tapped my throat with my index finger. The rough metal brackets scraped at my lips, threatening to break free.

"What?" Molly twirled the pink streak around a chunky ring on her index finger. I leaned closer. Was that . . . a *skull*?

I swiped Molly's day planner and ripped out a piece of paper from the back. Liv pulled a pencil from her messy bun and handed it to me.

L̶a̶r̶n̶g̶i̶

L̶a̶r̶y̶n̶g̶y̶

*Lost my voice. Dr. says I probably got some sort of throat
disease from your party.*

Molly gasped. "Kacey! I'm so SORRY!" She gripped
my arm and squeezed tight.

The sea of floating heads in front of us turned. Paige's
uneven bob cocked to the left. Sean turned off the television.

"Ladies? Problem?"

I shook my head quickly, my chipmunk cheeks flaming.

"Kacey lost her voice!" Molly squeezed my arm tighter.
"And she passed out and almost died. At *my* boy-girl
party." She lowered her head. I would have felt bad for
lying to her had my life not been on the fast track to
Geekville.

"You should get somebody to talk for you in class," Liv
decided. "Be your spokesperson, or whatever."

"I'll do it." Molly waved her arm. "And I'll take notes."

"She can still write, genius," Nessa turned around and
rolled her eyes at me.

I smiled, then slapped my hand over my mouth. The
pulsing pain in my gums was nothing compared to the
fear that I'd let my braces show.

"What are you gonna do about *Simon Says*?" Liv
planted her elbows on the desk. The row of silver spoons
she'd bent into bangles clinked together like wind chimes.

"And rehearsal this afternoon!" Nessa cinched the waist tie on her eggplant trench tight. "Are you dropping out of the show?"

Rehearsal. I hadn't even thought about the fact that as long as I played mute, Molly got to play me. But if playing the real Kacey Simon meant playing a lisping, braces-and-glasses-wearing freak show, maybe I didn't want the part anymore.

"Being authentic in your characters means committing to the role in every way," Sean announced at the beginning of rehearsal that afternoon. Most of the cast sat cross-legged in a circle onstage with notebooks and pencils, trying not to have boredom-induced strokes while Sean paced in front of us and read from a tiny square paperback. I sat between Molly and Quinn with my knees pulled to my chest, trying not to relax my trembling lips, which had been plastered over my braces for the last nine hours. "That means committing to your characters' voices, their emotions, and their movements."

A disgusting stink wafted from the cardboard cup Molly was holding. I glared at her, then at the cup.

"Liv made it for me," she whispered excitedly. "Some kind of herbal potion thing for my stage voice."

I flashed her an *ex-cuse me?* stare.

"In case you're not feeling up to it," she said quickly, lifting the cup to her lips.

Quinn elbowed me in the ribs, making my last remaining functional body part throb in pain along with the rest of me. "Sean's such a nerd, right?" he whispered. His shaggy bangs grazed my earlobe and would have made my entire body convulse with love shivers, if I hadn't been sweating from the organic wool neck warmer Liv crocheted during lunch to speed up my laryngitis recovery.

"Today we're focusing on movement." Sean closed the paperback and stuffed it in his back pocket. "As we go through rehearsal, I want you all to focus on being inside your characters, not only emotionally, but physically. Explore what your character's body *feels* like."

"Can I explore what one of the girl character's bodies feels like?" Brady Kane, one of the lighting guys, breathed over the sound system from the tech booth.

"Sexist," Nessa announced firmly, whipping out her notepad.

"I'll rephrase," Sean sighed. "What does it feel like to *be* your character? Does he or she have a limp? Perfect posture?" He clapped. "Everybody on your feet, and we'll get started."

I racked my brain for stall tactics. *Compliment his jeans. Ask where he got his stage presence. Pull him aside and ask for a repeat of that AMAZING lecture he gave last week on the Second Amendment.* Wait. All of these involved opening my mouth.

Molly leapt to standing. "Ready, Sean!"

"Kacey, I take it you're going to sit this one out?" Sean asked. "Let Molly step in for you?"

"I'm happy to help out!" Molly unhooked her hair from behind her ear. It slipped over her face, making a curtain between us that I couldn't penetrate with my death stare.

I sneered at the pink streak anyway. Suddenly all I wanted to do was sprint home, dive under the covers, and start the day over again. No. The week. The year. My *life*. What was I supposed to do? Let Molly star opposite Quinn? Or out myself as a lisping liar in *braces*? It was lose-lose.

"Kacey?" Sean prompted me gently.

My head felt heavy. I nodded slowly. There was no other choice.

"Awesome," Molly squeaked without even looking at me. "Oh, and I had some new ideas for blocking, that are, like, a little diff than what Kacey's been doing?"

"Okay, then. Let's give them a shot." Sean's glasses bobbed up and down before he turned his back to me and faced the rest of the cast. "I need Molly and Quinn onstage, please? Molly and Quinn."

Molly and Quinn. The combination made me want to puke more than Regis and Kelly.

"Everybody else, take a seat in the first few rows, please."

Liv came up behind me and looped her arm around my shoulder. "Let's go, sicko."

I avoided looking at Molly, or Sean, or anybody as we trudged down the stairs. Even with my back to the stage I could tell everyone was watching me. But instead of giving me the usual adrenaline rush, it made me want to crawl under the stage and die of metal poisoning.

"Wanna sit in the back?" Liv whispered. "I can fill you in on what you missed Saturday night."

I shook my head and dragged her to the front row of seats. If Molly was going to hit the stage, I wanted to keep an eye on her. Figuratively speaking.

"Really?" she asked teasingly, plopping down next to me in the center seats. "You don't even want to hear the part about Molly trying the nachos at the rink, and how she might be lactose intolerant?"

"Disgusting," Nessa added before she slid into the seat next to Liv. The dim house lights gave her wide brown eyes a naughty gleam. "You're lucky you missed it."

I practically had to weld my lips together to keep from

laughing. At least two-thirds of my friends knew what it took to make a girl feel better.

"Quiet, please!" Sean hopped off the stage and sat next to Nessa. The house lights dimmed and two spotlights skittered across the stage before they found Molly and Quinn. In the background, one of the trees burped. "Whenever you're ready, folks. We'll pick up in Havana, on the bottom of page forty-seven, with Molly's line."

Kacey's line! I wanted to yell. I also wanted to point out that Molly was definitely not supposed to be standing that close to Quinn. Why wasn't Nessa doing her job and directing her back a few steps?

"Still, you MUST think I'm a terrible PRUDE," Molly's voice rang out, clear and confident. Her fuzzy outline leaned closer to Quinn's fuzzy outline. So close she could probably smell his bodywash. I dug my nails into the wooden armrests, trying to conjure up the smell from memory. Nothing.

"I don't know *what* you are," Quinn flirted.

A *fake, backstabbing, scene-stealing, lactose-intolerant UNDERSTUDY!* Why was I always the only one who understood the truth about people?

"You *must* think I'm *something*." Oh, no. Molly was using the exact same voice she used to ask Jake Fields to the sixth-grade Halloween Hoedown. And they ended up disappearing for a good four minutes in the middle of the dance. When she came back? There was straw in her hair. Just saying.

"Yeah, you're *something* all buttoned up," Quinn observed, like the stage directions were forcing him to talk in the hottest voice ever. Quinn was acting like it didn't matter that I was dying of laryngitis, or that my best friend didn't need any convincing to steal my part. He was saying his lines like nothing had changed. "All except one button."

Then something bizarre happened. As Quinn's hand neared the zipper of Molly's black hoodie, the scene switched into slow motion. Instead of watching Quinn reach for Molly for two seconds, I had to watch it for at least eight. Which was probably why this happened:

"CUUUUUUUUUUUUUT!" I screamed. And then I was on my feet, and rushing the stage, and the spotlight was on Quinn and me, like usual. Only this time, Molly was standing between us.

Molly's jaw dropped and crimson invaded her cheeks.

"Kacey," she said to the floor. "Quinn and I are in the middle of a scene. You said you didn't want to do it." Even though she wasn't looking at me, her voice was stronger than I'd ever heard it. No abbreviations. No asking for a second opinion.

"Thought I'd give my *underthtudy* a little help," I spat, the spotlight coaxing sweat from my pores. *Oh, no. The lisp.* But it was too late to back down.

"Kacey?" More than anything, Molly sounded confused. "We'll talk. Later."

"*Later?*" When I sucked in, a few strands of my hair tangled in my braces. "You mean, after you wrap up *my* thene?"

"*What* is wrong with you?" Now she was looking directly at me.

"Are those braces?" Quinn shielded his eyes from the glare of my mouth. "Hard core." He chuckled. "Didn't know you were into heavy metal."

"I'm FINE." My fists clenched at my side. "And you? You're perfect for what you are . . . an UNDERTHTUDY. Don't forget that *I'm* the lead. And that won't change."

"Girls!" Sean stood up, as if anyone was going to listen to a government teacher at a time like this. "That's enough."

"Um, ew." Molly lifted the hem of her top and dabbed at her forehead, as if I'd soaked her with spit from my lisp. Drama queen. "Does anybody have some hand sanitizer?" she asked the crowd.

Laughter peppered the first few rows of the auditorium.

"Thtop it," I choked.

Now everyone was laughing. I tried to catch my breath, but couldn't. She wasn't doing this to me. She couldn't be, after everything I'd done for her, all the ways I'd helped her, including suffering a concussion to make *her* party cooler.

"Cut!" Sean yelled.

I shoved past Molly and Quinn and flew down the steps. *Please don't fall. Please don't fall.* From somewhere far away, Sean was calling my name, but I kept going. Molly could try all she wanted to humiliate me, but no one could force me to sit there and take it.

I shoved through the auditorium doors and made it into Silverstein before the tears came, making me feel even more stupid and completely alone. I hadn't cried since . . . since Dad left.

"Hey, Sarah Brown."

I whirled around.

"Thkinny Jeanth?" I wheezed, doubling over to catch my breath. My eyes teared up again and his blue streak ran like watery ink.

"Zander," he corrected me. He was wearing a Beatles T-shirt over a brown waffled henley. He might as well have worn a sign around his neck that read POSEUR. "And you're Kacey. Kacey Simon?"

Not anymore.

"So. Tough rehearsal, huh?" His voice was soft. He hooked his thumbs in the belt loops of his jeans and took a step forward.

"Whatever." I shrugged.

"Yeah," he said thoughtfully, like I'd just said something super deep and he had to think it over. After a while, he said, "I used to have braces, too. They're not so bad once you get used to them."

"Right," I snapped, finally looking at him. "Only by the time I get *uthed to them*, I'll be fired from the play."

"No way, man." Skinny Jeans said emphatically. "You definitely won't lose your part."

I shook my head. "You didn't thee what happened in there."

"So? I heard you singing the other day, and you're really good."

"Um, maybe you haven't heard my little thpeech impediment?" I hated myself a little more every time I opened my mouth.

"Oh, yeah." S.J. shrugged. "That goes away after a while. Plus, you don't have a lisp when you sing. It's weird."

My chin dropped to my chest. "Whatever. Do you have a point?"

"Actually, yeah." S.J. dropped his arms to his sides and took a step toward me. Was he going to *hug* me? Oh. My. God. "I'm, ah, looking for a lead singer for my band. You . . . interested?"

Worse than a hug. An invite to hang out with him and his freak friends. Not even I had sunk that low. I scanned the hallway to make sure no one had overheard the invitation. This was how terrible rumors got started.

Luckily, Silverstein was empty.

"Uh, no." I ducked past him. "I'm thwamped. Beginning now."

"Need company?" he called after me.

"Not from you!"

"Closest door's at the other end of the hall." His laugh was raspy, like he'd been yelling.

"I'm taking the THENIC ROUTE," I yelled back. Kacey Simon, getting a pep talk from *Skinny Jeans*? Please. Not in my lifetime. I picked up the pace, refusing to give him the satisfaction of looking over my shoulder. At least I could still make a decent exit.

A JURY OF HER PEERS
Tuesday, 10:05 A.M.

The next morning, I trudged down Hemingway alone, head down, while the rest of the student body herded to second period in groups. When no one was looking, I sneaked my glasses from my messenger back and slid them on.

In my defense, I *had* to. Mom made me triple swear on my broadcast career last night, after Sean called her to break the news about my rehearsal meltdown. She had told him about my glasses, so if I showed up to class without them, I'd be in serious trouble.

So I'd caved, and tried my hand at geek chic. I'd whipped my hair into a high, messy bun. My cropped black pencil trousers fell just above my silver Converse. I'd tucked in a white silky tank and cinched my fitted red cardigan with a skinny snakeskin belt.

And then, there were the glasses.

My steps slowed the closer I got to Sean's American government class. In the absence of some sort of miracle, I needed a mantra. Something to get me through the day until I figured a way out of this mess. Liv was amazing with mantras. But since she hadn't called or texted since rehearsal yesterday, I was on my own. So far, all I'd come up with was *I will never say any word that begins with, ends with, or otherwise involves the letter* s.

When I reached the door, I gave the metal handle a reluctant twist. I could feel the ugly brownish-orange frames on the bridge of my nose mocking me. Waiting to reveal themselves to the entire class. I took a sharp breath and stepped inside.

"Morning, Kacey." Sean looked up from his papers, but he didn't smile. "Feeling better, I hope?" His left eyebrow inched over his black-rimmed frames, broadcasting his disapproval.

"M-morning." My entire body went hot, then cold as I waited for my classmates to point at my glasses. But oddly, no one looked at me. Every single kid in the class was hunched over an iPhone, BlackBerry, or cell.

"Burn." Quinn Wilder snorted at his Droid screen.

In the back row, Molly squealed with laughter, her volume turned up about ten decibels too loud. Liv and Nessa huddled in close to her, snickering. Wait. Why was Nessa sitting in *my seat?*

What was going on?

As if she'd heard my silent question, Paige turned around and stared directly at me. Through her glasses, I could see her brown eyes widen, then seem to melt. She pursed her lips together in a small smile and tilted her head slightly.

My banana milkshake churned in my stomach the second I recognized the expression.

Paige Greene . . . pitied me.

I broke her gaze. This was the girl who used to hold protest marches in my kitchen on Saturday mornings when we ran out of orange juice. The girl who went on a hunger strike for a full forty-five minutes until my mom and dad both promised to vote in the neighborhood watch association's midterm elections. This was a girl who'd been wearing glasses for years, without even realizing they were ruining her life. Didn't she have enough causes to worry about without pitying me?

The seat next to Liv was empty. I sat down and, like the rest of my classmates, pulled out my cell and stared at the screen. Zero texts. Zero messages. Zero clues. Not only was my phone cold, it was silent, which was more than I could say for everybody else's. Jumbled sound was leaking out of various phones at different volumes. Liv leaned away from me, so far over Molly's desk that she was practically falling out of her chair.

"Hey." With the toe of my sneaker, I nudged her gold coin ankle bracelet. "What—up?"

I chomped down on my lip. *What up? Come on, Simon. Get it together.*

Liv straightened up immediately. "Oh, hey, girl. Nothing." Her eyes flitted across my face, resting everywhere but my glasses. "Cool . . . accessories?" she said uncertainly. If she thought I didn't see her kick Molly under the desk, she was wrong.

"Molly?" I pressed. "What're you guys looking at?"

Molly's head snapped toward us. She shuddered when her eyes fell on mine, like she'd just gotten a chill. "When did *those* happen?" she blurted, flicking her braided pink streak indignantly away from her face.

"Molly!" Nessa smacked Molly's desk, then shrugged apologetically at me.

"They're temporary," I said tightly. At least one of my friends had the decency to give it to me straight. "Like the brac— my . . . mouth problem."

Then I reached across Liv's desk and snatched Molly's phone from her grasp.

"You don't want to do that." Liv made a halfhearted

grab for the cell, but I turned quickly, using my body as a barricade. "It's nothing. Really."

"Morning, Marquette." My tiny image glowed in an open YouTube window. Liv's oversized flannel flower was bobbing in the bottom corner. "And welcome to this week's edition of—"

"*Thhhhhhhimon Thhhhhheettttttthhhh*," an unidentified female voice lisped over my moving lips. My banana milkshake did a three-point turn in my stomach and sped toward the back of my throat. I swallowed.

"I'm—"

"*Kaaaaytheeee Thhhhhhimon.*"

"—here to—"

"*Give you people adviiithhhhhhh.*"

I gripped the phone harder, the rhinestone snowflake decals pricking my skin like tiny blades.

"Okay. Phones off. Let's go ahead and get started," Sean said.

But I didn't budge. I wanted to. I wanted to throw Molly's phone on the floor and stomp it into oblivion. Torch it. Throw it out the window. Whatever I had to do to MAKE THE LISPING STOP. But for some reason, my body refused to listen to my brain. My eyes stayed on the razor-sharp image of my public humiliation. Why had I picked today, of all days, to start seeing clearly?

"Kacey. Phone off, please, or it's mine." Sean hovered over my desk, extending his outstretched palm. Seconds later, I felt the phone slide out of my grip, and then it disappeared into the pocket of Sean's khakis.

"Great," Molly hissed. "Thanks, Kacey."

Did I hear a lisp, or was my brain playing tricks on me? My glasses started to fog. *Stop. Don't let them do this to you.*

Sean headed for the white SMART Board behind his desk and uncapped a red dry erase marker. "Today, we're going to see what the court system looks like in action by reenacting a legal case study."

A few rows ahead, Quinn yawned, as if I hadn't just been ripped to shreds on the Web. How could a guy with hair that soft be so callous? The snakeskin belt around my hips felt like an actual python, squeezing the life out of me. Maybe Quinn didn't like me after all. Maybe he never had.

Liv nudged my chair leg apologetically, but I pretended not to feel it. *Traitor.*

"Under your desks, you have a mock trial transcript with your role highlighted in yellow." Sean rolled up the sleeves of his plaid button-down. "We'll act out day one of the trial and break into small groups for discussion tomorrow."

Everyone reached under their desks. My packet said *Witness #1.* On any other day, I would have believed I deserved a much better part, like the prosecutor, or the judge. Now, I wished I'd been assigned the role of *Invisible Girl.*

Sean pointed out everyone's places. Molly, the judge, settled into Sean's desk and Liv and Nessa huddled together in the jury box, while I crowded behind all the other bit parts at the back of the class.

"We'll start with the prosecution's opening statement," Sean said.

"That's me," Paige piped up, throwing her shoulders back. She turned to face the jury box. "Good morning, ladies and gentlemen of the jury." She overacted her entire statement, wrapping up with, "The prosecution calls Kacey Simon to the stand."

"*That'th you,*" whispered a guy's voice somewhere to my left. I stomped to the front of the room and slammed into the chair next to Sean's desk. My glasses tumbled down the bridge of my nose, and I shoved them back with my index finger.

"Raise your right hand?" Imran Bhatt the Bailiff said authoritatively.

I lifted my right hand. It was shaking.

"I, Kacey Simon, do solemnly swear . . ."

My vision blurred. *No. I can't use the letter* s. I pursed my lips over my braces, but my mouth wouldn't close all the way. The sharp metal dug into the backs of my lips.

"I, Kacey Simon, do solemnly swear . . ." Imran repeated loudly.

"I . . . K-Kaythee Thimon, do tholemnly thwear—" I half choked, half whispered.

The classroom went so quiet, I could hear the creak of the radiator under the window.

"To tell the truth, the whole truth, and nothing but the truth, so help me—"

A weird gurgling noise escaped my throat. I glanced pleadingly at Sean, but he just nodded.

"To tell the truth, the whole truth, and nothing but the truth, tho—"

Someone snorted in the back of the room.

"Order!" Molly whacked the edge of Sean's desk with her rolled-up script. "Let the witness . . . talk!"

I glanced over at her, grateful until I saw that her shoulders were shaking. Her lips were twitching, trying not to break into a smile. In the jury box, Liv and Nessa shielded their mouths with their scripts.

I stared, disbelieving, while Molly leaned back in her chair, drinking in my humiliation. Her blue eyes sparkled, the way they always had when I'd said something hilarious about one of the unfortunates at Marquette. And now, she was the one . . . *I* was the . . .

I couldn't even finish the thought.

The trial in Sean's class might just have gotten under way, but the trial in my head was already over. And the verdict was guilty. For everybody. Including my so-called friends, who hadn't even *faked* being mad about the You-Tube thing. How many times had I saved Molly from wearing some stupid horseback riding/parallel bars– flipping/figure-eight skating outfit to school? Or made one of Liv's designs so popular she completely sold out? Or helped Nessa study for a test so she could keep her one-hundred average?

"Okay, let's keep going," Sean said as a few more giggles rose at the back of the class.

My frames were burrowing into my skin, getting heavier with each passing second. I tore them off. But not before I caught a glimpse of Paige, standing alone behind the prosecutor's desk. She stared at me for a few seconds, then blinked like she might cry. Quickly, I lowered my eyes to the desk in front of me. MT RJ was carved in the very center.

It might as well have read U R OVR.

THE WRITING'S ON THE STALL
Tuesday, 3:13 P.M.

The door to the girls' bathroom had barely closed behind me when the tears started. Actually, they were more like choking sobs, magnified by the gray tiled floor and empty metal stalls. I stumbled into the second stall, locked the door, and curled onto the seat.

Somehow, I'd managed to get to last period without anyone seeing me cry. During lunch, I'd hidden away in the studio, picking out a *Simon Says: Greatest Clips* reel for Thursday's broadcast so I wouldn't have to show my face on air. But when last period came and I got a pink slip from the school psychologist's office in front of the whole class, I couldn't take it anymore. So I left. In the middle of class. Which would inevitably result in another pink slip. Fingers crossed, I'd get expelled.

The clang of the final bell cut through my gasps. I wiped my glasses on my cardigan sleeve and plucked the last remaining square of toilet paper from the roll. When I blew my nose, snot soaked through the tissue and slimed my fingers.

"Awethome," I muttered, wiping my hands on my jeans.

"—just *left* like that, right in the middle of class." The bathroom door creaked open, and noise from the hallway invaded my sanctuary. "It's like she's gone psycho or something."

Molly. Sucking in my breath, I lifted my sneakers off the floor and planted them silently on the toilet seat. Through the crack in the stall, I watched a pink streak and a sliver of a black mesh V-neck pause at the middle sink.

"She just suffered a major social trauma," Nessa's voice countered evenly. "Actually, she suffered, like, six."

Fresh tears stung the inside corners of my eyes.

"Psychologically speaking, it makes sense that she would wig out," she continued. A pair of high-waisted knit pants, her unfortunate souvenir from last semester's London trip, slipped past my peephole. What were those pants doing in daylight? Had I not explained that knits were even more unforgiving than I'd be if she ever wore those in public? Was she blatantly disregarding my fashion opinion? "Diagnostically speaking, I'd say she suffers from a raging case of P.U.F.D."

"What's that?" Molly giggled.

"Pretty Ugly Freak Disorder," Nessa said gravely. "There's no known cure. And it's contagious."

"Ew!" Molly gasped.

I swallowed a sob and squeezed my knees to my chest, wondering how small I'd have to make myself before I could disappear entirely. I couldn't believe Nessa would talk about me like that. My hands shook with rage.

Liv's ankle bracelet jangled as she hoisted herself onto the sink. "Don't you kind of feel bad for her, though? It's like The Universe is coming down on her."

"She *deserves* it!" The heel of Molly's moto boot collided with the floor. "Have you forgotten how mean she's been lately? Or, like, always?" Her voice grew louder.

Liar! I fought the urge to cover my ears, to block the sound of her voice from my brain. *I've never been anything but honest!*

"Nessa. Remember that time she told you it was a really good thing you spoke three languages, because it would help guys forget about the fact that you still don't have boobs?"

"I have a boyish figure," Nessa said tightly. "Kacey said it was *chic*."

"And then she e-mailed you a coupon for a push-up bra," Liv reminded her.

That. Was. A. FAVOR.

"And Liv," Molly said. "Remember when you wanted to start a style blog?"

"Yeah." Liv's voice was soft. I shifted forward in my seat. "She said nobody else would ever be able to pull off my style so I should stick to designing accessories. It was a compliment."

"No, she *said*," Molly went on, "that your accessories speak louder than your typos."

"Yeah! And didn't she say telling people to raid their grandparents' closets wasn't good 'style advice'?" Nessa interrupted.

"That's because their grandpas aren't as cool as mine," Liv grumbled.

I chomped down on the inside of my cheek. Of all people, my so-called friends should've understood. I'd always told them the truth because I loved them! Would a real friend let Nessa roam the halls with the body of a sixth-grade boy? No. And would a true gal pal let Liv blog about how she *chose* to wear her grandpa's clothes? Never!

"See what I mean?" Molly's boots squeaked across the tiles as she paced. "She says all this really mean stuff, and then tells us she's being honest for our own good. And we're supposed to thank her for it?"

A cold sweat had practically shellacked the shrink's pink slip to my palm. How could Molly be so ungrateful when we were supposed to be best friends? We'd even bought friendship bracelets last year without telling the other girls. Mine was on my bedside table. I wondered if Molly had ditched hers already.

"Not me," Nessa said fiercely. "Not anymore."

"I still say she's trying to help," Liv held out. "But . . ." She sighed. "What goes around, comes around."

"Exactly," Molly agreed. Finally, she stopped pacing. "And do you really want to be hanging around her now that it's payback time?"

I'd never heard Molly talk like this, ever. Her voice was so strong . . . so confident. Was she really trying to take over? To *replace* me?

"Honestly, girls? I'm done. And unless you want to go down with her, you will be, too."

"Done?" Liv echoed. The word hung heavy in the air. Suddenly, it felt like Molly had knocked the wind out of me. I couldn't breathe. *Done.*

"Do *you* want to end up on YouTube?" Molly asked.

"No," Liv said quietly. "But what if she—"

"Realistically, what's she gonna do now?" Nessa said.

"Yeah. Nobody cares what she thinks anymore, anyway," Molly observed. "Not after this morning."

"True." Liv hopped down from the sink. Her ankle bracelet sounded like shackles.

"Come on, girls. We're gonna be late for rehearsal." Molly shuffled toward the door and pulled it open.

Done. The Sharpie graffiti on the back of the stall door began to swim as a fresh batch of tears flooded my eyes.

Wait! I wanted to scream. *You have it all wrong!*

My lips parted slightly, but nothing came out. And then the door closed, and I was left utterly, completely alone.

THE DOCTOR IS IN
Tuesday, 3:42 P.M.

THE ONLY NORMAL PEOPLE ARE THE ONES YOU DON'T KNOW VERY
WELL.

Underneath the bumper sticker on the school psychologist's door was a scratched brass nameplate that read
PHILIPPA MEYERS, PSY.D.

"Come in!" A low, soft voice sounded from inside, even
though I hadn't knocked. "Door's open."

Was the shrink psychic? I bit my lip and pushed the
door open. If nothing else, maybe she could tell me if
there was a chance Molly would ever speak to me again.

Inside, the office reminded me of an incense store in
Edgewater that Liv dragged me to last year, when she
wanted to cast a spell on her middle sister for wearing her
favorite flats without asking. Woven tapestries hung on

the light purple walls, and a trickling stone fountain sat on the low table between the couch and the shrink's chair. Dusty stacks of books were piled around the perimeter of the room, and two framed prints that looked like giant ink spills hung over the couch.

The shrink sat in a tufted mustard-colored armchair. She didn't look up right away. She was reading the *Trib* (plus one—she kept up with the news) and sitting barefoot in lotus pose (minus one—that reminded me of Liv). A trio of candles burned on the side table next to her, releasing light wisps of lavender into the room.

"Hello?" I shut the door behind me and readjusted my glasses. Lavender was supposed to be relaxing, right? So why did I feel like I could throw up at any second? "I, um, got a pink . . . paper? I'm Kaythee Thimon?" I wiped my nose on the back of my cardigan sleeve.

"Kacey! Of course." The shrink hopped to her feet. Instead of a middle-aged woman dressed head-to-toe in Chico's, she was young. And short, close to my height. If I'd seen her in the halls, I'd probably have thought she was in ninth. When she smiled, a tiny diamond nose stud glinted in the dim light of the paper lanterns hanging over our heads.

I perched on the edge of the brown leather couch. Was I supposed to lie down and start talking about my mother?

The shrink settled back into her chair without saying anything. She just waited, like *I* was the one who'd pink-slipped *her*.

"Am I in trouble, Doctor . . . M?" I blurted out.

"Phil," she corrected me, propping her feet next to the brass Buddha on the table. "You can call me Phil."

I waited for her to laugh. She didn't.

"*Dr. Phil?*" I snorted. "No way."

"Just Phil." She wiggled her bare toes. "I've always hated my full name. Ever since I was a kid." She reached for a steaming mug on the side table. "But you were saying?"

"Nothing." I shook my head. "I have to go. I'm late for rehear— um, the auditorium." Even though the thought of seeing the girls and Quinn Wilder made me want to enroll in a Swiss boarding school, the play was all I had left now.

"Rough day?" Phil guessed.

I shrugged. "Whatever."

"Just a hunch." And then she winked. Ew. Was that supposed to make me like her?

She took another long sip from her mug and stared at me.

I stared back. Two could play this game, sister.

Finally, there was a knock at the door.

"Come on in, Sean," called Dr. Phil.

Sean? My head whipped toward the door.

"Sorry I'm late." Sean popped his head in. The wall hanging on the back of the door fluttered when he closed the door behind him.

"Mind if I sit?" he asked. As if the opinion of Witness #1 really mattered.

I begrudgingly scooted over. "Why aren't you in the auditorium?" I asked, eyeing him suspiciously.

He settled in next to me. "Actually, I cancelled rehearsal this afternoon." He opened his mouth like he was going to say something else, but didn't.

I glanced warily at Dr. Phil.

"Kacey," she began, "we asked you here because Sean has some news he'd like to share, and he thought it might be helpful for the two of you to process that news here, in the safety of the office." She propped her elbow on her knee and cupped her chin in her hand. "Sean?" she prompted. "Whenever you're ready."

I pinched a silver sequin on the throw pillow in my lap until it bent. My lips were getting drier by the second. I would have killed for some Burt's right about then.

"Kacey." Sean shifted to face me and clasped his hands together in his lap. His ugly brown corduroys blended in with the couch. "After yesterday's rehearsal . . . and class this morning . . . I've been thinking we should chat."

"Um, okay."

"I'm just not sure that with your latest . . . *changes* . . . it's in the best interest of the show for you to play Sarah Brown." Sean fake-coughed into his fist.

I jerked my head toward Phil, then back to Sean. He wasn't serious. He couldn't be . . . *serious*. Any second now, he was going to take it back. Apologize for making such a horrific joke. Tell me I was being punked for the school's new hidden camera show. I didn't care, as long as the role of Sarah Brown was still mine.

The room was silent. The second hand on the clock over the door mocked me with every tick. *Lo-ser. Lo-ser. Lo-ser.*

"You're *firing* me?" My voice was barely a whisper. "For having bratheth and glatheth?" It felt like a weight was pressing down on my chest, making it impossible for me to breathe. Didn't he understand? The play was the only thing I had left! If he took that away, he took away Quinn, and those little shivers I got every time I saw him. He took away inside jokes with the girls, hours spent hanging in the wings together trying on costumes and gossiping. He took away any chance of making up with them. Of things ever going back to normal. My body went burning hot, then icy cold. I shuddered.

"I'm so sorry, Kacey."

"Pleath." The sound of my lisp made my hands start to tremble. I hated myself for that stupid lisp. Sean was right: I didn't deserve the lead. Didn't deserve Quinn, or my friends. Pretty soon, he'd take away *Simon Says*, too. Not that I'd ever go on the air sounding like this.

"Listen, Kacey." Sean leaned forward earnestly, rubbing the dark chin scruff he'd been trying to grow all semester. "You have an incredible voice. Everybody knows it."

I shook my head. The day's humiliation welled up inside of me, hardening into anger. I stared at a tiny blue ink stain on Sean's shirt pocket.

"Under any other circumstances, I'd love to have you star in the show," Sean continued. He took off his glasses and wiped them on his shirt, leaving sweat stains on the fabric. "But . . . I'm thinking I should recast Molly as the lead."

"*Molly?*" I exploded, releasing the sequined pillow to the floor. Now he'd gone too far. Maybe I couldn't stop him from taking everything away from me, but handing it all over to *Molly*? Could. Not. Happen.

"She *is* your understudy," Sean reminded me.

"You *can't*! It'th not fair!"

"Kacey, I absolutely want you onstage," Sean insisted. "You know that."

I shook my head furiously, the frizzed ends of my loose bun whipping me in the face. Until five minutes ago, I'd known a lot of things. That I was the lead. The one and only girl in the seventh grade who could say she'd kissed Quinn Wilder. Rumor had it there was a girl in eighth who could make that claim. But real journalists don't deal in rumors.

"I've recast you in another role, if you're up for it," Sean offered weakly.

"*Up* for it?" Now he wanted me to *watch* Molly take over my life? I jumped to my feet, but was suddenly light-headed. The candles, and the humiliation, and the fact that I hadn't eaten solid food in days must have been catching up to me.

"Careful." Sean gripped my arm, guiding me back to the couch. "Listen. How about Dancing Die Number Three?" He said it brightly, like he was offering me the lead all over again. "I'm sure the other two would be happy to get you up to speed on choreography."

My breath caught in my throat. "*OVERTHITHED DANTHING DIE NUMBER THREE?*" I shrieked. "You want me to hop around in a giant foam rubber die coth-tume in the background?" I'd transfer first. Seriously. Switzerland. Or maybe a country that didn't start with the letter *s*. "Doeth Molly know yet?"

"She does," Sean admitted. "I told her this morning."

Suddenly, it all made sense. How Molly had gotten the courage to convince the other girls to defect. How she'd suddenly become so strong. She'd known she was about to be cast in the lead. She'd known the whole time.

"Kacey." Phil's voice dropped an octave. "Could I ask you to sit down, please?"

"Do I have a choith?" I wailed. I hadn't even realized I was standing.

Phil nodded. "Always."

Fuming, I dropped to the couch and stared at my bug-eyed reflection in the Buddha's bald, brass head.

"Have you ever heard the saying 'There are no small parts, only small actors?'" Sean asked me after a long pause. "You know who said that?"

"An underthtudy?"

"Konstantin Stanislavksy," Sean corrected me. "A pretty awesome director. His point is that every role is important. Think about that while you decide whether to take me up on the offer."

"Do you think you could do that, Kacey?" Phil leaned forward and caught my eye. Hers were a deep blue-green color, almost the color of mine when I wasn't wearing contacts. "Why don't you take some time to sit with this? Let Sean know in a couple days?"

"I've thought about it," I choked, standing up. "And my anther ith NO."

Without looking at Sean or Phil, I found my way to the door and stormed out. My head was throbbing; my eyes were dry. There were no more tears. I had nothing left.

TOGETHER AGAIN, FOR A LIMITED TIME . . .
Tuesday, 5:37 P.M.

At the Fullerton stop, I dragged my El card through the scanner and bumped my way through the turnstile. Rush hour had just started, so the stairs and icy platform were packed with commuters wearing dark overcoats and carrying shiny leather briefcases. I nudged my way through the crowd to the edge of the platform and checked my watch. If I didn't make it home in time to watch Ella so Mom could get to the studio, she'd kill me. Maybe that would be the easiest way out.

A bright white spotlight swung across the platform when the train sped down the track, reflecting off my braces. Liv would say The Universe was spotlighting me in the crowd, singling me out. Showing everyone what a gigantic loser I'd become.

The wind was brutal, sweeping through my sweat-matted hair and numbing my face. Even with the protection of my glasses, my eyes were starting to water. When the doors opened, I dove past a sour-looking woman in nude pantyhose to snag the first seat by the door.

The lady huffed loudly, highlighting the frosted beige lipstick caked on her two front teeth. It was the kind you'd find in the bargain bin at the drugstore that probably had a name like Iced Mocha. It made her teeth look three shades yellower than they already were. The old Kacey Simon would have suggested a nice tooth-whitening treatment, or a sheer berry shade. But the old Kacey Simon was slipping away.

"Hold the doors!" a frantic voice called from the platform. A few seconds later, a wobbly green foam board teetered into the car. The slogan GO GREENE: PAIGE GREENE FOR EIGHTH-GRADE PRESIDENT was printed neatly on the board with sweeping gold glitter. The board tilted to the left, then did a sweeping arc at the front of the car, backhanding Iced Mocha. "Oops! Sorry."

I cringed and sank low in my seat. I hadn't seen Paige since the mock trial, and if she shot me one more pitying smile, I was going to lose it in public.

"Kacey?" Paige dropped the giant poster and peered over the top. Her glasses were foggy from the heat of the car. "Hey!"

"Oh, hey." I pretended to read the backlit ads on the other side of the car. Mom's new promo shots were up, because unlike me, she was getting more popular by the second. The caption under her headshot read *Channel 5: The Station with the Sterling Reputation.* It would have been perfect. Except . . . I cleaned my glasses on the hem of my coat and looked again. Someone had given Mom a mustache with a gold marker. And—

"Is that a wart?" Paige wedged the campaign poster between the doors and my seat, gripping the nearest metal pole as the train lurched forward. Her glasses slipped down the bridge of her nose and settled at the tip. She shoved them into place again. "Because that qualifies as vandalism. Or, in Illinois, malicious mischief. Punishable by up to six years in prison." In addition to her political ambitions, Paige also planned on going to law school.

I didn't even have the energy to blow her off.

"Hey. Remember Benny Dorchester?" Paige waggled her scraggly brows.

I nodded. Paige's law school kick started back in kindergarten, when Benny D. vandalized her cubby with sidewalk chalk and Miss Elaine refused to do anything about it. Paige swore on the spot that the next time Benny felt like "expressing himself" on her property, she'd sue the sidewalk chalk right out of his chubby little fist.

"He still lives down the street, you know. He's actually kinda cute now."

"No way." I snorted. "He dyed hith hair with red Kool Aid and tattooed hith neck!"

"I have eccentric taste. Sue me!" She grinned, then reached into the sagging canvas tote hanging from the crook of her arm. She pulled out a plastic button with her face and campaign slogan printed on it. "What do you think?" She lobbed the button in my direction.

I surveyed Paige's photo-op smile, which was almost as crooked as her bangs. The button reminded me of the ones she'd made in fifth, right before I ditched her. Just like . . . Molly was ditching me now. I swallowed.

"Cool," I said, quickly tucking it in my bag. Back in fifth, I had worn Paige's pin. This was seventh. Things were different now.

"Kacey?" Paige nestled the tote bag between her sneakers and leaned toward me. "Are you . . . is something up? How come you're heading home so late?"

My cheeks flamed and I averted my eyes. "Meeting for the play."

"Oh. I thought I heard that you . . . had to leave the cast," she said carefully. The softer her voice got, the more it sounded like she was feeling sorry for me.

I clenched my jaw. News traveled fast—and wrong,

when I wasn't the one to spread it. "I wath offered a new role. Temporarily. But I turned it down."

"So now Molly Knight's the lead?"

"Temporarily," I repeated, a little louder this time.

"Okay." Silence. Specifically, judgmental silence.

"But I'm getting even with Molly," I said, suddenly desperate to make Paige stop looking at me like I was a stray puppy with a raging case of fleas. "Liv, too. All of them." I forced my mouth to close. Why did I suddenly care what Paige thought about me?

"How?" Paige's eyes narrowed skeptically behind her lenses.

"Um, by getting back the lead?" Why did that sound like a question?

"And then . . ." Paige prompted.

I stared out the window. City lights swam by in a liquid gold blur. I didn't remember the train ride ever taking this long. Not even the time I downed a sixty-four ounce Big Gulp after school and the train stalled on the tracks for twenty minutes. "What do you mean?"

"And then . . . what's your strategy?" she pressed. "Like, are you gonna sue them?"

"For what? Defamation of lithp?" The train finally slowed at Armitage, and I jumped up.

"A good campaign is all about strategy," Paige prattled

on as the train stopped and the doors opened. "You have to know exactly what you want, and what steps you're gonna take to get there. Plus, you have to have people you can trust in your corner. And it doesn't hurt if you can call in a few favors, either. You, especially. Your rep's taken a major hit, if you hadn't noticed." At the top of the stairs, she stopped to adjust her gloved grip on the poster. "Hold these," she ordered, extending the bag of buttons in my direction.

I took the bag with a sigh.

"So what is it you really want?" she asked in a clipped tone as we hustled outside.

"I told you. I want my part back." I braced myself against the cold.

"Wrong." Paige shook her head, her frayed ends flying around her face like one of those car wash mops. "You have to think big picture." She switched the poster board to her other arm and picked up the pace. "Like, you want your part back, but you probably also want your reputation back the way it was. Basically, you want your old life back. Am I right?"

I frowned. When she put it that way, it seemed a lot more complicated than just trading in my tortoiseshell frames for new contacts and learning how to pronounce the letter s again.

We rounded the corner onto Clark. "Don't feel bad. Not everybody can think like a politician," Paige assured me. "It's just because I'm used to it. Example: It's like, yeah, I want to get reelected for next year. But big picture? I want to be the first female president of the United States. See the difference?"

I didn't answer, but fell into step with the rhythmic jangling of the buttons at my side. For once, Paige was right. This was about way more than getting my part back. It was like Sean had said last week in rehearsal: Life imitates art. Meaning, if I was strong enough to reclaim my place as the lead in the play, I was definitely strong enough to take back the lead in life. I could get my friends back, my crush back, and best of all, my audience back.

When we reached our block, Paige gasped. "I just had," she announced, "a brilliant idea." She smacked the fence outside of her townhouse. The fence in front of our homes was still missing the third and fourth pickets from the time in fifth grade we knocked them out so we wouldn't have to mess with the finicky gate when we just had to see each other right away. "I could be your political strategist! Help you out of this rut!"

I opened my mouth to object.

"I could get you back to the top of the popularity food chain before opening night! It would be the biggest accomplishment of my political career." Her eyes shone with wild excitement.

"Paige," I scoffed. "*You* teaching me how to be popular again? Are you altho gonna teach me how to win a fifth-grade election?"

Paige recoiled.

It was a low blow. I knew it the second the words left my mouth.

"You don't have to get mad." I searched her face, but the glare from her porch light on her glasses made it impossible for me to see her expression.

"This," she said slowly, looking down at her scuffed black snow boots. "This is exactly why I decided . . . why we're not friends anymore." She didn't say it in a snarky way, like Molly would have. Instead, her voice just got soft. She sounded so small. Which somehow made me feel even worse. Still . . .

"*You* dethided?" I raised my left eyebrow. So I'd hurt her feelings. She didn't have to revise history.

Next door, light flooded the front stoop of my town-house, and Ella flounced through the doorway, wearing oven mitts on both hands. The tinfoil was gone, but Mom's old reading glasses were still propped on her nose, this time with masking tape wound around the bridge.

"KAYYYYCEEEEEE," she bellowed. "If you don't

come in right now, Mom's tightening your braces with the caaaaaan oooooopennnnnnnner!"

"COMING!" I yelled back.

"Heeeeey, Paige!" Ella waved, then slammed the front door.

"I'm doing it," Paige said sharply. "I'm getting you your part back."

I stared at her. "What? Why?"

"You'd have to do something for me, too. Quid pro quo. Once you're back in power, you have to use your popularity to make sure I get reelected. It's strictly business."

"Paige. You can't be theriouth." Not that it couldn't be done. It was just . . . me? And Paige? Did I really want to relive my elementary school years? Then again, if things kept getting worse, my elementary school years might start to look like the good old days. And peaking in elementary school would be million times worse than peaking in middle school.

"Quid pro quo." Paige shrugged matter-of-factly. "And then we go our separate ways for good." She stretched out her hand and leveled her eyes at me. "We'll meet at my house tomorrow night to plan. Do we have a deal?"

"Fine," I said, reluctantly shaking her outstretched palm. "Deal."

SAVING KACEY SIMON
Friday, 4:19 P.M.

Even with my eyes closed, I could feel Paige hovering approximately six inches from my chair. She smelled disgustingly sweet, which was what happened when you tried twelve different mall perfume samples at the same time.

"Okayokay," she breathed. "Opennnnn . . . NOW!"

I opened.

"Lemme thee." I grabbed the square handheld mirror Paige had swiped from the Sephora salesgirl at Water Tower Place, where we were in the early stages of executing Operation: Saving Kacey Simon. We'd spent hours in Paige's room the past few nights, crafting the perfect foolproof plan to get my popularity back. According to Paige, today was the day to strike.

I blinked at my hazy reflection. "I can't thee." Tiny drops of spit showered the glass.

"You need these." Paige rammed my glasses onto my face and my image sharpened.

I took a cautious second look. My auburn waves were perfectly smooth, thanks to the flyaway serum the salesgirl had recommended before she realized we weren't going to buy anything. Paige had dabbed dark chocolate eye shadow on the outer corners of my lids. It made the green in my eyes glow, so my glasses weren't even the first thing I saw.

"Well?" Paige leaned closer. Her black crocheted scarf smelled like a combination of honeysuckle, vanilla, and amber. My stomach turned. "Whaddya think?"

"I'm gonna need you to back up," I instructed my reflection. My cheeks were flushed from the cold, and I'd coated my lips with a sample of shimmery sugar gloss they were giving out at the front of the store.

If Mom had seen me, she would have killed me. In related news, I looked leading lady amazing.

I cracked a smile, but the reflection from my braces almost blinded me all over again. I groaned and closed my eyes.

"Would you stop? You look like a model." Paige's voice got a little louder, like it always did when she got excited about something. "A LensCrafters model, maybe."

I whacked her with the mirror.

"Listen, girls." The sleepy-eyed Sephora girl whose mirror we'd taken circled my chair for the fiftieth time. "Are you gonna buy anything, or . . ."

Paige jumped between us. "She's considering it. But just so you know? High-pressure sales situations don't work on us. I'm in politics, and she's in broadcasting. We thrive under pressure."

The salesgirl sighed and headed for the perfume wall.

I cracked up, showering everything within a six-inch radius.

"Ewwwww! Kacey!" Giggling, Paige leapt back, narrowly missing my spit shower.

I settled into the black vinyl makeup chair and kneaded the knot in my left shoulder, trying not to think about the last time I'd come to Water Tower Place. I'd been with Liv, raiding the sale section at Williams-Sonoma. The next day, she'd given me a gorgeous hammered-silver disc pendant made out of an antique-looking teaspoon. I only wore it on special occasions.

"Okay." Paige yanked up the sleeves of her black trench. "It's time for Phase One."

My stomach did a figure eight. I'd completely forgotten about Operation: SKS. Instantly, I felt humiliated and completely exposed. It was the same feeling I got after waking up from a nightmare where the curtain rose on Quinn and me on opening night. He was in costume. I was in nothing but underpants. Ella's *Sesame Street* underpants.

"Can't we jutht go home?" I stole one more look at myself in the mirror and lunged for a tissue.

"Nope." Paige shook her head vehemently. Then she pulled a folded piece of paper from the pocket of her trench and shoved it in my face. "Review."

Operation: Saving Kacey Simon (aka SKS)

PHASE ONE

Location: Water Tower Place, North Michigan Avenue
Time: 1600 hours
Targets: Molly Knight, Liv Parrillo, & Nessa Beckett
Sources: Facebook wall posts

Goal: Intercept ex-BFFs during cast party outfit expedition. Obtain binding verbal agreement on Phase Two from temporary group leader Knight (Code Name: Pink Poseur).

OBJECTIVES

- **Objective A:** Look amazing. Makeup and hair at Sephora by political image strategist Greene (Code Name: Prezzy G).

- **Objective B:** Appear cool, calm, and casual during "accidental run-in" with Pink Poseur. Try not to rip out her pink streak, trip her, or otherwise attract attention from mall security.
- **Objective C:** Fake being fine with temporary cast change. Lull Pink Poseur into false sense of superiority using any means necessary (flattery, bribes, etc.). Smile. Try not to rip out her pink streak, trip her, or otherwise attract attention from mall security.
- **Objective D:** AMBUSH PINK POSEUR.

MATERIALS

1. Map of Water Tower Place (enclosed) with likely hangouts for Pink Poseur and friends. According to confidential sources,* PP is searching for something "hard rock glam" to impress Z. Jarvis at cast party. Possible locations: Betsey Johnson, Bebe, Wet Seal, Forever 21.
   Stores to avoid: Chico's, Eileen Fisher, Everything Alpaca.
2. Blackmail materials if necessary, including embarrassing unretouched pics of PP after hair-scorching incident, "authentic" note from PP disclosing genetic predisposition to bacne, video footage of

PP's last skating competition, including slow-mo montage of falling scenes.

3. Proof of believable, nonhumiliating mall errand (winter clothes shopping list, permission slip to visit Sephora for on-air touch-up materials and/or stage makeup).

*Confidential sources = Pink Poseur's Twitter page, last updated 12:34 P.M.

"Paige. I don't know if thith will work." I stretched my lips tight over my braces. The odds here were not good. It was two against three. And Paige wasn't exactly an expert on popularity, so really it was one-point-five against three.

"Look at me." Paige gripped both my arms like she was going to shake me. "It's gonna work, as long as you *believe* it's gonna work. What's your motto?"

I glanced around the store. "Fake it 'til I make it," I mumbled.

"Right." Paige folded the plan and stuffed it back in her pocket. "Now let's move. According to Molly's last Twitter update, your friends will be here in . . ." She checked her watch. "T-minus three minutes."

"Ex-friendth," I corrected her miserably.

"Not for loooong!" Paige slipped her hand into mine and dragged me past the fake eyelash display and into the mall. My snow-caked sneakers squeaked against the shiny ivory floor.

We rode the escalator down three floors to Betsey Johnson, the setting on my stomach switching from mix to blend to liquefy. By the time we got to the second floor, it had reached turbo-powered purée.

The Betsey Johnson glass storefront displayed a row of mannequins flaunting silver-studded belts over loud, printed party dresses. At the entrance, two punk princess salesgirls hovered over a display of patent stilettos.

"Instructions: Find at least three items Molly would die for," Paige instructed, running her fingers over a row of jewel-encrusted handbags.

I lifted a hot pink dress with a black mesh sash from the nearest rack while Paige grabbed a purple taffeta mini dotted with tiny black skulls. Perfect. Molly was drawn to skulls like a magnet to . . . um . . . my mouth.

Once we were settled inside the biggest dressing room, there was nothing for me to do but wait. And try not to throw up. And breathe through my mouth to avoid the stench of patchouli-vanilla-hazelnut-sandalwood-cedar-mint perfume invading my personal space.

"Come on, try on your outfit!" Paige whispered, doing a quick twirl in front of the mirror. She winked at her reflection, then plopped down on the leopard-print calf-hair chaise against the wall. "It'll take your mind off things." In her sensible mousy hair, glasses, and skull-dotted mini, she looked completely mismatched. Like someone put the head of Scientist Skipper on the body of Disco-Punk Barbie.

". . . asked him if he wanted to come with me to the cast party, and maybe play a few songs." I heard Molly's voice, then the shuffle of footsteps and the crinkle of shopping bags.

"You actually said come with you?" Nessa sounded amazed and disapproving at the same time. "Gutsy."

"So? What'd he say?" Liv's vegan-friendly faux leather boots shuffled by.

"What do you think he said?" Molly sounded offended. The dressing room next door clicked open, then shut. "I mean, he said he was kind of busy, but he was obv just playing hard to get." Pause. "Ew. What is that *smell*?"

I stared at Paige, the blender in my stomach shifting into overdrive.

She blinked back, tapping the digital watch on her wrist.

Suddenly my shimmer gloss felt goopy, and the mascara on my lashes was weighing down my lids. I frantically shook my head *no*, but she just ticked numbers off her hand, like Carlos counting down to broadcast.

Three, two—

"REALLY?" she almost yelled, her lips just inches from the wall that separated our dressing room from my exes'. "Zander Jarvis asked you to be his lead singer? What'd you SAY?"

I coughed. "Um, I told him I'd think about it." Lie. "They're good and all, but I've had a lot of other offer—" *NO S's!* "—plural—and they'd be my fallback." *Lie.* "Quitting the play really freed me up for better opportunity—plural." *Lie.*

"Totally." Paige gave me a thumbs-up, her body quaking with silent giggles. But with every lie I told, my shoulders slumped farther down. What was I doing? Kacey Simon didn't lie to get ahead. She told the hard-hitting truth, even when it was uglier than skull-printed taffeta.

There was a heavy pause on the other side of the wall.

"Uh, K-Kacey?" Molly broke the silence first.

"Molly?" I widened my eyes in fake shock and met her in the dressing room hall. "What are you doing here?"

"We were just shopping for the cast party." Molly jammed her hands into the pockets of a pewter leather jacket, then took them out again and crossed them over her chest. "And Zander really loves this . . . kind of stuff." Her kohl-lined eyes flickered with uncertainty. "Right, girls?"

"Right, Mols." Popping out of the dressing room, Liv and Nessa answered in unison. Their voices sounded tired, the way Mom's did when Ella asked *but why?* a million times in five minutes.

"What?" Molly yanked her jacket zipper to her chin. "You don't think—"

"We're shopping for the cast party too," Paige cut her off, appearing at my side.

"Oh." One look at Paige, and Molly's face hardened. "So I guess extras are invited?" She flicked at her pink streak. "I wouldn't know."

Beneath her sleek pixie cut, Nessa's lips were pursed in a tight line, like she couldn't decide if she wanted to smile or frown. Liv rolled up the sleeves of her grandpa blazer, her eyes darting between mine and Molly's uncertainly. She looked like she was watching a tie-breaking lightning round at Wimbledon.

"So, um . . ." Molly unzipped her jacket, then zipped it again. "Did I hear something about you singing for Zander's band, or whatever?" *Unzip. Zip.*

I opened my mouth to respond. But my jaw locked when I saw the hammered silver teaspoon pendant around Molly's neck. I glanced at Liv, then Nessa. They each had one. My face felt hot.

"Yup," Paige jumped in loudly, throwing her arm around my waist. I tensed. "He's practically begging her."

"Paige." I forced an eye roll. The corners of my lips were starting to twitch with anger, and I pressed them together. Molly could fake cool all she wanted. But her flushed cheeks gave her away. "Haven't dethided."

"Do it," Molly said, too quickly. "Then maybe you guys could play the cast party. Since you probably won't get an invite otherwise."

I forced myself to take a deep breath and remain calm. *Big picture. Big picture. Big picture.*

"Oh, I'll be there," I assured her. "But you don't need me to get the band, right? Ithn't Zander your date?"

"Obv." Molly raked her fingers through her hair. When her skull ring got tangled in the ends of her extensions, she left her hand resting on her shoulder. "I mean, is that what he told you?"

"Ummmm . . ." I turned and squinted through my lenses at Paige, pretending to think. *One Mississippi, two Mississippi, three Mississippi.* I shook my head. "Nope," I said lightly. "Jutht begging me to be in the band."

Molly's face blanched.

"I'm sure he just forgot." Liv draped her arm over Molly's shoulder.

"*Forgot?*" Molly freed the ring from her hair, bringing a few long blonde strands with it and elbowing Nessa in the ribs.

"Ow!" Nessa snapped.

Just in time, the alarm Paige had set on my cell started buzzing.

I lifted an index finger, cutting off Nessa's whine. "Oh," I said, glancing at the screen.

"Who is it?" Molly said desperately.

"Lemme guess. Zander. Again," Paige jumped in.

"For like the tenth time today." I sighed and pocketed my cell. "I'll call him later."

Paige shot me a meaningful glance. "So . . . I should get changed. Meet you out front?"

"Yup." I tousled my waves as Paige shut the door to her dressing room. Then I tossed Molly a casual wave, fighting the urge to strangle her with her knock-off kitchenware necklace. "Good luck finding an outfit."

I spun on my heel and headed confidently for the door.

"Wait!" Molly squealed, right on cue. You could have wrung the desperation out of her voice. "So . . . um, Zander's really been calling you a lot?"

I turned back to face her. "And texting."

"Huh." Her brow crinkled. "Do you think . . . maybe you could give me, like, some pointersonhowtogethimtogowithmetothecastparty?" The last part she blurted out in record time.

Gotcha. Slowly, I held her gaze until her cheeks reddened again.

"I mean, I could do it on my own. But since he seems to value your opinion for whatever reason."

"I gueth. If I wanted."

Her face relaxed. "OhmygodTHANK—"

"In return for thomething, obv," I cut her off.

"W-what?" she blinked and looked down at the floor.

"I want back in. And I want the YouTube video gone."

"Umm . . ." Molly turned to her left and right, as if she was looking for Liv or Nessa to make the call. Typical.

"You're delusional." Nessa jutted out her chin defiantly. "Do you even know what's happened to your rep in the past few days?"

"The whole school saw that video." Liv looked genuinely confused. "We can't exactly erase their memories."

I ignored them. My business was with Molly. "We go back to normal," I informed her.

The recessed lighting highlighted Molly's fading pink streak. She bit her lip, tiny worry lines furrowing her brow. "Okaaay . . . but I want a date with him *before* the cast party, one-on-one. And I want him at the cast party, too."

"Done." I didn't care that my voice shook a little. The plan was working. It was actually *working*. "Not a problem. I'll get him for you."

"If you say so." Irritation pricked at Molly's voice.

"Getoutwhileyoustillcan!" Paige coughed from the dressing room.

Ordinarily, I didn't take advice from other people. It would be backward, sort of like the Rolling Stones asking Skinny Jeans for tips on the six string. But in this case I made an exception, and scurried out of Betsey Johnson before Molly Knight could change her mind.

BEGGARS CAN'T BE DRAMA QUEENS
Monday, 12:02 P.M.

The success of Phase One was a double-edged sword. On the bright side, Molly needed me now more than ever. And I had to give Paige credit: Using Skinny Jeans to lure Molly back to being friends with me was pure political genius.

On the downside, I'd completely forgotten how insufferable Paige got when she knew she was right.

"So you should review the Phase Two rundown again," Paige ordered Monday during lunch, as we hovered outside the double doors to the auditorium.

"My entire future dependth on it, Paige. I've got it down." I took a swig of grape Pedialyte, which was the only liquid Mom could find in the fridge that morning, and pressed my ear to the warped wood door. Silence.

"Didn't your Confidential Informant thay they'd be here

during lunch?" The fingerless metallic gold gloves Liv had knit for me last year were starting to make my palms sweat. Even though I'd decided on a strict no-LīVthreads wardrobe until she apologized, the gloves added a hard rock edge to my outfit, as did the fishnets under my ripped skinny jeans.

"They'll be here," Paige assured me. "My Algebra CI's never wrong. And she says the band rehearses in the auditorium every day during lunch."

I turned my back to the doors and slid to the floor.

"Are you sure you've got it?" Paige flopped down next to me and unzipped the front pocket of her backpack, pulling out a stack of green note cards at least three inches thick. They reminded me of Nessa. "I made cue cards if you need them. Maybe you should review one last time."

I sighed. Operation: SKS was almost as exhausting as rehearsal. Come to think of it, it was exactly as exhausting as rehearsal: lines to learn, props to remember, and a know-it-all director.

Operation: Saving Kacey Simon (aka SKS)

PHASE TWO

Location: Auditorium, Silverstein Hall, Marquette Middle

Time: 1200 hours

Targets: Zander Jarvis, Kevin Cho, Nelson Lund, and The Beat

Sources: Gravity Facebook page, Confidential Informant in Paige's Algebra II class

Goal: Accept Zander Jarvis's (Code Name: Zander) offer to front band, without appearing desperate. Fake being friends long enough to get him to date Molly.

OBJECTIVES

- **Objective A:** Flatter Gravity to butter them up. **Possible flattery points:**
- Hair dyed the color of blue crush berry punch is adorable and really brings out Zander's eyes. And the tapered pants? Slimming. In a . . . manly . . . kind of way.
  - Calling yourself by a name like "The Beat" is so not lame. It's kind of like Madonna, or Sting. And they're major rock icons.
  - Kacey just happened to be walking down the hall during lunch and heard what can only be described as musical innovation. WHAT? It was

Skinny Jeans's band? And they haven't signed a major record deal yet? Get. Out.

Objective B: Rock out hard enough that Zander totally owes Kacey a favor. Cash in said favor on Friday and Saturday nights, with a date for Molly (Code Name: Pink Poseur).

A cymbal crash clanged on the other side of the auditorium doors, followed by a drum roll and an electric guitar riff.

"It'th them!" I scrambled to my feet, my heart pounding.

"Commence Phase Two!" Paige thrust the deck of note cards into my hand.

"I told you, I don't need thethe." But I stuffed them in my back pocket anyway, my gloves soaking with sweat as I realized the enormity of my mission. What if Phase Two was a total flop? I had no backup plan, no other scheme to get Molly a date with Zander. My entire future rested on how the next two minutes played out.

"Kacey! Breathe," Paige ordered. "You got this."

I closed my eyes and took three deep, cleansing breaths until my pulse returned to normal. Okay. Gravity was no big deal. They were nothing, compared with the time Mom brought me as her dinner date for that fancy televised fund-raiser in New York and I accidentally (on purpose) TOUCHED MEREDITH VIEIRA'S HAIR during the second c-break.

"Meet me at Sugar Daddy after school to debrief." Paige whipped open the auditorium doors and shoved me inside. "NOW GO!"

I stumbled over the threshold into the seat closest to the doors. Most of the house lights were down, but a few spotlights glowed over the band onstage. Zander was lifting his guitar strap over his head, cradling the polished wood instrument like it was the Hope Diamond.

"So where do we want to start?" asked the kid hanging behind the keyboard. *Kevin Cho on bass, Nelson Lund on keyboard*, I reminded myself as Nelson bent over the keys and tried out a few chords.

"Pick up where we left off last night, Z?" Nelson shook a mussed blond curl out of his eyes. His gray T-shirt was ripped in three places. Probably on purpose.

"Yeah. Sure." Zander kept his head down, strumming a few chords.

"So you ever talk to that girl?" The Beat called from behind his black drum set. He tossed his drumsticks in the air and caught them without even looking up. "About the vocalist spot?"

I gripped the armrests.

"Yeah. Not interested," Zander said. "And she was kind of mean about it."

HONEST! She was honest! I squeezed the armrest even harder, until the feeling left my fingers entirely.

"Isn't she that drama queen on Channel M?" Kevin asked.

Top. Rated. Reporter. Not that I cared what these guys thought, but seriously. Get your facts straight, people.

Zander's lips thinned as he pressed them together. "Yeah. Not a good fit."

Why, because my hair color came from nature? I sucked in a deep breath and forced my fingers to uncurl. *Big picture. Big picture. Big picture.*

"Your call, Z." The Beat cracked his knuckles and picked up his drumsticks again. "And one. Two. Three. Four."

Gravity launched into a mellow piece with no vocals and I shifted in my seat, watching the guys jam out. Skinny Jeans had this strange, dreamy look on his face. His eyes were closed, and not once did he scan the stage to make sure he wasn't screwing up. It was like he didn't even realize he was playing in front of other people. I'd never seen anyone that relaxed on stage before. Not Mom at the news desk, not Quinn during our duet, and definitely not me. The whole point of performing was that you had an audience.

He looked so calm and at peace that suddenly watching him felt wrong, like I'd just walked in on him in his boxers or something. I focused my attention on the scuffed plate on the armrest, tracing the scratches in the brass until the song trailed off a few minutes later.

That was my cue. Gnawing at the cold sore inside my left cheek, I stood and moved slowly down the carpeted aisle, preparing for the biggest performance of my life. I debuted a close-lipped version of the Simon Smile. My character loved emo band boys, and it *so* didn't bother her when they talked about her behind her back. And she wanted to front this band more than she wanted these five-pound frames off her nose.

Aaaand . . . action.

I leaned against the aisle seat in the front row and tossed my hair over my shoulder. "I'm in."

Zander squinted down at me, his eyes flashing with something. Awe? Amazement? Annoyance?

"Well?" I pressed. "When are you rehearthing next?"

Zander rested his guitar gently against one of the speakers and tromped down the stairs. "What're you doing here?" His voice was clipped.

My left butt pocket sagged under the weight of Paige's note cards, and suddenly my mind went blanker than Molly's algebra homework before she wheedled Nessa into doing it for her. Why hadn't I reviewed the flash cards, like Paige suggested? What was I supposed to say again? Something about his hair? Tell him blue hair rocks. Hard. TELL HIM! TELL HIM YOU LOVE HIS COOKIE MONSTER BANGS!

But something in me was fighting the lie. Was it worth risking my journalistic principles, my reputation, on the off chance that he'd eventually agree to date Molly? I couldn't do it. I couldn't lie. So I said something I actually believed.

"You'd be much better with a lead thinger."

"Yeah, well." Zander unsnapped the worn leather cuff bracelet on his wrist, then snapped it again, his gaze fixed on my feet. "Thought you weren't interested."

"Ummm . . ." I kicked at a worn spot in the carpet with the toe of my sneaker. "I changed my mind."

Onstage, the rest of the band went quiet, clearly eavesdropping.

"Yeah, well, maybe I changed my mind, too." He glanced up at me. I'd never noticed his eyes before. They were a steely gray—hard and unforgiving. Immediately, I wished he'd kept staring at my shoes. "We need a musician. Not an on-air gossip with a mean streak," he said in a flat tone. "This is a drama-free zone, Simon."

"What did you thay to me?" Spit from my lisp leapt across the space between us and spritzed his ratty Jimi Hendrix tee. I cringed.

The kid at the keyboard coughed, and The Beat hid a smile behind a cymbal.

"You heard me." Zander shrugged. "You know, for a girl with a rep for dishing out the truth, you don't really know how to take it."

"For a drama-free guy, you're doing a pretty good job of creating it," I shot back, putting my hands on my hips.

"So, are you this mean to everybody, or just people you don't know?" His voice was low and steady, but it felt like he was screaming.

"I'm not mean!" My voice cracked, and I instantly regretted letting him get to me. "I tell the truth. Not the thame thing."

But from the skeptical look on his face, he didn't believe me. It was time to step it up.

"Okay. You're right. But I haven't been hanging out with my old group anymore." I plucked a piece of lint off my gloves. Now I was the one who couldn't look him in the eye. "I've changed. Really. I'm . . . different . . . now." My voice trailed off.

"Whatever." He turned away, retracing his steps to the stage.

"Zander!" I croaked. What else did he *want* from me? But he didn't hear me, or he pretended not to.

"I'm . . . thorry." The words were barely a whisper.

I dropped into the nearest seat and took off my glasses, rubbing my eyes. *Okay. This can't be it. The real Kacey Simon doesn't take no for an answer. The real Kacey Simon pushes until she gets exactly what she wants. The real Kacey Simon . . .*

. . . disappeared when I got braces and glasses.

"Hey. You okay?" Skinny Jeans's voice boomed over the microphone.

I shoved my glasses on and headed toward the door. "Fine," I sniffed at the carpet.

"Audition's at four thirty at my place. Get off at Berwyn and take Broadway to Balmoral."

I jerked toward the stage.

"*Audithon?*" It was a major slap in the face. "You want me to *audithon?* But—"

Zander's face hardened. "Forget it."

"WAIT! OKAY. Four thirty."

He lifted his guitar. "Any drama, and you're out. Got it?"

"Right. Thank you. Thankth," I babbled, backing up the aisle.

"Oh, and you see those records in my bag?" He nodded at the beat-up leather messenger bag slung over a chair in a middle row. A handful of colorful albums peeked out of the top.

I lifted the flap and inspected the titles. *Purple Rain,*

Time Out of Mind, Déjà Vu. I hadn't heard of any of them. And they smelled like Mrs. Weitzman, my ancient next-door neighbor.

"Listen to those before you come. Especially Dylan. He's a freaking genius."

Homework? I bit my lip and tucked the albums under my arm. "'Kay."

"Four thirty," he repeated as I headed down the aisle. "Don't be late."

WHO'S YOUR SUGAR DADDY?
Monday, 3:20 P.M.

Walking into Sugar Daddy alone that afternoon felt surreal. It had been my friends' hangout since the very first day of sixth. We'd been looking for a place to debrief after the final bell that day, and had fallen in love with everything about the tiny bakery: the creaky wooden floors, the vintage student desks and colorful chairs, and the turquoise leather couches in the back.

This afternoon was the first time I'd ever walked through the frosted glass doors alone—and the first time I'd ever seen the couches in the back unoccupied.

Those couches had history. It was where we'd been lounging when Nessa found out she'd gotten into that super exclusive French language camp in Avignon last summer. Where we'd thrown Liv a surprise after-school birthday party, complete with vegan cupcakes. Where Molly had tried the triple espresso hot chocolate and discovered that Molly + caffeine = Bad Idea.

"You're late." Paige was already sitting at the two-top next to the Frost-It-Yourself cupcake bar in the center of the bakery. A half-eaten carrot cupcake topped with cream cheese frosting sat next to the chrome napkin dispenser.

I tossed my messenger bag under the table and propped Skinny Jeans's albums between the napkin dispenser and Paige's plate. "You're looking at the lead . . ." I paused, trying to find another non-*s*-word for *singer*. Vocalist? Nope. Voice? Not that one either. ". . . *you know what* for Gravity."

"So we can check that off the list," Paige replied without looking up from the *Marquette Gazette*. "Do you want the bad news first, or the worse news?" Her foot shook at warp speed under the table, making the red ceramic cup and saucer in front of her clink like a minor earthquake had just struck Lincoln Park.

"Huh?"

"I'm just gonna give it to you straight." Finally, Paige looked up. Her brows scrunched together like one giant, hairy caterpillar. "It's not looking good." She snapped the paper in half and slid it across the table. "On the bright side, you made the front page."

I scanned the headline.

UNDERSTUDY TO STAR IN SATURDAY'S PRODUCTION OF *GUYS AND DOLLS*

And in smaller letters beneath the headline:

RISING STAR: "FATE AND ORTHODONTIC DIFFICULTIES BROUGHT ME TO THE STAGE"

The newsprint swam in my field of vision. But the candid shot of Molly standing alone onstage, gazing into the spotlight, glared back at me in gritty black and white. That was supposed to be *my* front page shot! How could she possibly have made it above the fold before I did? I whipped off my glasses and sent them skittering across the table.

"Big picture," Paige admonished, stabbing her cupcake with her fork. "Our new buzz phrase is *damage control.*"

"Don't you think we're a little late for that?" I felt torn between finding and burning every copy of the *Gazette* in the greater Chicagoland area, and reading the article until I had every word memorized.

Paige shook her head. "This is just a mock-up of tomorrow's paper. So if we can get our own story in by deadline tonight, we'll be okay. We've just got to think." She lifted a pen next to her mug and started making notes in the margins. "Maybe we could do a blurb about how you're in the band now, or something. What do you think?"

"Wait. How'd *you* get a mock-up?" I'd never been able to get the next day's headlines this far in advance.

Her eyes darted back and forth behind her black frames. There was a smudge of cream cheese frosting on the left lens. "Do you get how full of yourself you sound, or is everyone else too scared of you to point that out?"

"Excuuuthe me! Do *you* get who you're talking to?" I pointed to my face, for emphasis. The *Kacey Simon, former and soon-to-be-reinstated seventh-grade advice guru, star of the stage, and object of Quinn Wilder's affections* part was implied. So I'd hit a little bump in the road. A BRIEF detour. But as soon as I picked up a lead singer gig and ditched the lisp (and Paige) everything would be back to normal.

"Who I'm talking to?" Paige took her glasses off, then slid them back on. Then she did it again. "I'm talking to a girl whose approval rating dropped forty percentage points since last Monday." She reached for her water glass and chugged half its contents in one gulp. "A girl who doesn't seem to get that the entire school, with the exception of yours truly, is, shall we say, enjoying your new look. It's called payback, Kacey."

"The entire school?" I wrapped my palms around my own sweating water glass to lower my spiking body temperature. "No way."

In the old days, Molly would have shut up and dropped the subject. But Paige just kept going. "Who cares if you're in a band if you've been a complete jerk and now everybody's over you? Hello? John Mayer?"

Just then, the bell over the front door jangled, and in walked someone carrying a crooked stack of *Gazette* mock-ups. Molly.

When she saw me, she stopped in her tracks. One beat later, so did Liv and Nessa. Had the four of us always looked that choreographed?

"Oh." Molly's voice was sweeter than double-fudge frosting. "You saw it. Totally Sean's idea. You know. For publicity." She lowered the stack onto our table.

"Can I see?" Paige made a sudden, jerking movement toward the papers. Her teacup tipped and rolled, soaking Molly's slate-gray micro-mini with dark liquid. "Oops. Sorry."

I bit my lip as the stain expanded.

Molly sucked in a deep breath. She ripped a handful of napkins from the dispenser and started blotting her crotch. "Phoebe, right?"

"Paige, actually."

"Whatever." Molly dumped the soaked napkins in front of me and wrung out her "vintage" I'M WITH THE BAND T-shirt. "BTW? The only reason Kacey's hanging out with you is because she doesn't want to hang alone." She flipped her blonde extensions over her shoulder. "So I guess you're better than nothing."

My chair screeched as I scooted back from the table.

"BTW?" Paige jumped in before I could. "The only reason Kacey *used* to hang out with you is because she needed someone to hold her purse with one hand and stroke her ego with the other! Got it, Millie?"

Hey! I wanted to yell. *That's not fair!* But part of me wondered if it was.

"It's Molly." Molly crossed her arms over her chest, a new shade of crimson saturating her entire face. Liv's mouth fell open, and she nudged Nessa with her elbow.

"Listen, girls." Paige interlaced her fingers on the table. "You're gonna have to find your own table. Kacey was just telling me about her plans with Zander later." She shooed Molly and the girls away with an easy flick of the wrist.

"Wait. Zander?" Molly glanced at me again. This time, there was the slightest sliver of hope in her eyes. And something else. Jealousy?

"Yup." Casually, I plucked a chunk from the side of Paige's cupcake and popped it in my mouth. The sugary crumbles immediately lodged themselves in my braces. Worth it.

"So . . . buh-bye, now." Paige blinked.

Without a word, the girls turned on their heels and stalked across the floor.

I shook my head at Paige and slow-clapped. "You. Are. Brilliant. And. Brutal." I hoped it half counted as an apology. I wanted to ask her if she'd been serious, about Molly only being there to stroke my ego. But my lips couldn't form the sentence.

The bell over the door clanged again, and I watched my friends leave me behind. Once they were outside, Liv slid her arm around Molly's shoulders and squeezed, while Nessa's purple mittens gestured wildly in the falling snow, like she was conducting an orchestra. When really, all she was doing was . . . gossiping about me. I turned away.

"I don't get it." Paige folded a stack of soggy *Gazettes* and dropped them on the floor. Then she rested her chin in her cupped hand, searching my face. "All this work, just so you can hang out with *them*?" I could tell from the tiny wrinkles around her eyes that she wasn't being mean. She was truly confused.

It's not that I wanted to be with them right at that moment, exactly. But they were acting like they didn't even miss me a little. Like everything was just as good without me—better, even—although without them, my world was crashing and burning.

"They're not . . . that bad." I plucked a napkin from the dispenser and picked at the edges. I checked the window again. They were gone, and the white flakes were starting to fall harder.

Paige stayed silent, but what she wasn't saying weighed heavily on me. The pile of shredded napkins in front of me was growing into a small, snowy mountain.

"Gotta go," I said finally. "Rehearthal in twenty."

Paige gave me a tiny smile. "I'll leak the story that you're in the band for tomorrow's paper. Damage control, right?"

"Right." I smiled back, then jumped up and tugged at my slouchy cream sweater. "I look hard rock, right?"

"Hard rock. Right." Paige rolled her eyes. "Where'd you get that sweater, Anthropologie?"

"But I'm wearing it with fith-netth!" I protested. As payback, I swiped the rest of her cupcake for the road. "I'll text you after."

"Good luck." Then Paige said something under her breath that sounded a whole lot like, *"You'll need it."*

16

YOU CAN TAKE THE GIRL OUT OF LINCOLN PARK. . . .
Monday, 4:28 P.M.

I made it to Skinny Jeans's house with less than three minutes to spare before my nonnegotiable call time.

At least I thought it was his house. Checking the number inked on my palm, I tilted my head back and stared up at a two-story brick warehouse with the words JACOB HARVEY & SONS stamped in peeling white block letters on the electric blue loading dock door. A row of tall, rectangular windows reached from the top of the door to a flat tin roof.

As far as I could tell, there wasn't a front entrance. So I tromped around the warehouse, where I found a regular-sized blue door. It opened before I had the chance to knock.

"Hey. You found it!" Zander crouched in the threshold, holding back a giant salt-and-pepper-haired dog with pointy ears. "People usually think they've got the wrong address. Used to be a furniture warehouse, or something." He tossed his blue streak out of his eyes.

"And you live here?" I asked, trying to send chill, confident vibes in the dog's direction. Nessa volunteered at the Humane Society on Sunday afternoons, and once she told me that dogs could smell fear. I wondered if they could also smell social desperation.

"Yup." Zander clapped the dog on its side and rose. "Oh. This is Hendrix."

Hendrix bared his teeth and glared at me with one brown eye and one lazy, pale blue eye. Awesome. Even the lazy-eyed dog hated me. Maybe Paige was right.

"Come on. I'll give you the tour." Zander ushered me into an open square room with a ceiling that must have been forty feet high. Two spiral staircases and a green wooden ladder led to lofted bedrooms on both sides of the warehouse. Since there were no walls dividing the room, the concrete floor was painted in sections: a silvery gray for the living area, dusty violet for the kitchen, and eggshell beneath the brushed copper dining room table. Just being there made me feel cooler.

"Moved in three months ago, and we still haven't totally unpacked." Zander nudged a worn cardboard box marked *Miscellaneous Junk XIV* out of our path. He fiddled with a stereo on the table by the door, and some kind of heavy metal blasted from every corner of the loft. Hendrix whined and scrambled under the dining room table.

I examined the framed photos on the exposed brick walls: black and white, color, landscape, panoramic. Everything from posed family reunion portraits to an up-close candid of Zander strumming his guitar. I giggled at a small three-by-five shot of a little girl about Ella's age in a Grateful Dead T-shirt, flashing a toothless grin and the peace sign. "LITTLE THITHTER?" I shouted over the music.

Zander nodded and adjusted the volume. "Roz. She's a trip." He ambled across the room to the kitchen. "You want something to drink?"

"Water would be good." I dropped my bag on the leather couch in the living area, my voice bouncing off the exposed pipes that snaked in a maze around the ceiling. "How many photographth are in here?" By my count, each wall held at least one hundred.

"I know, right? Mom's a photographer. Mostly for ad campaigns and stuff." He jerked open the stainless-steel fridge door and pulled out two bottles of water. "Her passion's people, so she shoots a lot of the fam." He kicked the door shut with his heel. "Heads up."

I caught the water bottle as it sailed toward me. "Thankth."

He nodded. "We rehearse back here," he said, leading me into a tangerine sponge-painted breakfast nook next to the kitchen. A drum set, two acoustic guitars, and a keyboard were set up behind a few microphone stands.

"Your mom and dad don't care?"

"Nah. They're at work. Plus we're the only loft on the block. We can totally let loose and nobody cares." Zander took a seat on a metal stool behind one of the mics and adjusted its height.

"Cool." I picked up a drumstick and tapped a beat on my thigh.

"So. Straight up. How come you changed your mind about the band?" Zander caught my gaze and stared directly into my eyes. He had an annoying way of doing that, just like Paige.

Before I could inform him that staring was rude, the rest of the guys herded through the side door, backpacks slung over their shoulders. They dumped their gear next to the couch and headed straight for the fridge. I dropped the drumstick.

"I'm saying, though," argued The Beat. He was holding a small, blinking camcorder, which he shoved in

Kevin's face. "It's like you haven't experienced music till you've heard the acoustic version. Disagree?"

I cracked open my water bottle and took a swig.

"Exactly," chimed the keyboardist with the blond curls. *Nelson.* He tugged off his army-green cargo jacket and slung it on the ottoman in front of the couch. "That track, like, changed my world."

Kevin shook his head. "No way. They sold out, man." Even with a metal bar through his lip, he had no lisp. Unbelievable.

"You think everybody's a sell-out, Cho," laughed Zander, sliding off the stool.

"Yeah." Kevin shrugged, then stopped to look directly into The Beat's camera lens. "'Cause they are. You all are."

"Dude." The Beat dropped his camcorder on the kitchen counter. "How am I supposed to get any good publicity footage for the website if you keep badmouthing our fans?"

"It's controversy, man," Kevin argued. "Controversy sells."

"Whatever." The Beat ducked into the refrigerator and emerged with a plastic bottle of orange juice. Then he unscrewed the green plastic top and chugged straight from the bottle.

"Dude!" Zander exclaimed. "My mom drinks from that."

"My baaaaaaaad," The Beat belched.

"Dithguthting," I muttered into my water bottle. Wait. Did that qualify as drama? I zipped my lips.

The guys turned to look at me in surprise. It was the longest anyone had ever taken to notice me, ever. Maybe I really was becoming invisible. I scratched the back of my neck, not knowing where to look.

"Oh. Hey." Nelson pulled a box of granola from the pantry and stuffed his hand inside.

"Hey, guyth." The plastic water battle crinkled beneath my grip.

"Cool accent," Nelson said over a mouthful of cereal. "Where you from?" A dried cranberry shot out of his mouth and pegged Kevin in the cheek.

"Lincoln Park," I said flatly.

Kevin wiped his cheek and lifted his hand in a semi-wave. "What up."

The guys convened in the breakfast nook and took their places behind their instruments. I stayed pressed against the wall, unsure where to go. Unsure of my place.

"You ever sung lead vocals before?" The Beat asked.

Did the shower count? "I, uh, wath the lead in the play." My glasses were starting to slip. I shoved them back into place.

"Oh, yeah. The musical." Kevin didn't even try to hide his disdain. He glanced meaningfully at Zander, who was fiddling with his mic stand. "The middle school musical."

"Yeah?" I said defensively.

"Pretty mainstream." When he bent over his bass, I swear I heard him mumble "Sellout." I cut my eyes to Skinny Je— Zander, to see if he'd heard. How did that not qualify as drama? Or just plain mean?

"She's really good," Zander said quickly, tuning his guitar. "Awesome range." He plucked the same string over and over, twisting the silver knobs at the top of the instrument until he seemed satisfied.

I swallowed, my cheeks burning. The ripped skinny jeans and fishnets were doing nothing for me, other than making my sweaty thighs itch like crazy.

"So we're working on some original material for the album." Zander strummed a few chords. "I just started this one. Not quite done yet. You sight read, yeah?"

What? I blinked as Zander thrust a few pages of sheet music into my hands.

"I wrote it in triple, but we're slowing it down to four-four."

"Uh, great." Even my eyelashes were starting to sweat.

"Okay, so just jump in whenever." He nodded his head toward the mic stand on his right. "You're over here. By me."

I took my place behind the mic, suddenly feeling faint. Too bad I was about to make him look terrible in front of his friends. He didn't deserve that, even with his blue hair and girl jeans. I felt a stabbing pain in my stomach. I never should have swiped Paige's cupcake.

The Beat counted off. "One, two, three, four."

While the band rocked a guitar-heavy intro, I stared at the music in my grip. I may as well have been trying to read Japanese. Sure, we were supposed to learn the sheet music for *Guys and Dolls*. But downloading the soundtrack on iTunes was faster.

This world spins round and round
The sun goes up and down
They said this would get easier
But it keeps getting harder . . . somehow

I actually kind of liked the lyrics. They had feeling, without being sappy or dramatic.

"Whenever you're ready, Mainstream," The Beat said into his mic.

No drama. No drama. No drama. I cleared my throat, instead of pummeling him with my mic stand.

"This world spins round and round." Stunned, I whipped away from the mic and stared at Zander.

"Told you," he said without looking up. "You don't have a lisp when you sing."

"The sun goes up and down." Sweaty shivers ran up and down my spine. Even without my lisp, this sucked. Standing in the middle of a group of guys I didn't know, staring at music I didn't understand. Every note bringing a brand-new chance for me to humiliate myself.

But nobody was laughing, or making snotty comments into the mic. The band just kept playing. Was it possible that . . .

. . . I *didn't* suck?

I leaned a little closer to the mic, feeling the vibrations in the music buzz from my hands through the rest of my body. "They said this would get easier." My voice was getting stronger, bolder. "But it keeps getting HAAA—"

Without warning, my voice cracked like a sixth-grade boy's. Horrified, I slapped my hand over my mouth. Pain reverberated through my gums.

"Hold up," Zander instructed, shaking his head. "Let's take it back."

The band trailed off, and Kevin let out an exasperated sigh.

"Thorry." I stared at the floor, seized with the urge to take my glasses off. To make everything in my world blurred around the edges again.

"No problem," Zander assured me. "But maybe you can try it a little more from the diaphragm this time?"

"Thure," I mumbled, my cheeks burning. Why had I ever thought I could do this? I belonged onstage, or on the air. Not here. I was an imposter. A poseur.

The Beat counted down again.

"Here we go," called Zander over the opening chords. "You got this."

I stepped toward the mic. "This world spins round and round. The sun goes up and down." I closed my eyes and visualized a dark stage with velvet curtains. Opening night. Kacey Simon, unplugged, in front of a spellbound audience. "They said it would get easier . . ."

"DO IT, MAINSTREAM!" yelled Nelson.

This was it. My last chance. No holding back.

"But it keeps getting HAAAARDER, SOOOME-HOW!" I belted. My voice echoed throughout the loft, clear and strong.

"Yeeeaaaah!" Zander cheered. "ROCK! ON!"

I gripped the mic, fresh energy pulsing through my body in time to the beat. It felt like my sixth sense, only amplified. As I sang, everything but the lyrics started to melt away. Molly's snide comments, my plummeting approval rating, the recast: For just a few minutes, nothing mattered. Nothing but the music.

THREE'S COMPANY, SIX IS A CROWD
Tuesday, 12:06 P.M.

I rode my hard rock high all the way into lunch period the next day.

"And after we were done, we tried out a few trackth from the Bob Dylan album I borrowed," I told Paige. "No lithp there, either. Can you believe it?" I cracked open my açai berry smoothie and surveyed The Square from my new lunch spot: an ivy-infested iron loveseat shoved in the corner between Silverstein and Hemingway.

The Square was starting to fill, but the old stone bench I used to share with the girls was deserted. Directly diagonal from our corner, Quinn, Jake, and Aaron were lounging next to the sixth graders' dead Earth Day garden, playing paper football.

"Sounds fun." Paige bent over with her head between

her knees, digging for something in her backpack. "Wait 'til you see this." Her voice was muffled.

"Mm-hmm," I said absently, momentarily hypnotized by the way the sunlight seemed to pour through the greenhouse ceiling and land in a perfect halo around Quinn's head. He leaned against the brick wall and flicked a field goal, laughing at something Jake had just said. His teeth were so white, I had to close my eyes for a second. I fantasized that Quinn hadn't laughed at the YouTube spoof the week before. I imagined that instead, he'd told off the entire class and we'd stormed out together, then headed to Sugar Daddy for our first official date.

Paige snapped her fingers in front of my nose. "It took a little bargaining with the features editor, but . . ." She produced a folded newspaper and rattled it excitedly.

"Wait." It took a few seconds of staring into Paige's giant, unblinking eyes to jog my memory, but our conversation at Sugar Daddy finally came flooding back. "We made the front page?" I lunged for the *Gazette*, but Paige leapt up, holding it just out of my reach. "I can't believe you waited to tell me!"

"I can't believe you forgot to ask!" Paige laughed, making the paper dance just inches from my glasses.

Well, I wasn't completely sure you were gonna be able to pull it off. I managed to swallow the words.

Paige cleared her throat. *"Marquette's Broadcast Queen Down with Gravity."*

"No way!" I stashed my smoothie under the bench and commandeered the paper before she could stop me.

"Read the part about how you overcame hardship!" Paige screeched. "That's my favorite line."

"Hey! It's Gravity's newest supah-stahhh!" I glanced up from my promo to see Zander slinking across the courtyard. He was wearing slouchy brown cargos, a thin waffled orange hoodie, and a T-shirt with icons of a baby chick and a horseshoe magnet on it.

I waved, then went back to the piece.

"What's going on?" When Zander raised his palm, his leather cuff bracelet peeked out from beneath his henley.

"Hey. I'm Paige." Paige gave him a high five.

"Yeah. I'm voting for you." He grinned. "Zander."

But Paige had already refocused on the promo. "Let me read it. Nobody can understand you with that lisp, anyway." She snatched the paper and smoothed it against her thigh. "It says . . . 'Although public humiliation has been haunting the journalist since she lost her looks to braces and glasses last week, she's not crawling under a rock and dying, like this reporter would do. Instead, she's working to overcome her hardships, taking a brief hiatus from the stage and the airwaves to conquer an entirely new industry: rock music.'"

"Sweet!" Zander punched my shoulder, making my glasses bump down my nose.

"Keep going!" I squealed.

"Simon confirmed to the *Gazette*: 'I'm joining forces with Marquette's newest musical powerhouse, the band Gravity. I'm way pumped about this new phase of seventh.'" Paige surfaced and took a huge breath. "No. Wait. *This* is my favorite part. 'And I was happy to ask my friend Molly Knight to take my part in *Guys and Dolls*. Even understudies deserve a chance.'"

I snorted. "Nithe TOUCH, Paige!"

"Here at the *Gazette*, we suspect Miss Simon might just be making a COMEBACK. And THIS reporter—" Paige's eyes fluttered shut and she recited the rest from memory. "*Wants front. Row. Seats.*"

"Ahhhhhhhh!" I ignored the saliva sprinkler spritzing from my mouth and threw my arms around Paige's lanky frame. "No way!"

"Nice work." Zander nodded his approval.

"Wait." I pulled away. "How'd you get the reporter to print it? I hadn't made the band by then."

Paige folded the paper gingerly and slipped it back into her portfolio case. "So Zander," she said brightly. "She was really good last night, huh?"

"Yeah, she was," Zander took a swig of his lemon Honest Tea. "Awesome. The rest of the guys thought so, too." He lifted his palm to shade his face and smiled at me.

"Thankth." Back to the point. "Paige. Come on." I whacked her pilled black sweater.

"Ow! Fine." She patted her bangs self-consciously. "It's possible . . . that I swore to double the paper's budget when I get reelected."

"Paige!" I snorted, impressed. "You can't do that! Hello, corruption?"

"What if you don't get reelected?" Zander squinted, looking genuinely concerned. "I mean, you probably will. You did great in that debate on Channel M last month. But—"

"Oh. I'll get reelected." Paige shot me a meaningful look, then winked. "Quid pro quo, beh-beh."

I burst out laughing, reaching under the bench for my smoothie. Instead, I found my messenger bag. "Oh! I wanted to give you thith." I pulled out the album I'd tucked in my bag and flung it at Zander like a Frisbee.

He caught it. "Elton John. 'Rock and Roll Madonna.'" He inspected the worn sleeve. "This is killer! Where'd you get it?"

"Home. It wa . . . well, my dad had it." I chewed at the inside of my cheek.

Paige pressed her lips together.

"Awesome. Thanks. I'll take a listen tonight." Zander tucked it carefully under his hoodie. "Which reminds me. We're doing rehearsal a little later today. I'm taking you someplace after school."

"Where?"

"You'll like it," he promised evasively. "And it's a surprise."

"Ooh. Tell me!" Paige begged. "I love surprises. As long as they don't happen tomorrow night. We're working on my campaign speech." She glanced at me for confirmation. "Right?"

I nodded.

"Okay." She bent over in her seat. Zander cupped his hand around his mouth and bent to whisper something in her ear.

"Heyyy, Kayth— uhh, Kacey."

I looked up in surprise to see Jake Fields standing over me and holding a plastic Gatorade bottle. Aaron and Quinn were right behind him. "How's it going?" He bit his lip, looking down at the ground. His hunched shoulders were shaking slightly. It reminded me of Molly's posture during the mock trial.

"Hey," I said tersely.

Next to me, Paige tensed.

"We were just headed to the auditorium." Aaron nodded, stealing a quick glance at Quinn. "Sean called a quick cast meeting. You coming?"

"I quit the play, duh." I looked over at Quinn, who was studiously avoiding my gaze. An uneasy feeling sloshed in the pit of my stomach. I told myself it was just the açai berry.

"Oh. I forgot!" Aaron smacked his forehead.

"Guys." Zander stood, his eyes turning to steel. "We're kind of in the middle of something, so—"

"Hey. Easy, dude." Jake lifted his hands in surrender. "We're just trying to help out."

"Come on," I said tightly to Zander and Paige. "Let'th get out of here." I stood.

But Jake blocked my way. "Hold up. Thought you could use this." He extended the Gatorade bottle in my direction. "Seems like you're losing a lot of fluid with . . . all that spitting."

"Ohhhhhh!" Jake punched Aaron and Quinn in the shoulders, and Quinn finally looked up. And cracked a smile, which turned into a slow, easy laugh. His light blue eyes seemed to illuminate and his cheeks lifted. Like . . .

. . . like I was nothing more than a punch line to him. Standing at the edge of the packed Square, I'd never felt so alone.

Zander and Paige jumped up.

"Come on, Kacey," Paige said quietly. She gripped my arm and squeezed. "Let's go."

"Yeah." Zander rolled his eyes. "These guys aren't worth it."

I glanced up at Zander and Paige's determined faces, and just like that, something inside me snapped. I *wasn't* alone. I had Zander and Paige, and they had my back. My embarrassment melted into anger as the guys nudged one another and laughed. Quinn was such a coward. He couldn't even look at me while he was dissing me.

"Hey, Quinn," I said, my voice surprisingly confident. "Could you alert Dumb and Dumber here that they're about a week too late on the lithp joke? It aired on You-Tube, if they didn't catch it."

"Whatever, Simon." Jake chuckled uneasily.

"Oh. And while we're on the topic of YouTube, I've been meaning to mention." I amped up my volume, snagging the attention of a curious group of girls just a few feet away. "I wath in the Channel M tape room the other day? And I found really great uncut footage of the three of you in the auditorium, getting ready for rehearthal. Makeup, and everything."

"Dude." Aaron glanced nervously at Quinn.

"Duuuude." I nodded knowingly. I could feel Zander and Paige's smiles. "Don't you think it would be enlightening for everyone to watch? I mean, who knew that Jake wore unicorn boxerth?"

"They're horses!" Jake hissed, turning bright red.

"Or that Aaron added an extra coat of cheek thtain when he thought no one wath around?" I broke into a broad grin, braces and all.

The girls nearby burst out laughing.

"Stage lights wash me out." Aaron's voice was barely audible.

When my eyes fell on Quinn, I felt something strange. It wasn't power. It was more like . . . pity. Pity that Quinn was so weak that he couldn't even stand up to his sidekicks. Pity that he still couldn't look me in the eye—that he could only stand there, shoulders stooped, head down. And suddenly, I didn't feel like humiliating him in front of his friends anymore.

Briiiiiiiiiiiiiiiiiiiing!

The sound of the bell echoed throughout The Square. Looking relieved, the guys ducked past us and scampered for the door to Silverstein.

"Whoa." Zander's jaw dropped. "I mean . . . whoa."

"KACEY!" Paige threw her arms around me and squeezed tight. "Way to stand up for yourself."

I leaned into her, ignoring the tiny, guilty knot that had formed in my stomach. Those guys deserved the humiliation. The warning that I was still there, underneath the braces and glasses. Ready to fight.

CULTURE CLUB
Tuesday, 3:35 P.M.

After school, I let Zander lead me all the way to Andersonville before I started bugging him about our surprise field trip.

"Come onnnnn. A hint," I insisted, dragging my saffron cutout ankle boots against the cracked sidewalks. I'd lived in Chicago all my life, and never really explored any of the neighborhoods on the north side. It felt different up here, more urban than Lincoln Park. Chain-link to my wrought iron. Above-store lofts to my townhouses. Grunge to my pop.

Basically, Zander to my Kacey.

"Almost there," Zander promised as we crossed over Foster. My cardio cramps turned to hunger pangs as we passed hole-in-the-wall coffee shops and Swedish bakeries that smelled of warm butter and cinnamon. I gazed long-ingly at the window displays of flour-dusted biscuits, muffins, and pancakes glazed with lingonberry jam.

"Okay. Close your eyes," Zander instructed me.

"Nope," I huffed. My breath made a frosty cloud in the air between us.

"Suit yourself." We slowed in front of a small gray storefront with a red door labeled:

"Vinyl Dethtination?" I said skeptically.

"Uh-huh." Zander sidled in front of me and pressed his thumb against the brass handle. "Think of this place as the first stop in your grand tour of rock culture," he announced. "If you're gonna be part of the band, you can't just sing rock 'n' roll. You gotta live it."

I rolled my eyes at the back of his head. Was he serious?

"I'm Zander, your tour guide. But you can call me . . . Master of Rock."

I could think of plenty of other things to call him right then.

"Am I even cool enough to get in?" I quipped. "Not too, and I quote, 'mainthtream'?"

He turned, pretending to be deep in thought. "Good point. Hold on." He unsnapped his leather cuff bracelet and looped it around my wrist. It slid halfway to my elbow. "There. So cool I hardly recognize you."

"Great."

He turned back toward the door, ramming it twice with his shoulder to get it to open.

We stepped into a musty, fluorescent-lit store with dingy white walls. And records. Stacks of records, everywhere. Piled in listing columns on the cluttered oak tables. Shoved under the ripped leather armchair in the back corner. Stacked next to the sets of cushioned black headphones dangling from wall hooks all around the store. Propping up the adding machine on the speaker by the door. I sucked in, to preserve space. And oxygen.

"Z?" A guy's voice sounded somewhere to the right. "That you?"

"Hey, Elton." Zander reached for a dusty Pink Floyd album on a stack by the door and blew on it. A fine layer of dust curled into the air. I sneezed.

"You come here a lot?" I reached for the nearest record sleeve. A woman's gaunt, faded face was printed on it in various shades of blue.

"Yeah. It's like this . . . rock 'n' roll mecca." A peaceful smile spread over Zander's face. It was the same faraway look he had when he was playing. He looked down at the album in my hand. "Joni Mitchell. *Blue*," he observed. "Nineteen seventy-one. Not as good as *Clouds*, but definitely solid. Oh. And these." He scooped up a pile of Led Zeppelin albums balanced on the radiator under the window. "I don't think I really *got* rock 'n' roll before *Physical Graffiti*, you know?"

"Not really." I wondered if I'd ever heard him say this many words at once.

"The newer stuff's in the back." He disappeared into the maze of record stacks, and I hurried to catch up so I wouldn't lose him.

"How'd you find thith place?" I asked, gluing my arms to my sides and shimmying around a random speaker planted in the middle of the floor. There was a coffee mug on top with something white and furry floating in it. I stifled a gag.

"There's a café next door, and they do open mic nights," he called over his shoulder. "We played there when—" He stopped mid-stride and turned to face me. "Wait. How'd I find this . . . what?" he asked slowly. The skin around his eyes creased. "I didn't hear you."

"PLACE," I said loudly, cupping my hands around my mouth like a megaphone. "PLACE."

Zander shot me a huge grin.

"Place," I repeated a third time, feeling a jolt from my pinky toe to my earlobe. "My lithp!" *Relax the tongue.* "My . . . lissssp!"

"Told you!" he exclaimed. "Cheesy slo-mo victory five?"

I glanced around to see if anyone was watching. Since we were walled in by columns of records taller than we were, it wasn't a problem.

"Yes, please." In sync, we wound up and sent our hands arching slowly toward each other. I swallowed a giggle as we pressed our palms together in mid-air and held them there. His was soft and warm, like the leather bracelet on my wrist.

"Nice." He laughed. Our hands dropped to our sides, and I felt a surge of excitement. It was really happening! My lisp was disappearing! And soon, my glasses would be gone, too. Things were actually falling into place. The Universe was smiling on me, reinstating me to my rightful place. At the top. With Molly at my right han—

Molly.

I mentally smacked myself in the forehead. Time for Phase Three.

"Come on." Zander gripped my wrist and dragged me through the record maze. "You gotta hear this one album. Oh. And this other one." Without warning, he turned a corner and stopped. I almost tripped over him.

"Fourth on the left," he murmured to himself, kneeling down in front of one of the piles. His lips moved slowly as he counted silently from the bottom. He looked up at me. "Hold this?"

I steadied the column, and he slid a lime-green album sleeve carefully from the bottom of the stack. "Aaaaahhhh . . . got it."

"Who ith it?" Oh no. The lisp was back. My forehead crinkled in disappointment.

"Cut yourself a break." He nudged me in the shin. "It'll take some time. Probably fade in and out a little."

"I gueth."

His face suddenly got serious, and he stood up. "You GUETH?" he said. "Well, I am THHHHHHERIOUTHLY THHHUR that you'll be THPEAKING WITHOUT IT THHHHHHOOOPER thoon."

"Thut up, Thander." I flushed, nudging him back.

"OHHH, KAYYTHEEEE," he belted out.

Wait. Was he breaking into *song*?

"You hard roooock lady.

Don't be tho thhyyyyy

Says thith hard rockin' guyyy!

Let go and beeee craaathy.

Yeah, hard rooooock Kaythee."

He was soaking the stacks with spit showers, and I ducked out of the way to avoid getting drenched.

"THANDER!" I mock scolded him, gasping with

laughter. "Thpitting in public ith THIMPLY thothally unacctheptable. Thometimes? It'th thmart to care what people think."

He dropped his head in faux-shame. "Thorry."

"Just don't let it happen again." I wiped tears from the corners of my eyes with the back of my hands.

"Aaanyhoo." He waved the green album in my face. "These guys are hard-core. My all-time favorite. Acoustic Rebellion. Ever heard of them?"

I shook my head. "Are they on iTunes?"

"I'm gonna pretend I didn't hear that." He shoved the record in my hands. "Actually, they're coming to town Friday night. Pritzker Pavilion."

"And you're going?" I scanned the track listing on the back.

"Definitely. I've had my tickets for months now." He paused. "You'll like track five. Although, it's kind of like you won't get the true experience unless you hear them, you know, live."

"Oh." My eyes snapped up and met his. I was experiencing what we call a "lightning bolt moment." Watch and learn.

"Ohmygod." I smacked my palm to my forehead. "Did you say ACOUTHtic Rebellion?"

He nodded.

"I knew I recognized that name from somewhere. That's Molly Knight's favorite band!"

Impressive, no?

"Seriously?" Beneath the blue streak, his forehead wrinkled. "'Cause she doesn't really seem like the type who likes . . ." He paused, like he was trying to think of the answer on a test. "Deep . . . stuff."

"Oh, totally," I gushed. "Molly loves . . . deep . . . stuff. But especially Acouthtic Rebellion."

"Really?" His eyes narrowed.

I nodded so hard that my glasses skittered down the bridge of my nose. "She may not look all deep and alternative, but inside, she . . . so . . . is."

I took a breath. This was it. The hard sell.

"It's really sad, though, because people who aren't open-minded sometimes think she's ditzy, or boy-crazy, or something." I pretended to scan the record stack in front of me, but cut my eyes in his direction.

He shook his head slowly. "Yeah. Close-minded people suck."

"For real. Anyway, she has all their albums, and—"

"They've only done one."

"She has their album, and she follows them on Twitt—"

His face darkened.

"—in *Rolling Stone*, all the time."

"Wow." His dissolving forehead wrinkles meant he was buying it. I moved in for the kill.

"Now that I think about it, you guys have a lot in common," I said thoughtfully. "Maybe you should hang out."

"In common?" he repeated, missing my hint by a mile. "Like what?"

"Liiiiiiiiiiike." I cocked my head to the side, racking my brain. "You both have colorful hair. And you're both rock 'n' roll affith—" I started over. "Affith—"

"Aficionados?" he said with a smile. But it wasn't a mean smile.

I nodded. "Yup. She's pretty much a rock 'n' roll trivia buff."

"Has she ever been to the Rock and Roll Hall of Fame? In Cleveland?" Zander perked up.

"YES!" I slapped his arm. I hadn't felt this pumped since the girls and I went on a Sugar Daddy bender after exams last semester. "Rock and Roll Hall of Fame!" *Mall of America!* "In Cleveland!" *Minneapolis!*

"Dude. I've been wanting to go there forever."

"Dude. You should totally ask her about it," I advised. "It's one of her favorite subjects."

Zander was quiet for a second. "I guess she doesn't really seem to care what people think about her outfits. That's kinda cool."

"Right?" *Do it! Ask her out! You're my last hope!*

"Yeah. Okay. So maybe I'll ask her to go?" His face flushed suddenly, like I'd just caught him writing in his journal about love—or unicorn boxers. "So . . . we should get to rehearsal."

I resisted the urge to throw my arms around him. Who knew that Zander Jarvis from Seattle would be my ticket back to the top? I could hardly believe this was actually working, but if everything went as planned, I'd be back on the air by next week. No more reruns. Just hard-hitting journalism, the way it was meant to be delivered. By me, lisp-free. "Yeah. Rehearsal," I said. Totally calm, like this was just any other day.

I followed Zander down the block. With every step, I was getting closer and closer to the old Kacey Simon.

MOMENT OF TRUTH
Wednesday, 3:44 P.M.

I decided not to tell Molly right away that Zander was planning to ask her out. Let the anticipation drive her a little crazy. For the first time in over a week, I was actually enjoying passing her in the halls and seeing her in homeroom. It was something about her expression. Beneath the layers of disdain and pride, there was something familiar in her eyes: just the tiniest glint of need.

Besides, I had more important things to do than text Molly. Mom had called me over lunch, telling me that she'd just gotten a call from Dr. Marco's office.

"What did he th—say?" I'd asked, my stomach seizing at the mere mention of his name.

"Just that he wanted to check on you. I made an

appointment for you this afternoon." Pause. "You *have* been using the drops, haven't you, Kacey Elisabeth?"

"Mooom!" I groaned. But the feeling of unease had grown, like there was a stampede of elephants doing a step routine in the pit of my stomach. What if Dr. Marco had misdiagnosed my infection? What if it was some horrible, eyeball-disfiguring disease that would ultimately leave me blind? What if my eyes were scarred forever and I'd have to wear glasses for the rest of my life?

By the time I arrived at Dr. Marco's office after school, I had to crank up the volume on my iPod to chase away the What Ifs roiling around in my brain. Oddly, the pounding fusion of punk and classic rock in Acoustic Rebellion's title track, "Sound Mutiny," which I had digitally recorded from the album, relaxed me. I settled into the exam chair and flicked a snowflake from my dark-wash jeggings.

Dr. Marco appeared in the doorway in his fake lab coat and mouthed something I couldn't quite make out.

I jerked the earbuds out of my ears and dropped them in my lap just as AR's lead guitarist started shredding an insane solo. This was Zander's favorite part. I hit Pause and made a mental note to tell Molly to memorize it. At least they'd have one thing to talk about. "Sorry, what?"

Dr. Marco chuckled and closed the door behind him.

"I said, firrrst you almost blind yourself, and now you're working on going deaf?"

"Hilarious," I said, shoving my iPod in my bag. "Although technically, I only went blind because you gave me bum contacts." I grinned to let him know I was joking. Sort of.

"You got braces since I saw you last! Cool rubber bands. Hot pink?" He took a seat next to me.

The grin morphed into a scowl.

"My daughter hates hers, too." Dr. Marco folded my frames and balanced them on his knee. His beachy cologne was extra strong today, smelling like sand, coconut oil, and just a trace of dead fish. But as long as he told me that I could wear contacts again one day, he could smell like whatever he wanted. "Have you been using the drops this time?"

I nodded. "Twice a day." Or four. Whatever.

"Good." He pulled his mini-flashlight out of his coat pocket as the chair went higher. "This is going to be bright, but I need you to keep your eyes open for me."

I opened wide, staring up at the tiny cracks in Dr. Marco's forehead. Inside my gray suede boots, I pointed my toes. Then flexed them. Pointed. Flexed. I braced myself for the dreaded *tsk*.

Instead came the rare: "Mmm-hmmm." Dr. Marco slid his flashlight from the left eye to the right.

I drummed my fingertips quadruple-time on my legs. "I swear, I used the drops."

Finally, Dr. Marco clicked off his flashlight and sat back. He pressed a button on the side of the chair, bringing it downward.

"So . . . how does everything look?" I asked. *Point. Flex. Point. Flex.*

He stared at me for what felt like an entire commercial break, then broke out into a smile. "Everything's looking great!"

My body relaxed instantly, like I'd just stepped into the mineral bath at The Drake spa. "Really?"

"Really," he confirmed. "You'll be back in contacts by Saturday."

"Saturday! Woo! Hoo!" I shouted, sitting on my hands to keep from bear-hugging my eye doctor.

He unfolded my glasses and handed them over. When I put them on, everything looked sharp and shiny. I grinned. Today was the first day of the rest of seventh grade. I could feel it. Tonight, I'd help Paige write the best campaign speech ever delivered. Tomorrow, I'd show up to school with a disappearing lisp. Friday, Zander would fake interest in Molly at the concert. And by Saturday, I'd be onstage. Comeback complete, baby. It had all the makings of a made-for-TV movie.

"Tell your mother I said hello." Dr. Marco smiled kindly, then headed for the door.

My face was starting to ache, and I realized I'd had a wide grin plastered on it. I could hardly wait to text Paige and Zander. Or maybe I'd just surprise Paige when she came over to work on the speech, and send Zander a picture text later. So many options! So little time!

"THREE DAYS, BABY!" I squealed, shimmying off the chair as the door closed with a click. Three days. Seventy-two hours. And then, finally, I could be me again.

20

IT'S NOT WHAT YOU SAID,
IT'S THE WAY YOU SAID IT
Wednesday, 7:15 P.M.

"You want the truth, Marquette?" Paige challenged. "Well, you won't get it from Imran Bhatt." She paced back and forth in front of my clear pink computer desk, stepping over open takeout containers, rolls of green crepe paper, and a bunch of half-finished campaign posters pushing voters to *Go Greene*. On the wall behind her, a muted newscast glowed on the flatscreen.

"Say 'my opponent,'" I interrupted from my spot on the bed. "Otherwithe people will get Imran's name in their head." I cracked open my fortune cookie and stole a glance at the slip of paper inside.

YOUR LUCK IS ABOUT TO CHANGE.

I rested the fortune carefully on my bedside table, next to the framed photo of me holding Ella the day she was born.

"Right." Paige snagged a green ballpoint from my desk and made a note on her palm. "My opponent thinks you can't handle the truth."

"Booooooooooooo, 'ponent." Ella jumped on the bed, waving a finger-painted poster board declaring her allegiance to *Generation P*. The springs in my mattress groaned under her weight.

"Okay. Keep going." I reached for the bottle of Vivid Violet nail polish next to my alarm clock, rolled up my oatmeal-colored lounge pants, and started painting my toes.

"But with Paige Greene, you get a straight-talking candidate with a record that speaks for itself." Paige's nostrils flared with political passion. I think I even caught sight of a nose hair.

"Wooooooooooooo! Hoo!" Ella cheered, bouncing even higher. Her masking-taped reading glasses fell to the bed.

"So choose the candidate for student body president who knows you CAN handle the truth. Choose to Go Greene."

"Ohhhkay!" Ella giggled as she karate chopped the air, her sweaty curls matted to her face.

Paige's shoulders relaxed, and she tapped her untouched stack of index cards against her thigh. "So? What do you think?"

"The truth?" I watched Paige's eyebrows arch hopefully over her black plastic frames. The speech was . . . fine. Good enough, probably. And Paige had been slaving over it for the past hour, while I made a few much-needed editorial adjustments to her campaign rally video montage on gogreene.com. So what was the harm in telling her what she wanted to hear?

"Perfect. Couldn't have done it better myself." The second hand on my watch ticked loudly, like a gavel sentencing me to life for journalistic misconduct.

"Perfect?" Paige parroted skeptically. Her lips hardened into a thin line as she shuffled the note cards accusingly. "No notes. No feedback. Nada."

"Nope." I wheezed, feeling my heart rate start to spike. "Sounds great." I looked over her shoulder, pretending to study the campaign strategy diagrams and colorful slogans tacked to the wall between my desk and the photo booth in the corner.

"Huh." Paige sauntered over to the door and flipped the switch next to my floating wall shelves. White light spilled over me. "So . . . nothing about my delivery bothered you? You know, as a *broadcast journalist*, I'd think you'd at least have some pointers on—"

"WHEN YOU GET REALLY EXCITED, YOUR NOSTRILS FLARE LIKE MISS PIGGY'S!" I erupted. "I'm sorry, but that is NOT natural. There." My middle toe twitched involuntarily, smudging the polish. Ugh. Ruined.

"I KNEW IT!" Paige yelled back.

Ella scooted closer to me, burying her face in my lap.

"And when you do the whole 'You can't handle the truth' bit? You actually sound like that creepy old guy from the movie, which freaks me out even more than your Piggy nostrils." I collapsed onto my bed and stared up at the ceiling. There. I could breathe again.

Ella gasped. Paige was silent. I blinked at the plastic glow-in-the-dark solar system above me.

"Say thomething," I ordered Jupiter.

"You really don't get it, do you?" The floorboards creaked, and then Paige was sitting on the edge of the bed. She tucked her bob behind her ears, revealing two jeweled purple studs I'd never noticed before.

"Don't get what?"

She flopped onto the bed, her head making a giant dent in the cluttered collection of pillows piled against my headboard. "You don't get what's wrong with saying everything you think, all the time."

I took off my glasses and rubbed my temples. "Paige. *Real* journalists—"

"—don't have any stories to break if they're mean to all their sources," Paige said quietly. "You have to figure out how to be honest with people without making them hate you for it."

"People didn't used to care that I was honest," I pointed out.

"Yeah, they did. They were just scared of you before." Paige turned onto her side and looked at me. The static from my pillows made her hair flutter around her face. I searched her eyes for a sign that she was kidding. But her expression was serious. I felt a pang of something in my gut. Guilt? Remorse? Mu shu pork?

"Your Miss Piggy comment," Paige said. "Ow."

"Sorry." I shrugged. *It was true.*

"No, you're not. But you should be. That's really mean. Especially when you could have said something like 'Paige, your enthusiasm's great, but you might want to take it down a notch.'"

I sighed and wrinkled my nose. "Paige. Your . . . *enthusiasm's* great, but you might wanna take it down a notch." The words felt foreign in my mouth. Wrong, like I'd bitten into a hunk of tofu when I'd ordered steak.

"Okay. We'll try something else," she said, sitting up. "This is gonna hurt, but it's for your own good." She closed her eyes and swallowed. "I . . . have something to tell you. Ever since my presidential bid in fifth, you've been so mean I've actually *avoided* being seen around you."

"What?" I snapped, lunging for my pink throw pillow. "That's a lie. *I* ditched *you!*"

She jumped off the bed and pushed herself onto my desk, gripping the edge. "Nope. I was embarrassed to be seen with you." Her voice softened as her knuckles whitened against the wood. "I even told somebody that your mom used to pay me to walk to school with you, because everybody else was too scared to be your friend."

Ella turned to me, her eyes wide as saucers. I could feel myself flushing, and I wanted to cover Ella's ears with my hands. But it was too late.

"Okay. I get the point. Be nicer. Whatever. Can we move on?" I said quickly. I hated it when Ella looked at me like that.

"Not yet." Paige put her hands on her hips. "Because I could have said all that like this: 'Kacey. My feelings were really hurt in fifth when you didn't support me after I lost the election. It made me feel like we weren't real friends. I'll really miss you, but I just . . . can't hang out with someone who cares more about popularity than people.'"

My throat tightened. Behind her lenses, Paige's eyes turned down at the corners.

"Paige—" I stopped and swallowed.

I was suddenly overcome with the urge to go back in time and prove that Paige was wrong. To show that all my advice, all the times I'd told the truth, had been to help people, not hurt them. The only difference between me and everyone else was that I said what I was thinking to people's faces. And if I showed up to school, like Molly had once, wearing boots covered in hot-pink fur, I'd rather hear it from a friend than learn later that everyone had been talking about the dead Muppet strapped to my feet.

Because the truth was, if someone had pulled me aside when I was younger and said, "Hey, Kacey, just so you know, one day your dad's going to pack up and leave," then maybe I wouldn't have felt so blindsided and stupid and devastated when he'd gone. The truth may hurt, but it was *always* better to know. Always.

"Paige," I started again. It came out sounding like a whisper.

Downstairs, the front door slammed. "Girls?"

My head snapped toward the stairs. "Mom?" My voice sounded breathy and hoarse, like I'd just sprinted from The Square to the studio and back.

I heard the thunk of pumps being kicked off and deposited in the entrance hall, and then light but slow steps as they got closer. Seventeen. Eighteen. Nineteen.

Mom popped her head in and smiled, her eyes heavily lined. It always seemed strange to me when she didn't take off her show makeup before she got home. It took time to find her under all those layers. "So how are things in the war room?" she asked.

"Good." I caught Paige's eye and tried a small smile. My face felt stiff, as if I'd just been crying.

"Hey, stranger." Mom pulled Paige in for a side hug. Then she leaned over the foot of the bed, kissing Ella on the forehead. Finally, it was my turn. She smelled like perfume and bad coffee.

"Gearing up for the good fight, I see." She sat on the edge of the bed and ran her fingers through my hair, which had deflated from rocker chick to baby chick.

"Want a campaign button, Sterling?" Since Paige grew up next door, she's always had a free pass to call Mom by her first name. She grabbed a spare from the pile of buttons on my desk and chucked one in Mom's direction.

"I thought you'd never ask." Mom caught Paige's underhand pitch and pinned the button to her cream blouse without flinching at the holes she was making in the silk. "How does it look?" She scratched my scalp slowly, the way she used to do when I was a kid and I couldn't fall asleep.

"Lookin' good. Maybe you could wear it on the air?" Paige suggested.

Mom smiled. "That wouldn't be very neutral, would it?" she asked. "What about my reputation as an unbiased newswoman?"

"Oh." Paige shrugged. "Right."

Mom swallowed a yawn. "Okay, munchkin," she said to Ella, pulling her onto her lap. "It's time." She plucked a piece of green Silly String from Ella's curls. "Past time, in fact."

"But I want"—Ella yawned mid-sentence—"to watch the show." She rubbed her eyes.

"Tomorrow," Mom promised. She scooped Ella up with a groan and carted her across the room. "Night, girls," she called as she headed down the steps. "Don't stay up too late."

"Niiiiight," we chimed in unison as they disappeared down the stairs.

"I just got this weird feeling," Paige announced, before I had to think of something to say. "Like déjà vu, or something." Her eyes fell on the stack of records piled on my desk chair, and she jumped up and started riffling through them. "Remember when I used to spend the night over here when your parents went out? And your dad would sneak party food back in a napkin and—" She stopped and gnawed at her lip.

"Paige." I took off my glasses and rubbed my eyes. "It's fine." Why didn't anybody get that the only thing worse than not having a dad was feeling like you couldn't even mention him? I used to love those nights when Paige would sleep over, when Dad would heat up hors d'oeuvres on a paper plate and serve them to us on the living room couch. Mom would slip out of her dress shoes and they would curl up together with glasses of wine.

"Where'd you get these?" Paige was quick to change the subject, and I let her.

"That record store in Andersonville." I yawned. "Hey. Put on the Joni Mitchell one. The record player's on the floor there, by the photo booth."

"So Zander's date with Molly's all set up?" Paige kneeled on the floor next to the booth. She lifted the needle on Dad's old RCA, the one I'd just recently pulled out of hiding, and slipped the album from its worn sleeve. It crackled for a few seconds before the low, easy sounds of the first track filled my room.

I shook my head. "He's asking her tomorrow." Which reminded me. I reached for my cell on my bedside table and typed a quick text for Molly.

TOMORROW A.M., A LOCAL ROCK GURU MAKES MUSIC WITH A NEW LEADING LADY. MEET AT LOCKERS 4 DEETS. 7:15 AM– HAVE TO BE IN THE STUDIO BY 7:30.

"Awesome." Paige beamed.

"Oh, and I did I tell you Carlos wants me back for a

broadcast tomorrow morning?" I yawned, like it wasn't a big deal. "He texted and said ratings are down and he heard my lisp was fading, so . . ."

"See? Told you everything was gonna be fine," Paige said knowingly. "And you're gonna be nicer, right? Like I showed you?"

"Leave the broadcasting to the pros, Paige." My eyes fluttered shut. I'd only been off the air for a week, but it felt like years since I'd womaned the desk.

"Kacey?"

"Paige?"

"It's really working. Our plan?"

"It really is." My eyes still closed, I broke into an enormous metal-mouthed grin.

REUNITED, AND IT FEELS SO GOOD
Thursday, 7:17 A.M.

Early the next morning, I found Molly sitting with her back against my locker, looking like she'd camped out in Hemingway the night before. Her hair was pulled back into a messy low ponytail, and her black glitter eyeliner looked smudged, like she'd accidentally fallen asleep with it on. It reminded me of the time she'd passed out at ten at one of my sleepovers, and Nessa and Liv and I got through half a makeover before she woke up and wigged out. The photo booth pictures from that night were priceless. And tacked next to my locker mirror, until last week.

I wasn't sure why, exactly, but I slowed as I got closer to her. It wasn't that I was nervous; I'd rehearsed everything on the El ride to school. How casual and lisp-free my voice would sound as I dropped cryptic hints about

Zander. And my back-to-the-airwaves outfit oozed power and control: my skinniest skinny jeans, the equestrian-style boots Nessa helped me pick out over winter break, and my cream cashmere sweater with the funnel neck and asymmetrical buttons. My high, tight ponytail meant serious business.

"Kacey! Hey! Okay, tell me everything." Molly jumped to her feet and pawed a few layers out of her face. Her pink streak was fading, and her natural white blonde was starting to peek through again. Her eyes widened, pleading for help.

"Hey." I gave her a small smile. For the first time since everything had happened between us, I didn't want to strangle her with her own metal-studded dog collar. Something about how helpless she looked, waiting for me, needing me, made me want to throw my arms around her and squeeze. I wanted to tell her that soon everything would be fine. And then smack her for everything she'd put me through. "Um—"

"No!" she said, a little too loudly. "Wait." The fluorescent overhead lights made her eyes look wild. "Is it bad?" She lunged toward me like she was going to grab me, then took a step back. "If it's bad, I don't wanna know."

"Well—"

"I knew it." She backed up to the lockers and let the

crown of her head rest in defeat against a painted metal vent. "He *would* be the only guy at the school who doesn't love me."

I let that one go. "Mols," I said gently, releasing my messenger bag to the floor.

"Yeah?"

I took a seat on the checkered floor and patted the square next to me. "It's not bad."

"'Kay." She slid down my locker and plopped onto the floor. Then she turned her head and rested her cheek against the locker. "So." She grinned. "Start from the beginning before I. WIG. OUT! What are you WAITING for?"

"So you know how I'm in the band now?"

"Yeah." She sniffed, like she wasn't the least bit jealous.

"So yesterday, Zan— Skinny Jeans and I were hanging out at this record place, and—"

"Name?"

"Vinyl Destination. You've been there, you love it. Your favorite section is the Best New Artists wall in the back room."

"Check." Her gaze fell on my wrist, where Zander's bracelet peeked out from beneath the cuff of my sweater.

I yanked my sleeve over my hand. "Anyway, while we were there, he . . . said he was thinking of asking you out."

So I took a few artistic liberties with the truth. Paige *had* told me to be nicer.

"He just *happened* to bring it up." She braided the fading pink streak, then undid it and started over.

"Mm-hmm," I said through pursed lips.

"OhhhhhmyGOOOOOOODKacey! You're the BEST!" She side-tackled me with an enormous hug, smashing her cheek against mine.

"Owww!" I laughed, spitting out a clump of her hair, which tasted like pineapple pomade. "Get OFF, nut job!" But she held on tight, smashing my glasses into my cheekbones.

"Start from the beginning. Tell me everything, like, word for word." She pushed herself onto her knees, looking petrified and exhilarated at the same time. "Verbates."

"There's not that much to tell," I said, holding back a smile. I'd never seen her get this flustered over a guy before. Though I'd never admit it aloud, guys were the only thing she understood a little better than I did. It made sense if you thought about it, since she had a half-brother in college and a dad at home. To be fair, I didn't have that kind of study material. "Except he said he thought you seemed pretty cool, and—" I dug into my jeans pocket and pulled out the shimmery peach gloss I'd been using to shellac my lips together. "Here."

She grinned and swiped it, slathering on a thick coat. "And?"

"And I said you *were*—cool, I mean—"

"Oh. Uh, hey."

Molly had been so busy body-slamming and quizzing me that neither one of us had noticed Zander heading toward us, spiral notebook in hand. On the back cover was a bumper sticker that read *Mean People Suck*.

We scrambled to our feet.

"Wanted to wish you luck on the broadcast." He glanced at my wrist and smiled.

"Oh. Thanks." I nudged Molly in the ribs.

She flicked her hair over the shoulder. "Hey, Zander Jarvis from Seattle." Her voice sounded almost as raspy as Nessa's great-grandma's, a lifelong smoker with chronic emphysema.

Zander gave a crooked half smile, then raised his eyebrow slightly at me. I blinked back at him, sending him psychic vibes to ask her out.

"Uh, hey . . . Molly . . ."

"Knight," Molly purred. "From Chicags."

"So, what's up?" I asked quickly. *Ask her! Ask her now!*

"Actually, I uh, wanted to talk to Molly," he said. "I, uh, heard you were a die-hard fan of Acoustic—"

"Obv!" Molly turned back to Zander. "They're so raw, so . . ." Her voice faltered, like she was getting distracted by Zander's face.

"I'd say the band's more like . . . unconventional," I offered. Listening to their album for twelve hours on loop had left every single note practically ingrained in my brain.

Zander's eyes lit up, turning from gray to silver.

"*Right?*" Molly said a little too loudly.

Zander and I turned to look at her. She batted her lashes, and I felt a surge of something in the pit of my stomach. Guilt? Irritation? No. More like . . . unease, or something. She and Zander had zero in common. They really should have been chatting about how annoying it was to wait the full twenty minutes before they washed out their hair dye.

"So, ah, I have to get to homeroom." Zander hooked his thumbs around his backpack straps. "But I wanted to check if maybe you wanted to go see the band at Pritzker tomorrow after school?"

"Pritzker?" Molly backed into the lockers, pressing her palms against the metal. "Totes."

"Um . . ." Zander looked to me for help. "What?"

"Totally," I translated.

"Right on." He looked at the ground and scratched the left leg of his jeans with his right sneaker. "Okay, so . . . later."

I fought the urge to fist-pump. The plan was working! Things were starting to feel right with Molly, my lisp was gone, and in TWO DAYS my glasses would be too. *My glasses.* My hand flew to my face, to be sure they were still there. Lately, I hadn't even noticed. Because I had more important things to worry about, not because I was getting used to them.

"So?" I turned to Molly and cocked an eyebrow as Zander walked away. "Simon Saaaaays . . . you've got yourself a hot date."

Molly shook her head back and forth in tiny, jerking movements. "I . . . don't know." She crossed her arms over her chest. Sweaty palm prints glistened on the locker behind her.

"I don't knoooow . . ." *How to carry on a conversation with Zander without my help? How to lead our group the way I could? How to pick a hobby and stick with it?* I shook my head to erase the mean thoughts.

"It's like he's . . . different from other guys." She cast her eyes downward so all I could see were her lashes, coated with plum-colored mascara. Suddenly she looked like a scared little kid who forgot to brush her hair and accidentally got into her mom's makeup drawer. "I dunno. Maybs this wasn't such a good idea?"

My stomach fluttered. She was looking to me for advice, needed me to guide her. Just like old times. "You just need a few pointers before tomorrow, is all." Pointers. Advice. From *me*. The sudden burst of hyper I felt had nothing to do with the hot chocolate I'd had at breakfast. I was needed again. Necessary.

"You've gotta help me," she begged. "Come over after school?"

"I've got band rehearsal." I shrugged, turning toward my locker to hide my smile. "You wouldn't want me to blow off your crush, would you?" I could feel her eyes on me as I twirled the dial on my locker padlock and yanked open the door. In fact, I could feel lots of eyes on me. As homeroom neared, the halls were getting louder and more crowded.

"So come afterrrrr!"

I located my French book under a lone gym sneaker along with my emergency mini flatiron.

"Actually, I'm supposed to, um"—I slammed the locker door—"meet Paige after, to work on her campaign."

"Please." Molly ducked between the locker and me, planting both her hands on my shoulders. "Paige *Greene*?"

I scanned the halls for any sign of Paige. Honestly, I could use a few hours playing with clothes and makeup, instead of mock debating with Paige over things like vegetarian lunch menu choices and the unconstitutionality of forcing people to participate in dodgeball. "I did promise, though."

"Kacey. Seriously? I need"—Molly's eyes flitted to the left of my ear—"this."

I couldn't help the grin that spread over my face. "Yeah, you do," I said crisply, play-shoving her out of my space. "And you know what else you need? To lose the black eyeliner. You look like you're auditioning to be a Kardashian."

As we started to walk down the hall together, Molly slipped her arm into mine. In the midst of the morning chaos, a path slowly cleared for us as we made our way to Sean's. I scrunched my eyes shut and opened them again, almost afraid it was a dream. But it was just my life, finding its way back to normal.

"Oh. Almost forgot," Mols said. "Sleepover tomorrow after the concert, with the girls. My house. 'Kay?"

"'Kay. I've got to get to the studio. First broadcast back." A nervous shiver bolted through me. Was it going back on the air that was making me anxious? Or the idea of hanging with the girls again?

"Break a leg, Kacey." The softness in Molly's sapphire eyes proved that she meant it.

"Thanks." Maybe the shiver was my sixth sense, alerting me that everything was falling magically into place. That soon, the four of us would be back together again.

Without warning, a few doubtful whispers surfaced. I nudged them to the back of my mind. After all, my sixth sense had never been wrong.

JUST LIKE RIDING A BIKE
Thursday, 7:43 A.M.

"I had to pull an old letter from our archives," Carlos said as I sank into my anchor chair with less than a minute to air. Avoiding my eyes, he handed me a baby-blue sheet of paper.

"No letters this week?"

One of the camera guys snorted behind his tripod.

My pulse tripled. "What? What's wrong?"

"Nothing," Carlos said, too quickly. "We got letters. They were just—we couldn't use them."

"Prank letters," clarified Camera Guy Two.

"Just . . . pranking the station." Still, Carlos refused to make eye contact. "They were stupid."

"What kind of loser has nothing better to do than prank-write the station?" My laugh was overly loud, and

Carlos flinched ever so slightly. The rest of the studio was silent, but not in the usual way. Even Camera Guys One through Four seemed nervous, like they were prepared to cut to black if I started lisping up a storm.

"Okay, guys. Have a good show." *You've got this, Simon*, I pep-talked myself. I pushed away from the desk and swiveled around once in my chair. But instead of injecting my hair with volume, it just made me nauseous. Under the desk, I pinched the cuff bracelet on my left wrist. It comforted me, almost as if Zander were there rooting me on.

"Thirty seconds to air." Carlos droned like he was announcing his own death. Depending on how the show went, he might have been announcing mine. "Aren't you going to read through the letter?" It sounded more like a command than a question.

I shook my head vigorously. "We need some energy around here," I insisted. "I'm ad-libbing this one." I flipped the paper over so I wouldn't be tempted.

"Super," Carlos dead-panned, leaning back in his director's chair. "Does anybody know where Abra is?"

"Laryngitis," Camera Three piped up. "Kacey'll have to go long today." He said it like I wasn't sitting directly in front of him.

"Roses." Carlos thunked his head against the wall in slow, agonizing rhythm.

"CAR. LOS." I stiffened, suddenly feeling more defensive than nervous. I couldn't force him to look at me, but he couldn't stop me from staring him down. No way was I going to let myself be embarrassed by a shrimp in ironed jeans and a starched button-down. "Who won the M-my in every possible category this year except 'Best Rookie Broadcaster'?"

Carlos crossed his legs. "You," he huffed.

"Because—" I prompted.

"You're not a rookie."

"Exactly." Someone turned up the lights, and I lifted my face slightly, letting them warm me, energize me. "So maybe you could trust me a little."

Carlos opened his mouth to object. But I wasn't finished.

"And *maybe*, instead of being such a downer, you could do your job and direct my show. Unless you're more interested in finding a new extracurricular? Maybe Math Club historian?" I tightened my ponytail and straightened my glasses. "I hear they have an awesome 'Dress Like Your Favorite Mathematician' costume party every Halloween."

"And she's baaaack." Camera Guy Two's eyes widened.

"You know it." I beamed. "Now let's do a SHOW, people!"

Carlos straightened up and yanked his wireless headset

into place. "Fine." He sniffed. "HERE WE GO! In five, four—"

Trembling with anticipation, I flipped over my script and stared deep into the camera lens in front of me. But something moving around near the doors in the back caught my eye.

"Three, two—"

Paige. She'd just sneaked in and was standing next to the doors in the back. She flashed me a thumbs-up sign and a giant grin.

One. Carlos signaled me with his index finger and I flashed the Simon Smile, braces and all.

"Morning, Marquette. And welcome to this week's edition of *Simon Says.*" I swear I heard orchestra music swelling somewhere in the background. The kind they play in feel-good movies when the heroine (me) has overcome every tragic obstacle imaginable to kick some serious butt while her nerdy sidekick (Paige) cheers her on from the wings. "I'm your host, Kacey Ssssimon, and from all of us here at Channel M, apologies for last week's hiatus. You have my word that it won't happen again."

I glanced down at my script. The words were clear and crisp, even if the paper was trembling in my hands. "Today's letter comes to us from Picked On in P.E. Picked on writes: 'Dear Kacey, ever since I started middle school here, I'm having a really awful time. Kids aren't that friendly here, especially if you're new or different—'"

My throat caught on the word *different*, and the words swam together on the page in front of me, as if I'd taken off my glasses. Frantically, I scanned the page for my place.

"Um, 'especially if you're new or different. And I'm really having a sucky time in P.E. I'm always the last one picked for kickball, and last week somebody stole my gym shoes and shorts, so I had to run the cross-country mile in my socks and my brother's SpongeBob swim trunks. Someone even posted a picture on Facebook.'"

I swallowed a laugh. *It's not funny. Think about You-Tube. Think about YouTube.*

"'I want to transfer schools again, but my mom won't let me. What can I do to fit in better?'"

The second I stopped reading, the studio seemed to flood with silence. Paige hovered expectantly in the back, probably waiting for me to give the poor loser a virtual hug and tell him everything was going to be fine. That he'd be Homecoming King before the semester was out. But I couldn't do that, could I? Lie to the kid, just for the sake of making him feel better?

I gripped the script so tightly, I could hear the paper crinkle. No. I was a *journalist*. A good one. And I couldn't sacrifice my principles just because Paige thought they were mean.

My eyes snapped back to the camera. "Dear Picked On," I started slowly. "First of all, don't feel bad about the bathing suit. My little sister has SpongeBob pajamas, and they're super cute on her." I paused and shook my head slowly at the camera. "Of course, she's six. And you're in sixth."

Carlos clapped his hand over his mouth.

"See the diff—"

I was halfway through an eye roll at the camera when Paige ducked into my line of sight, shaking her head so violently, it looked like it might spin off. I could practically hear her words from the night before: *Ever since my presidential bid in fifth, you've been so mean I've actually avoided being seen around you.*

The same feeling I'd felt the night before seized my stomach and kneaded it like silly putty. But this time, I couldn't blame it on the mu shu.

"Um . . ." I glanced at the countdown clock, the red digits ticking away second after second of dead air. I could always give Paige's way a shot, right? Go back to my way if her way bombed?

Please. One more slip on the social ladder, and I'd be a goner.

Then again, Paige had been dead on with her strategy so far. . . .

You've been so mean I've actually avoided being seen around you.

I bit my lip. And the proverbial bullet.

"Dear Picked On," I said in my most serious broadcaster voice. "Do you have any idea who you're talking to?"

I could hear Carlos's palms rubbing together in excitement.

"You're talking to a girl who has spent almost two weeks at Marquette with giant tortoiseshell glasses and an accent that's rivaled only by Daffy Duck's. And you think *you've* got it bad?"

Cameras One through Four started laughing. When I narrowed my eyes at them for kicks, the laughter turned to coughing fits.

"Count your lucky stars, Picked On. At least you only made it to Facebook. As far as I know, my YouTube spoof has been translated into fourteen different languages."

Paige's giggles rose over the camera guys' coughing fits.

"I set off metal detectors with nothing but my mouth, still can't handle solid foods, and weigh an extra four pounds with my glasses on," I continued. "So, Picked On—" I stopped to savor the familiar feeling of victory. "So," I said again, softer this time. "I know what you're going through. And the best advice I can give you is this: Hang in there. It might suck for a while, but eventually, you'll find friends who like you for you. And in the meantime, join the yearbook staff so you can make some friends and delete that pic. Oh, and ditch the SpongeBob shorts. This has been Kacey Simon. Until next time, Marquette." I gazed into camera two until the lights above me dimmed.

"Aaaand, we're out!" Carlos announced. He slid out of his chair and walked briskly across the set to my desk. "*That*, Kacey Simon, was pretty genius."

"What'd I tell you?" I grabbed my messenger bag.

"Nice work." Camera Guys Three and Four high-fived me as I shimmied between their cameras.

"Thanks, guys. See you next week." I felt like I could have flown out the door to homeroom.

In the back of the studio, Paige was waiting for me.

She wrapped her arms around me and squeezed. "I knew you could do it!"

I hugged her back, and we stumbled through the double doors still linked together.

"And I was thinking? Maybe you could work it out with your producer so that we could televise the next presidential debate? You could even moderate!"

"Sign me up, Pres—"

"Uh, hey." Standing just outside the studio doors, with

his hands stuffed awkwardly in his pockets, was Quinn Wilder.

I stopped, and so did Paige.

Excitement buzzed through me, followed by confusion, and then a general ate-too-much-Halloween-candy-and-now-I-think-I-might-puke kind of sensation. I didn't know what to do or say, so I just stared at him, hoping I was shooting him a dirty look. And that my lenses magnified it.

He was wearing perfectly faded jeans, sneakers, and a ripped Hard Rock Cafe Chicago T-shirt under a pumpkin-colored hoodie. It was my favorite hoodie, the one he'd been wearing at Sugar Daddy when he'd ordered the exact same cupcake as me.

"Hey." I inhaled. Not because I wanted to see if he still smelled minty fresh, or if the smell of butterscotch still lingered on his sweatshirt, but because I had to breathe. I didn't really have a choice.

He did, coincidentally, smell minty fresh. With a hint of butterscotch.

"What . . . what are you doing here?" Suddenly, my power outfit seemed all wrong. The high neck on my sweater was making my neck itch, and my boots were pinching my toes.

"I, uh—" Quinn glanced at me, then at Paige.

"I should get to homeroom." Paige said hurriedly, untangling herself from my arm. She caught my eye for a split second, questioning if I wanted her to stay. I double-blinked *no*.

"So." Quinn's voice was husky, like he belonged in some sort of rugged cologne ad. It was almost enough to make me forgive him. "I guess she, uh . . . she's probably kind of mad at me."

"Huh?" My head jerked up, and our eyes met. Or my eyes landed on the spot where his should have been. But he was overdue a hair toss, so all I could see were his soft, sandy-colored bangs.

"I mean, I just wanted to . . ." Now Quinn was the one staring at his feet. "I'm really sorry I didn't say anything at lunch the other day. Those guys were being really lame."

"Yeah. They were." *You were.* I tried to sound mad, but the part in Quinn's hair was adorably off-center. I wondered what kind of shampoo he used to make it fall like that.

"And uh . . . it really wasn't cool. So . . . sorry." Quinn coughed, then hair-tossed. In the brief second that his eyes were visible, they burned with irresistible remorse.

"'Kay." I could feel my cheeks starting to get hot. "So, uh . . . we should get to homeroom." But for some reason, my feet wouldn't move.

"Yeah." Quinn took a step closer. "And, um, one more thing. I, uh, think your glasses are cool. They make your eyes look pretty." The lighting in the hall washed over his chiseled features. It was like he was a perfect boy statue, posed in the middle of the Louvre, or something. All I could do was stare like an idiotic, fanny pack–wearing tourist.

Say something witty. . . .

"Well, don't get too used to them." I tried a hair toss of my own. My ponytail whipped me in the cheek. "Ow. They're coming off in two days."

"Bummer." Quinn grinned, tilting his head slightly to the right. And then he leaned in closer. So close, his warm breath was tickling my nose.

I froze. Was he going to *kiss* me? In the middle of *SIL-VERSTEIN?* But I hadn't had the chance to Google *making out with braces* yet! My throat went completely dry, and my pits were suddenly drenched with sweat.

Briiiiiiiiiiiiiiiiiiiiiiiiiiiiiiiiiiiiiiiiiiiing! The homeroom bell sliced through our movie moment, leaving me with my head tilted slightly and a tiny trail of drool threatening to trickle down my lip. In under a second, we both snapped upright.

"So . . . uh, see you later?" Quinn said into his hoodie.

I mumbled something about getting to homeroom and

bolted, feeling dizzy and sweaty and completely crazed, like it was all a dream. Only it wasn't. It was my life. And Quinn Wilder seemed to want back in. Seemed to like me. *Me.* Braces, glasses, and all.

ONCE MORE, FROM THE TOP
Thursday, 4:39 P.M.

Hendrix greeted me at Zander's door that afternoon with
a quick flash of his incisors, but no bark. I took it as a
sign of progress.

"Sorry I'm late." I hit the toes of my boots against the
cement stoop, knocking frozen chunks of dirty snow from
the treads. Inside, Zander, Nelson, and Kevin were setting
up in the breakfast nook. The Beat was filming them with
his camcorder. In the center of the coffee table, a cedar-
scented pillar candle smoldered, making the entire loft smell
like boy. "I stayed after to watch the tape of the broadcast."

I shimmied out of my coat and draped it across the
leather sofa arm. When I yanked up my sweater sleeves, I
couldn't shake the feeling that Zander was watching me.
Staring, even. I ran the back of my hand across my lips.

Could he tell that Quinn had come centimeters away from kissing me?

"Oh, yeah?" Instead of laying into me for being late, Zander wandered into the living area. "And?"

"And . . ." I squinted into his eyes. This afternoon they were a light gray, and it looked like tiny flecks of gold danced around his pupils. Was he laughing at me? "And I think it went pretty well," I finished lamely.

"Yeah, it did." Finally, he broke into a grin. "Guys in my homeroom thought it was gutsy, ragging on yourself like that. And it was cool to see you cut the kid some slack and give him real advice, for a change."

"*Real* advice?" A defensive note crept into my voice. *For a change?*

Sensing a footage-worthy debate, The Beat rotated his camcorder in our direction.

"You know. Like, *nice* advice. Stuff he could actually use." Before I could argue that *all* my advice was *stuff people could actually use*, Zander refocused on my wrist. "Like that cuff bracelet, huh?"

"Oh. Yeah. Sorry." I scrambled to unsnap it, embarrassed. It wasn't like I was wearing it on purpose. I kept putting it on in the morning so I'd remember to give it back once I got to school. But then I'd forget and have to start over again the next day.

"Leave it," he said. "Looks cool."

I rubbed the leather between my index finger and thumb. "I'll give it back at the end of practice."

"Whatever." He shrugged and sat on the arm of the sofa. "So'd you listen to the Fleetwood Mac I left in your locker yesterday?"

"Yeah, and I wanna do a cover of 'Go Your Own Way.'" I nudged him over and sat down next to him. "Acoustic."

"You'd totally rock it." Resting his forearms on his thighs, he cocked his head to the side to look at me. "We could work on some harmonies." His expression glazed over, the way it always did when he was playing or talking music. When he closed his eyes, I could almost see the notes flying around in his head.

"Hey!" Nelson looked up from his keyboard, his hands flying over the dials on the body. "What's the holdup, kids?"

"Coming." I hopped up.

Zander, Hendrix, and I crossed to the nook, and I took my place at the mic while The Beat set up his camcorder on a tripod.

"Act natural," he instructed me. "I wanna get some good behind-the-scenes footage for the site."

I nodded. I was used to the camera. Hendrix circled in front of me a few times, then dropped to the floor and rested his chin on his paws.

"Anybody have an extra copy of the sheet music?" I tilted the mic down slightly and yanked the ponytail holder out of my hair, giving it a good shake.

No answer.

I looked up. "Hey. Guys. Sheet music." My post-practice plans with Molly were the first we'd had in a while, and being late wasn't an option. "I need it."

The Beat took his place behind me on the drums. "Not today, you don't," he said mysteriously.

"You did good last week, but we need a lead who has rock in her soul." Nelson closed his eyes.

"Today, we rock freestyle," finished The Beat. "You up for it?"

"*Freestyle?*" My voice was starting to sound panicky. No lyrics? No sheet music? What next, no instruments? "You want me to make up lyrics. On the spot." My eyes darted to the blinking camcorder.

"You didn't think we were gonna let you in the band that easy, did you?" Kevin scolded. "We gotta make sure you can jam."

I clenched the mic stand in my grip, twisting my fists back and forth. I was going to *kill* Zander. This was how he thanked me for hooking him up with the second-most— uh, the most—popular girl in school?

"So here's the deal," Zander explained. "The Beat

starts us out, and then we all jump in when we feel it. Other than that, no rules. Any questions?"

Hendrix lifted his head and grinned at me, his tongue lolling out of the left side of his mouth. He was loving this even more than the rest of them.

I nodded tightly, glaring at the dog. My glasses were starting to mist over with a thin layer of fear. I'd already ad-libbed once today and rocked it. Why push my luck, when things were just starting to get back to normal?

I skipped the cleansing breaths and visualized myself strangling Zander with his own guitar strings.

"Here we go." Zander nodded at The Beat.

No! Wait! I quit! I gripped the mic tighter to steady myself, but they slipped down to the stand. I wiped them on my jeans and tried again. No luck.

When everybody else was making last-minute adjustments to their instruments, Zander shot me a secret smile. In return, I shot him a death stare.

"And ONE! TWO! ONE! TWO! THREE! FOUR!" The Beat yelled. He started off with an easy, steady rhythm, accenting every other beat.

"Called a backbeat! Emphasis on two and four. We'll hang here for a while."

I ignored him, racking my brain for words. Any words that made sense. But my mind was completely blank.

Soon, Nelson's fingers were flying over the keyboard, and Kevin and Zander were rocking out, too. Nobody seemed the least bit concerned that THIS WASN'T A SONG.

"Jump in!" Nelson said it like it was just a casual, optional invite.

Any. Words. At All.

"I don't know what to sing!" I wailed. "I can't just make something up!"

"Yeah, you can!" Zander tapped his bare left foot against the floor. "Whatever comes to mind. Try not to think so hard!"

"Nobody cares if it sucks," offered Kevin oh-so-helpfully.

My breath caught in my throat. *Step one. Open mouth.*

"Just use whatever's going through your head!" The Beat picked up, well, the beat.

Fine. If they wanted ad-lib, they'd get ad-lib. I took a deep breath.

"Gravity . . . weighs down . . . on me," I started.

"There she goes!" Zander hooted.

"Met this . . . blue-haired guy, and I can't deny,

In his skinny jeans, ohhhhh,

Looks like girls I knooooow—"

"She got you, dude!" Nelson burst out laughing.

Hendrix lifted his snout and howled along.

"You asked for it." I smiled into the mic while The Beat switched to a slower tempo, and everybody followed. Out of the corner of my eye, I glanced at Zander, just to make sure he knew I was joking. To tell the truth, I didn't mind the skinny jeans so much anymore. They were kind of his trademark, like his version of the Simon Smile.

Without warning, he leaned into his mic.

"Yeah, she's got frames, but they're not to blame,
For all the change, she's seein'.
And she rocks 'em out, yeah she rocks so mellow,
She's our Buddy Holly, she's our Elvis Costello."

I laughed, leaning over and giving him a high five. The longer we rocked, the more the vibrations from the music massaged the tension from my body, transporting me to a whole new place where I could just be myself.

CHEAT SHEET
Thursday, 9:03 P.M.

After scarfing down a quick dinner at home, I took the Red Line to Molly's house to pick out a date-night outfit and quiz her on her Zander Jarvis knowledge. For a girl obsessed, she was failing miserably. I vowed not to leave until she had something intelligent to say about Acoustic Rebellion or looked so cute it didn't matter. Whichever came first.

"Lightning round!" Stretching out on my stomach on her king-sized bed, I rested my pack of index cards against a sparkling silver knit throw. "You ready?"

Other than a boot heel stomping against the hardwood floor inside her walk-in closet, I didn't get an answer. I propped my chin in my hands and took a look around, bobbing my head to the low thrum of Acoustic Rebellion's latest track.

For the most part, Molly's room looked the same as the last time I'd seen it: The ivory tulle canopy was still draped over the gigantic mahogany bed; the window seat across the room still offered a tiny peek of Wrigley Field if you pressed your nose against the glass and looked all the way to the left. Twinkling holiday lights were still strung across the ceiling, between her bedposts and the curtain rod over the window. But the details were different. The picture of the four of us that used to be taped to the painted vanity mirror next to her bed had vanished. The riding helmet that used to hang on one of the bedposts had been replaced with a black feather boa. And there was a hot pink bumper sticker pasted to the back of her bedroom door that read ROCK REVOLUTION. Was that a band Zander hadn't told me about yet?

The new touches in the familiar space made me feel like an outsider. It reminded me of the time I'd gotten back from summer camp, homesick and dying for my room, only to find that Mom had moved Ella's bed where mine used to be and changed the lampshades. Mom had accused me of being dramatic when I insisted we move the furniture back. But she didn't get it. Those details mattered.

"Mols!" I called again. "Lightning round!"

"Hit me." Molly's voice was muffled by the closet door.

I plucked an index card from the center of the deck.

"In the third track of the album, what contributes to the bluesy quality of the music?" Pumping up the volume on Molly's iPod dock, I found the third track that I'd copied from the vinyl. Instantly, an eerie, sad sound floated through the room.

"Are cowboy boots still in?" A pom-pom from Molly's cheerleading day (singular) sailed from the closet and landed in front of the bed.

"Are you even paying attention?" I groaned, settling on my back and staring at the ceiling. The twinkle lights shone dully through the tulle canopy, making it feel like I was staring at stars in a foggy night sky.

"Totally," Molly said. "Ummm . . . the major chord."

I sat up when Molly emerged from the closet, wearing a denim miniskirt, a too-tight Acoustic Rebellion tee, and cowboy boots over shredded tights. "What do you think?" She hopped over the outfit graveyard between us and did a little spin.

"Wrong. It's the minor key." *And I think that's almost the same outfit you wore last Halloween to be a slutty cowgirl.* "So . . . you actually want my opinion now?"

Molly blushed. "Obv."

I leaned over to her bedside table and turned down the volume on the iPod dock. *I think Zander was right: You really don't care what people think of your outfits.*

Also, I think this guitar riff is amazing.

"Hey." Molly finger-snapped me out of my solo haze. "For real. What do you think?"

"I—" I froze, Paige's words of wisdom blaring in my brain. "I think, maybe . . . try it without the band shirt or the tights?" It sounded like a question. I sucked in and held my breath.

Molly's forehead crinkled. Then she turned to face her reflection in the full-length mirror behind the door. "Wait. Is this my slutty cowgirl costume?"

"YES!" I exhaled. "DON'T DO IT!"

"So how come you didn't SAY anything?"

"I know. Sorry." My cheeks were suddenly flaming. Maybe Paige didn't know everything there was to know about truth-telling. Maybe some people liked other people the way other people *used* to be.

"What's his dog's name again?" Molly hurried over to her vanity and started removing her thick black glitter liner with a Q-tip.

"Hendrix. As in Jimi." I slid off the bed and riffled through the clothes pile on the floor. A slinky bronze tank and long-sleeved chocolate shirt caught my eye. "Here. Wear the tank over the shirt, with jeans and the boots, and lose the tights. Plus, we have to do something about that pink streak. It looks like you took a highlighter to your head."

In the reflection of the vanity mirror, I caught the look of relief flooding Molly's face. "Ohmygod. You're right."

"I know. Don't worry. We'll fix it." The longer I spent in Molly's room, the more it felt familiar. This was where I belonged. No matter what had happened between us, it was all in the past. Soon, we'd forget about the last two weeks, and all the girls would remember how much they needed me.

Molly and I caught each other's eye in the mirror and semi-smiled. Our reflections looked weird, mine standing behind hers, like a before-and-after shot for *Extreme Makeover: Geek Edition.*

On the bedside table, my cell pinged.

PAIGE: HOW'S IT GOING W/M?

KACEY: SO FAR, SO GOOD. ALTHO SHE SUCKS AT LIGHTNING ROUND.

PAIGE: OR: SHE COULD USE SOME IMPROVEMENT IN LIGHTNING ROUND.

KACEY: SUUUUUUCKS. ☺

PAIGE: CAN WE WORK ON CAMPAIGN TMRW?

KACEY: CAN'T. SLEEPOVER AT MOLS. SATURDAY AM?

"Who's that?" Molly demanded, turning around.

"Zander," I blurted. I didn't know why I'd said it, exactly. "He says he's psyched to hang with you tomorrow night."

"Nice." Molly flushed. "Tell him same, but don't put a smiley face or anything." She swiped my wardrobe choices from the crook of my arm and disappeared into the closet again. "I'm gonna try on the new outfit."

I snapped my phone shut and tossed it on the bed, reaching for my note cards. "The next category is pre-show conversation topics," I called. "Name two of Zander's three biggest musical inspirations. In under ten seconds. Readyyyyyyy, GO!"

"Wait!" Molly shrieked. "Brain freeze!"

"Eight!" I called. "Seven! Six! Ohhhhhhhhmygosh this is the longest awkward silence in the middle of a date eeeeever! Four! Three! Two! Your second date depends on this one—"

"WHO ARE THE JONAS BROTHERS?" Molly tripped over a pair of ice skates and stumbled into the middle of the room, sweaty and only half-clothed.

"Wrong!" I shouted. *Marley! Hendrix! Dylan!*

"Whatevs." She giggled, collapsing on the bed and batting the tulle away from her face. "He's, like, super lucky to be going out with me, anyway."

"Yeah. I bet he's always wanted to date a slutty cowgirl." Okay. I could have said something a little more . . .

Paige-approved. But Molly deserved a little grief.

"Bite me, four eyes." Then she rolled onto her side and looked at me. But it wasn't like she was staring at my glasses or making fun of me. It was sort of like . . . she saw the old me. "So Quinn Wilder totally misses you at rehearsal."

"For real?" I sat up. "He said that? When?" Had he told her about our near kiss in the hall?

"Please. He didn't have to. Who reads boys better than anyone you know?" she said confidently.

"Youyouyou. Now spill." I leaned forward.

"So we were at Sugar Daddy yesterday after rehearsal, and Quinn was trying to decide what to order, and what was that cupcake you guys used to get?"

"Butterscotch with dark chocolate frosting and mini-marshmallows."

"Right." Molly blew a few rogue strands out of her eyes. "So anyways, he orders plain chocolate with peanut butter frosting."

I waited.

"Get it?" Her eyes sparked with pride.

"Spell it out for me," I said flatly.

She sighed. "He obv couldn't order the butterscotch one, 'cause it was too emotionally *painful*, you know?"

"Nice try." I snorted.

My phone pinged again.

MOM: SCHOOL NIGHT. TAKE A CAB BACK–IT'S DARK.

"I gotta go." I jumped up. "That's Mom."

Molly's eyes widened in alarm. "But we haven't even gone over my witty comebacks and date laugh!" She reached for the note cards scattered on the bed, but I swiped them away.

"You've got this," I promised. "He'll love you. He's a guy, isn't he?" I half believed what I was telling her. Zander *was* a guy, despite the girl jeans and the fact that he was just . . . different from any guy I'd ever known. There was a part of me that thought Zander wouldn't fall for Molly's flirt tactics the way every other guy did. Or maybe at the core, all boys were the same.

Molly bit her lip and smiled. "Yeah. I guess you're right." She shook her head back and forth, like she was shaking off any remaining doubt.

"So you're coming to the sleepover tomorrow, right?" she asked as I gathered my stuff.

"Yeah." I bit the inside of my lip, to keep from smiling too wide.

"Good." Molly sighed. "Liv and Nessa are getting kind of annoying."

"Yeah?" I probably didn't have to sound so happy

about it.

"Like this morning, Liv picture-texted five times, asking which one of her grandpa's ties would work best as a shoulder strap for her new line of bags."

The yellow striped one.

"And it's like, I'm not your mom. Make a decision for yourself."

"Sounds like you need a break," I said sympathetically. "So . . . um, good luck tomorrow." I reached for the door handle. But before I could leave, Molly bounded over and squeezed me tight.

"I'm so glad we're talking again," she said into my hair.

"Me, too," I said. And of all the honest things I'd said that day, I meant that one the most.

SAME AS IT EVER WAS
Friday, 8:01 P.M.

The next evening, I hugged my sleeping bag to my chest with one arm and pressed the doorbell above the tacky ceramic HOME SWEET HOME sign Molly had made in second grade. As the doorbell chimed, I willed my right eye to stop twitching. My nerves had nothing to do with Molly and Zander's afternoon together, even though we *had* all decided last year that I'd be the first in the group to date. It had everything to do with feeling like anything was possible tonight. And not in a good way. Maybe Molly had softened a little—after all, she owed me for the date with Zander *and* the fashion advice—but Nessa and Liv were another story. What if they didn't want to make up?

"I gooooot it!" On the other side of the door, Molly's

shoes clacked across the hardwood floor. Those were definitely not cowboy boots.

"Hey, Kacey!" she chirped after she threw open the door. "Liv and Nessa just got here. Almost before I did, 'cause I ended up chilling with Z the whole afternoon."

Nessa's wedge booties. Leggings. An oversized guy's shirt, probably from Liv's collection.

And black. Glitter. Liner.

Stop. Rewind. Play.

I didn't know what annoyed me more: Molly's blatant disregard of my outfit advice, or her acting like Zander was her new BFF, when I'd been the one hanging with him every afternoon after school.

"Like the threads?" Molly did a quick twirl to showcase the boots, then pushed open the screen door so I could step into the foyer. "Last-minute decision. Zander was hanging in the den with my mom, and all of a sudden, the other outfit just wasn't working, so . . ."

I ditched my sleeping bag and backpack in the middle of the entrance hall and stepped over them. I wanted to ask her a million questions, like whether she'd texted Nessa to ask outfit advice. Or whether she'd showed Zander her room. Or what she thought was so wrong with the outfit *I'd* picked out. "You mean, Zander picked you up?"

"Yeah." She cocked her head to one side. "It was a

date." She whirled around on one heel and we headed down the narrow hallway to her room. There was a signed Acoustic Rebellion poster hanging on her closed door, and the CD blared from the stereo. It was the sixth track, the first one Zander ever learned on guitar. I had to give it to her: The girl didn't waste time.

For some reason, I felt a wave of anger. My hands curled to fists, but I uncurled them instantly. What did I care if she and Zander got to go backstage?

Molly's room smelled like fresh chocolate chip cookies, which somehow made me want to dry-heave. Liv and Nessa were sitting on the edge of Molly's bed, staring at her laptop screen. They looked different somehow. Like a year had passed, instead of just a week, and I was completely clueless about their lives. Did they have crushes on any new guys? Did Liv still like incense? Was Nessa still into all things French?

I hesitated in the doorway. "Hey, girls."

In theory, I was going for breezy/casual. In practice, it sounded more like anxious/nauseated, with just a pinch of hostility. I shrugged off my coat and draped it over the knob on the closed closet door.

Liv and Nessa looked up, but the tulle canopy obscured their faces. My skin suddenly felt dewy with sweat.

Finally, Liv broke out into a smile. "Hey!" She whipped

the canopy out of the way. The forest green bindi on her forehead matched her eyes, and she'd flatironed her black hair and center-parted it. She looked like she belonged in ninth, at least.

Nessa stood. Her pixie cut was slicked back, making her dark eyes and prominent cheekbones stand out even more. "Nice work with the whole Zander thing. Didn't think you could pull it off."

Was that supposed to be a compliment?

Liv's round cheeks flushed. "Seriously impressive, Kacey."

"Uh, thanks," I said awkwardly, still hanging by the door.

Silence.

"Molly was just showing us her Facebook album from the date," Liv announced. She tucked Molly's laptop under her arm, looking like she wanted to show me something but couldn't bring herself to take the first step.

"Already?" I forced a laugh and unwound the scarf Liv had knitted for my eleventh birthday, but my throat didn't feel any less tight. I mentally kicked myself for wearing one of Liv's designs to the sleepover. Did it make me look desperate?

"That's what *I* said." Nessa wrapped Molly's silver throw around her. "Mental, right?"

"Restraining order worthy." I sat on the edge of the window seat, grabbing a cookie from the plate next to me even though I wasn't hungry. Liv sat next to me and opened the laptop.

"The fourth one's my fave." Molly was checking her ends in the window instead of looking at the screen, meaning she'd memorized the slideshow. "We got so close to the stage, I think the lead guy spit on me."

"Disgusting." Nessa joined us by the window. The four of us fit on the cushion perfectly. It felt like a sign. I took a cautious bite of my cookie.

Liv handed me the laptop and I clicked through the first few pics. I had to admit, number four was a cool shot. Zander and Molly had their backs to the funky silver stage, so you could see the band in the background, rocking on what looked like an enormous space-orbiting satellite. Zander had taken the shot with his left hand and had his other arm looped around Molly's shoulder. Molly's eyes were so wide and her smile was so big, she looked possessed.

And really, really happy.

The bite of cookie churned in my stomach.

"He's just . . ." Molly got this faraway look, like she was posing for one of those terrible engagement pictures in the Sunday *Trib*, where the couples hugged prom-style and gazed into their future. Then she sighed. "You know?"

"What'd you guys talk about on the way there?" Nessa pulled her lanky legs to her chest.

"Everything," Mols said. "Mostly how much we have in common, though. Like how we both love Johnny Hendrix, and traveling the world, and whatever."

Jimi. Jimi Hendrix. I eyed her skeptically. I knew for a fact the farthest Molly Knight had ever been was Arizona to visit her grandparents, and that definitely didn't qualify as "traveling the world, and whatever."

"And he was telling me about how he really doesn't care what anybody thinks." She paused, probably for emphasis. "He said that's what he liked about me. That I do my own thing." She glanced quickly at me.

"Totally. You totally do your own thing," I reassured her.

Nessa shook her head. "Please. Everybody cares what people think. It's human nature."

"He really doesn't," I said. "It's kind of weird." Now that I thought about it, it was actually one of the things I liked best about him.

"I think it's cool not to care," Liv argued, twisting a turquoise ring around her finger. I'd bought it for her when she got her tonsils out last summer.

"You *would* think that." Nessa rolled her eyes.

I leaned back against the window, the chill from the glass seeping through my mini sweater dress. "It's like . . . when Zander's playing music, he's in his own world, and nothing else matters."

"So hot." Molly fanned herself with her palm. "I felt the same way at the Mall of America."

"So are you going out with him again?" Liv pressed.

"Obv. I mean, he said he was coming to the show tomorrow night." Her eyes darted over to mine uncertainly.

"I'm sure he'll be there," I assured her. Then I lifted my cookie in the air in a toast. "Cheers. To . . ."

"Getting back together!" Liv finished my thought for me.

"Geek chic!" Molly giggled.

"No more lithp!" I proclaimed boldly.

"Hot dates with the new kid." Nessa lifted her own cookie.

Molly flushed. "And to one more thing," she said quickly, glancing between Nessa and Liv. They smiled into their cookies.

"What?" I asked, an odd tingle making its way up my leg.

"So I was thinking about it, and I decided I'm gonna need time to focus on my new relationship. Which means I prob shouldn't star in *Guys and Dolls*," Molly said slowly.

I inhaled a lungful of cookie crumbs, then bent over, wheezing. Liv whacked me on the back.

"The show's for one night, Molly," Nessa reminded her.

"A good girlfriend focuses on her relationship." Molly sounded like she was reading out of *Ladies' Home Journal*.

"What is this, 1950?" Nessa challenged.

"You're quitting?" I sputtered. Was this a joke? I scanned the room, looking for a tell-tale red light. Had she just lured me here to make fun of me, film it on some sort of nanny cam, and broadcast it all over again?

Molly grinned. "I already talked to Sean and told him your lisp was gone and everything. He says it's fine by him. I can still be one of the background dancers. And besides, you really are meant to be the lead."

"But—" My tongue was moving at half the speed of my brain. Was she stepping down because she felt guilty? Did Sean fire her? No way was Molly Knight giving up a night in the spotlight for a guy. I cursed myself for being so quick to trust her again. It was just like Paige had said. You couldn't get something for nothing. *Quid pro*—

"Course, I'm gonna need you to do something for me." *Quo.*

I swallowed. Hard. "What?"

"So I can't really have my new boyfriend—"

"Boyfriend?" I interrupted.

"—*boyfriend* hanging with another girl every day after school."

"So?" I asked, not getting the point.

"So . . . you should prob quit the band." Molly blinked innocently, like she had just asked to borrow an unflattering sweater I didn't really care about.

Liv and Nessa looked at me expectantly.

"So?" Molly blinked. "The band, or the show? Choose."

The air in Molly's room seemed hotter than ever. Leave Gravity for one night onstage? For Quinn Wilder? For a steamy stage kiss and the adoration of the entire school? For my comeback?

To regain my rightful place at Marquette. On top with my girls, where we belonged.

The choice should have been easy. So why did I have no idea what to say?

NOW THAT'S COLD

Saturday, 7:27 A.M.

I woke up the next morning to a text from Zander, asking me to meet him at the Millennium Park skating rink. I dressed in the dark and slipped out before the girls woke up.

The rink was deserted. The ice stretched in front of me, white and smooth as glass. Beyond the rink was The Bean, the huge mirrored silver statue in the shape of a bean that reflected the Michigan Avenue skyline. And farther east was Pritzker, the pavilion where Molly and Zander had gone on their date. *Their date.* I shook the image from my head, the wind whipping in my ears. If it wasn't for that stupid date, I wouldn't have to make this choice.

"Hey!" Zander sat at one of the tables on the far side of the rink, facing the towering buildings on Michigan

Avenue. His guitar case leaned against the edge of the round table, and a silver thermos peeked out of the bag at his feet. He waved me over.

"It's zero degrees out," I informed him, hurrying around the rink and plopping down next to him. My houndstooth coat sleeve brushed against his wrist, and I suddenly felt jumpy. "What are we doing here?" I shaded my eyes with my palm as the sun lifted higher in the sky, casting gold shadows over the ice.

He shrugged. "I come here sometimes in the morning to think. It's quiet, you know?" His breath curled in smoky wisps in front of us.

I nodded. When Mom and Dad started fighting a lot, I used to sneak off to the seal tank at the Lincoln Park Zoo. The underwater observatory was dim, and almost completely silent. It was the only place I could go to think.

The morning cold was seeping through my coat, and I leaned a little closer to Zander.

"Here." He leaned over and pulled the silver thermos out of his bag. I unscrewed the top. Rich, sugary steam rose from inside, and I took a giant gulp of hot chocolate. It burned sliding down my throat.

"Okay. For real," I sputtered. "What are you doing here?"

"Fine." He laughed a little and stared down at his lap. There was a giant hole in the left knee of his jeans, but he didn't seem to notice. "Sometimes I come and try out new songs here. I sort of . . . pretend I'm playing Pritzker." The winter flush in his cheeks deepened. "It's stupid. The grounds people are cleaning up over there anyway, so I had to settle for the rink."

"It's not stupid," I said earnestly. "Sometimes I do live election coverage in the shower."

"Really?" But he didn't laugh. He just smiled this small, knowing smile, like he was taking in my secret and holding it safe.

I looked away. "So, uh . . . you have a new song?" I wrapped my hands around the thermos and squeezed.

He nodded. "Part of it."

"Can I hear?"

He stared out at the buildings on the other side of Michigan Avenue, like he hadn't even heard me. I followed his gaze, tried to find the apartment Paige and I had sworn we'd live in when we grew up. But none of the buildings looked familiar.

"So you know that footage The Beat filmed at rehearsal the other day?" Zander finally said.

"Of my terrible freestyling?" I snorted.

He grinned. "He posted it on our website—"

"ONLINE?" I whacked him in the arm.

"—and we got a call from this talent scout," Zander finished with a proud smile. "He's setting up a showcase at that coffee house next to Vinyl Destination. It's for a bunch of up-and-coming bands."

"What?" My shriek echoed over the ice.

"It's called Rock Chicago. And he wants us to perform."

"Like a real gig?"

"Like a real gig." He lifted his sticker-covered guitar case and unsnapped the hinges.

A showcase? Meaning . . . me and Gravity on a stage, with spotlights and a real, live audience?

"This is amazing!" I held out my gloved hand and he slapped it.

"I know! We have to get a set together, like now. The show is next Friday."

The cold from the bench seeped through the thin fabric of my jeans, slowly freezing me from the outside as Zander's words sank in. *Next Friday.* But I might not even be in the band the next Friday, not if I dropped out like Molly wanted.

Zander pulled out the guitar and began to strum. "I don't think this new song is ready yet . . . but here goes."

The opening chords were slow, and there was even a little hesitation between them. It was the kind of music that made you breathe a little easier. The kind that made you forget the life-changing decision you had to make, if only for a little while.

When Zander finally started to sing, his voice was softer than usual.

And it's so
easy to see
what you
thought she would be
but you
just didn't know what was underneath.

And she's
proving you wrong
with every
breath, every song
like she's
known all along that you would see

who she could be,
who she would be,
when she was free.

257

I didn't realize I'd been holding my breath until the last chord faded.

My eyes snapped open, and I stared straight ahead, watching taxicabs weave in and out of traffic on the glinting street below. But I couldn't hear the cars, or the honking horns, or the screeching of the train on the tracks. The only thing I could hear was us, Zander and me, breathing in and out together.

"That's uh, all I've got so far," he said, breaking the silence. "It's just a first shot, so I'll probably end up scratching the—"

"It's good," I said quickly, still staring straight ahead.

"Yeah?" He sounded hopeful. "You like it? You don't think I should change—"

"Nope." I shook my head. And it was true. I, Kacey Simon, had absolutely no advice to give. None. The song *had* to be about me. *With every breath, every song?* Molly wasn't the one belting out Gravity tunes every day after school.

"Anyway, she's all yours." Zander lifted the guitar and rested it carefully in my lap.

"What?" I cradled the body so it wouldn't slip to the ground. "What are you talking about?"

"She's yours," he said again. "I got a new one yesterday. So you should have this one. Learn to play on it, if you want."

"Oh. Wow," I said stupidly. I held the fret board tightly, feeling the tension of the strings beneath my fingertips. The gift wasn't a huge deal, right? Zander was just being nice. It didn't mean . . . anything. "Thanks." I still couldn't bring myself to look at him. Something inside was warning me not to.

"Um, Kacey?" Zander leaned toward me, and I flinched. Even in the bitter cold, he smelled like warm leather and guitar polish. "Is . . . everything okay?" He rested his hand on my arm, forcing me to turn.

When I did, our faces were just inches apart. He was so close I could feel the heat coming off his body. A voice in my head was screaming at me to run. But I was completely powerless, drawn in. I searched his face, and his eyes met mine, warm and soft. It felt like someone had tied our souls together with steel cables. And no matter how hard I tried, I couldn't pull away. I didn't want to.

Because I, Kacey Simon, had a *raging* crush on a BOY IN SKINNY JEANS.

The realization burned inside me like subzero temperatures. My stomach bottomed out, and I suddenly had the sensation that I was falling, like in a dream. I grabbed the edge of the table and gripped it tightly to steady myself. *No. I take it back*. I couldn't like Zander. Not now. Not when things were just starting to get back to normal.

259

Not when I had a shot at the lead again, onstage and in seventh. Not when I was just starting to be Kacey Simon again.

It dawned on me that Molly was right: I had to choose. Zander and music, or the old me. The real me.

"Kacey?" Zander shook my arm, bringing me back to reality. His eyes widened, trailing over my features. "Seriously. You okay? You don't look so good."

Seeing the open, caring expression on his face made me want to burst into tears. "I—I can't be in the band." The words left my mouth before they'd even registered in my brain.

Taking in his shocked expression, I expected to cry, or laugh, or do something. But I felt nothing but numbness. Heard nothing but awful, heavy silence.

"Wait. What?" Zander squinted, confused. "That's not funny."

I slipped my hand underneath my glasses and rubbed my eyes. "I'm not joking." My voice was flat, emotionless. It didn't even sound like me.

"But . . . why?" He was close enough that I could feel his breath start to quicken. "If you don't want the guitar—"

"It's not that. It's just . . ." I felt like someone was wringing out my insides until there was nothing left.

"Sean said I could take over Molly's spot in the play, and I'm gonna be really busy, and—"

"The play?" His voice cracked a little, and his bottom lip trembled. "But the play's over tonight! You can do both!"

"Zander!" I snapped, my fists curling into a ball in my lap. "I said I can't, okay? So let it go!"

We were silent for a while.

"Oh." Finally, Zander shoved his chair back. The scraping sound of the chair legs against the concrete sent shivers down my spine. "I get it." His eyes hardened. "Now that your lisp is gone, and you're hanging with your old friends again, we're not good enough."

"What? No!" I exclaimed helplessly. The numbness evaporated, and emotion brimmed up inside of me, threatening to overflow. I felt sick.

"Whatever, Kacey." He looked completely disgusted. "The least you could do is admit it."

Admit what? I wanted to scream. That every time he opened his mouth to sing, I got lightheaded? That I'd never laughed so hard in my life as I'd laughed with him? That I was too dense to figure all this out until *after* my best friend went on a date with him?

THAT I KIND OF LIKED THE BLUE HAIR, OKAY?

"Or are you a liar, on top of being a social climber?"

He jumped to his feet and started pacing back and forth in front of the rink. The wind whipped around his coat, making it flutter behind him.

"Zander!" I croaked, gripping my left wrist with my right palm. The leather cuff had hardened in the cold. Hot tears slipped down my stiff, frostbitten cheeks. I wondered how long I'd been crying.

"You know what?" Zander raked his hands through his hair, like it was giving him a splitting headache just to be near me. "I don't even care. I gotta get out of here." He leaned toward me and snatched the guitar out of my lap, shoving it in its case. His eyes were downcast and slightly red. Disappointed. All because of me. I wanted to stop him, to explain that I couldn't be in the band because that would mean betraying my best friend. Only wasn't that exactly what I was doing right now?

"I-I'm sorry," I whispered. "I have to."

He didn't answer. The only sound in the rink was the gusting wind, and two clicks as I unsnapped his bracelet and handed it over.

"Here." I stood up and thrust it in his palm, refusing to torture myself with one last glance.

Silently, he stuffed the bracelet in his pocket, grabbed his bag, and headed for the street, leaving me alone.

Deep down, I'd actually thought he would understand,

that he'd be there to help me through this. That he'd be the one person who wouldn't desert me. I cursed myself for being so stupid. Of course he'd left. It was like I told Paige. People leave. They move on. And Zander was no exception.

I reached for my cell to text Molly my final decision.

OPENING (AND CLOSING) NIGHT
Saturday, 6:40 P.M.

I applied a final coat of mascara, then slid on my glasses. The second I blinked, tiny black mascara polka dots deposited themselves on the lenses. I groaned and started over.

Wearing jeans and a boyfriend blazer, Mom sat cross-legged on my unmade bed, watching me apply my stage makeup. Probably to make sure I didn't overdo it. "Ella and I made something special for your big night." She caught my eye in the mirror. "Feeling ready?"

"I guess." My mouth parted slightly as I reapplied the mascara. "It's not that big of a deal."

"Kacey?" Mom's voice had that annoying *is there something we need to talk about?* twinge. "Everything okay?"

"Yeah. Fine." I swallowed, trying to force the memory of my early morning with Zander from my mind.

"Yeah. Fine," Mom repeated skeptically. That's the thing about moms. And journalists. Nothing gets by them. And when you have a mom who's also a journalist . . . forget it.

"Just a little nervous," I lied. I bent over slightly to ease the pains in my stomach, but they just sharpened. I wished I was wearing sweatpants instead of my black pencil pants and fitted silver tank.

"I get it. It's a big night," Mom acknowledged. "Especially since you weren't planning on performing this role."

Yeah. That's it. I nodded convincingly.

"But playing this part is something you've been looking forward to, right?"

"Right." It seemed like ages ago that the girls and I had crowded outside the auditorium doors to catch the first glimpse of the cast list.

"So whatever it is that's giving you second thoughts . . ." Mom came up behind me and gave me a squeeze. "Do the best you can to let it go for tonight. This is your night to shine, baby. I would hate to see you miss it."

I closed my eyes and leaned in to her, wanting to tell her everything so she could help me fix it.

"Mooooooo—" The piercing shriek of the kitchen smoke alarm cut Ella off.

"Oh, for crying out loud." Mom turned and sprinted for the stairs. "Your dinner call's in five, Miss Simon!"

I checked my reflection one last time. Mom had helped me with the chocolate liquid liner, since my first two attempts ended up looking like Ella had done them left-handed. Even with my glasses on, the liner made my green eyes pop. Pale peach blush accentuated my cheekbones, and creamy scarlet lipstick definitely drew the attention away from my braces. Mom had let me use her curling iron, so my hair fell in loose auburn waves around my face.

A certain somebody would have said I looked like a total fake. A phony. A lying, social-climbing, band-deserting monster.

But most people would have said I looked amazing.

I grabbed my coat and bag and reached for my cell. Four new texts.

PAIGE: U MISSED OUR CAMPAIGN MTG THIS AM!!!! WHERE WERE U?

P.S. IS HANDING OUT CAMPAIGN FLYERS AT INTERMISSION TACKY?

MOLLY: BREAK A LEG. CAN'T WAIT 2 C U.

LIV: REMEMBER DEEP BREATHS. PEACE, STAGE GODDESS.

MOLLY: P.S. DID U TALK TO Z ABOUT THE DATE? NEED INFO B4 CAST PARTY.

NESSA: ASK URSELF: WHAT'S MY MOTIVATION? (HINT – IT'S NOT KISSING Q. THAT'S JUST A BONUS.) YOU'LL B GR8.

Nothing from Zander. Not that I expected anything. I'd started about fifty different texts to him, but none of them seemed right. It didn't matter, anyway. There was nothing I could say to make him understand, unless I told him the whole truth. And that was one hundred percent impossible.

"We're ready!" Mom called.

"Coming!"

Downstairs, Ella stood in the doorway of the darkened kitchen, holding a cake with sparklers for candles. The fizzing, popping lights reflected off the lenses of her reading glasses. "SURPRIIIIIIISE!" she bellowed.

"Happy opening night," Mom said from her spot at the table.

"Thanks, guys!" I took the cake and carried it to the table. The pink icing read: CONGRATULATIONS, KAC.

"We ran out of icing." Ella wiped a smear of frosting off her nose.

"I'm sure it'll taste yummy." I kissed Mom on the cheek.

"Ooh! Me!" Ella stuck out her plump cheek, and I kissed it, too.

"Okay, let's get started," Mom said. "We don't want you to be late for your call."

The sparklers burned down and Mom flipped on the lights, revealing a rectangular box tied with a pink bow at my place setting. The attached note said: TO MY SHINING STAR, ONSTAGE AND OFF. LOVE, MOM.

"Mom!" I cried, yanking the ribbon off the box and pulling away wads of sparkly pink tissue paper. There, nestled inside, more welcome than the world's largest diamonds, was a pair of clear contacts and a small bottle of drops. "Contacts?" I'd completely forgotten.

"Your sentence is over." Mom smiled. "I picked these up from Dr. Marco so you'd have them in time for the show."

I shoved back my chair and tackled Mom. "Thankyou-thankyouthankyouthankyou!" I breathed. No lisp. No glasses. I was so ready for the stage.

"You're welcome." She laughed, squeezing me back. "Glad you like them. And by the way, if you don't use those drops, it's glasses from here on out."

"I will. I promise." I plopped back down in my chair. "I love them."

Solemnly, Ella removed her reading glasses, folded them, and placed them next to her plate with a sigh.

"Go put them in," Mom said. "We've got to leave soon if we want to get to the school on time."

"'Kay!" I flung off my glasses and dashed for the hall bathroom.

"Kacey—" Mom started.

"Right!" Back to the table. Glasses on, one last time. *Then* to the hall bathroom.

The contacts were most definitely a sign. My glasses days—my Zander days—were over. And there was no better place to make my debut than onstage, in front of the entire school. In the spotlight, where I belonged.

WILL THE REAL KACEY SIMON PLEASE STAND UP?
Saturday, 7:29 P.M.

"Heyyyy, Simon!"

When I burst through the auditorium doors, the first person I saw was Quinn Wilder, standing onstage and cupping his hands around his mouth like a megaphone. He was already in costume: His black pin-striped suit was perfectly tailored, and his bright red tie popped under the stage lights. His sandy bangs had been slicked back, making him pure leading man perfection. Behind him, the stage was crawling with tech crew, extras, and a few randoms I didn't recognize.

I swallowed. "Hey, Wilder," I called back. With my new crystal clear super-vision, I could see just how kissable his lips looked from all the way in the back. So how come all I could focus on was the sound of someone tuning a guitar in the orchestra pit?

"Nice . . ." He paused, like he wasn't quite sure what to say next. "Face."

I moved slowly down the aisle, letting my curled ends cascade over my green peacoat in the flirtiest way possible. "Thanks." I hurried up the steps to the stage, dying to get a whiff of Quinn's winterfresh essence.

"So. No more glasses, huh?" Quinn said. At the exact same moment, someone slid a gold film onto one of the stage lights, flooding Quinn with a heavenly glow and making him look like a stage god among mortal middle schoolers.

"Nope. Back to the old me." I leveled my eyes at him with confidence. He stared right back, and we locked eyes for at least two beats. Four, in a two-four time signature. Right? Zander would know. I shook my head, banishing Zander from my thoughts. I'd made my choice.

"Looks good." Direct, and to the point. Exactly how a guy should be, so there was no room for confusion. No sweet but ambiguous song lyrics that could drive a girl clinically insane.

"So I was thinking." Quinn's eyelids lowered to half-mast. "Since I've been rehearsing with Molly, maybe you and me should run through some of our lines before the show."

You and I, I corrected him silently. I breathed in deeply, through my nose. "Meet you backstage after I get into my costume?"

"It's a date." He grinned, making my entire body tingle with anticipation.

I turned and exited stage right without another word, maneuvering through the noisy, made-up crowd with total control even though my insides were as jittery as ever. I didn't have to turn around to know that Quinn was staring.

Just outside the girls' dressing area, Liv had arranged rolling racks of costumes: one for the leads, one for the extras, and one for the dancers. I found the hangers with my name taped to them, and lifted my maroon miniskirt and jacket from the rack.

"YOU. LOOK. AMAZING."

I started at the sound of Molly's voice.

"Seriously. You look like a total rock star."

Rock star. I felt a twinge in my stomach. But my stress turned to giggles the second I saw Molly's background dancer costume. She was dressed as an oversized dancing die: a giant white rubber foam cube that obscured her entire body, except for her legs. Tiny eyeholes had been poked out of the black marks on the front face of the die.

"Maaaaaaan in the wings!" Nessa charged into the

girls' dressing area, balancing a stack of programs on her clipboard. "Everybody dressed?" She'd gone Broadway director chic in head-to-toe black.

And a pair of cat-eye glasses embellished with tiny rhinestones.

"Yeaaaah," everyone chorused. I stared, openmouthed, at my friend.

She lowered her lips to the mic in her cordless headset. "All clear."

"Okay, girls, listen up!" Sean's voice boomed through the backstage area. Instead of his usual jeans uniform, he was wearing khakis and a button-down with the sleeves rolled up. "We've got twenty minutes to curtain and a packed house out there already, so I need everybody in costume and ready to rock and roll in no more than ten minutes! Got it?"

There was a brief moment of silence, and then everybody went back to what they were doing.

"Kacey? Is Kacey Simon back here?" Sean scanned the crowd until his eyes fell on me. His eyes widened slightly, like he didn't recognize me.

"Here." I blinked, kicking off my sneakers and reaching for the matronly oxfords that went with my costume. I smiled to myself when I saw the toes: glittery silver hearts, just like the ones Liv had drawn on my Converse two weeks ago. Hearts that only I could see onstage. I ran my thumb over the bumpy bling.

"So." Sean smiled. "Molly says your, ah . . . *speech problem* is all taken care of?"

Translation: *Say something with an s in it so I can be sure I don't get laughed out of the director's chair.*

He could have just come right out and asked. Since he didn't, I decided to have a little fun with him.

"Yup. Completely cured. All better." I ducked around Molly's left side and flashed an enthusiastic thumbs-up.

"Good. Great. Glad to hear it." He hovered awkwardly by the costume rack, trying to think of something else to say.

I let him squirm for a while. Then: "Um, I need to change? Into my co—" I caught myself just in time. "Play . . . outfit?"

Molly snorted inside her costume, finally catching on.

"Right. Of course. Okay." Sean rubbed the back of his neck. "Well . . . see you out there? Break a leg."

"No doubt. And I'm grateful for the . . . encouragement."

Sean stared at me for a second, confused, then escaped to the boys' side of the stage.

"Okay, so see you in a sec?" I shot Molly a grin.

"Def." Before I had the chance to arc around her, she

grabbed my left arm, and held on tight. "Hey. Is . . . Zander out there yet?"

My stomach clenched. This time, it was definitely guilt. "No. Not yet."

Her eyes darkened. "But I saved him a seat in the front row!"

"He'll be here," I assured her. "I saw him this morning, and he said he had a really great time with you yesterday," I lied.

"For real?" Her eyes lit up again.

I nodded. "I'll fill you in at the cast party, 'kay? I have to change." I scurried off before she had the chance to sniff out my crush or my lie.

I did a quick change behind the folding screen and then set out to find Quinn. I didn't bother looking for a mirror first. I could tell from the whispers, wide-eyed stares, and flickers of admiration and fear in the other kids' eyes that I looked . . . back to normal.

"Hey." A strong hand grabbed my arm and whirled me around, taking my breath away.

"Hey." It was nothing short of a miracle that I managed a greeting. With a fedora and silver tie pin added to his costume, Quinn looked the hottest I'd ever seen him look. I smoothed my maroon jacket, just to have something to do. But my hands were shaking, and not from stage jitters.

"THREE MINUTES TO CURTAIN, EVERYBODY!" Nessa yelled.

"So you wanna run lines real quick?" The *GQ* cover model standing across from me still hadn't let go of my arm. It was irrelevant, since I'd lost all feeling in my body anyway.

I nodded.

"Come on."

I let him drag me deeper into the wings, around the mannequin and changing screen to the very back, where there was nothing but a mop propped in the corner and one of those big yellow mop buckets with a picture of a stick figure slipping and falling on the side.

Quinn kicked the bucket out of the way, and it started to roll. "So, I'm glad you're back to normal, you know?" he murmured, backing me gently into the wall.

"Yeah." The traces of ammonia drifting from the mop bucket were making me dizzy. My breath quickened. "So, what scene did you want to run? We only have a—"

And then he kissed me.

It was a total movie kiss. Slow motion and everything. It's like one second I was saying something, and the next MY LIPS and QUINN'S LIPS were hurtling through space, desperate to meet. His lips were even softer than his hair, and I could even feel the flutter of his Maybellinelength lashes against my cheekbones. He gripped my face with his hands, making every nerve in my body explode like fireworks.

"Hey, has anybody seen—"

"Ohmygod. What are you doing here?" I gasped.

Zander stared at me for what seemed like hours. My entire body felt hot and tingly, but not in a good way.

"Uh—I was looking for Molly." He lifted a bunch of yellow roses, his face turning bright red. He glared at Quinn, then at me. His lips parted slightly, but nothing came out.

"What?" I crossed my arms over my chest, feeling like Zander had just walked in on me in a string bikini: completely exposed and totally humiliated.

"I mean . . ." Zander shook his head slowly. "Are you serious? This guy?" He jerked his thumb toward Quinn.

"What up, dude." Quinn nodded.

"What do you care?" I snapped. "You're with Molly!"

"I don't care."

"Good."

"Good."

"CURTAIN, EVERYBODY!" Nessa's voice sounded far away. "*I need Kacey Simon, ready for entrance! Kacey! Simon!*"

Quinn grinned and squeezed my arm.

"That's you."

I'LL HAVE WHAT SHE'S HAVING
Saturday, 9:30 P.M.

By the time the final curtain fell, I'd almost completely forgotten that Zander had ruined my first real kiss. The cast got a standing ovation, and all the performing left me jonesing for a custom cupcake with a side of brand-new boyfriend.

Sean had rented out Sugar Daddy for the night, and it looked amazing. The overhead lights were dimmed, platinum confetti dusted the tables and the floor, and gold star balloons hovered over every chair. The cast and crew were packed around the tables, reliving key show moments over platters of frosted cupcakes.

The girls and I had chosen the small square table in the center of the bakery, since it was the perfect see-and-be-seen spot. There was only one "problem": Since Liv,

Nessa, Jake Fields, and Aaron Peterman had taken four of
the five seats, Quinn and I had to share a seat.

Nessa used her knife and fork to dissect her red velvet
cupcake. "By the way, this is for you guys to sign." She
dropped her utensils and shoved a play program toward
Quinn and me. "They're auctioning it off at the end of
the night."

I reached for a pen and signed with a flourish. "So is
Mols on her way?" *And will she have her overly dramatic
spy of a boyfriend with her?*

"She texted she'll be here in a minute," Liv said over a
mouthful of vegan chocolate crumbs.

I swallowed. Maybe on the way to Sugar Daddy, Molly
and Zander would get into a fight over whose hair dye
was uglier and break up. Then Zander could go home
before he had a chance to ruin the cast party.

"You rocked it," Quinn said. His lips were just inches
from my ear. "Seriously. You were amazing."

"So were you," I flirted back, forcing myself to hold
his stare.

Under the table, he intertwined his fingers with mine
and squeezed. His hand was a little sweaty, but I told
myself it didn't matter. People were watching and it felt
amazing.

"Finally!" Nessa exclaimed, looking over my shoulder.

I whirled around. Molly was standing behind me, in jeans and a neon yellow hoodie the color of banana bubblegum. Zander's Acoustic Rebellion hoodie. Zander emerged from behind her. He did not look happy to see me.

"Soooo sorry we're late. But Z and I got . . . distracted." Molly scurried away before her words could sink in.

Distracted?

"Hey, guys. Good show," Zander said. My stomach plunged faster than the night's final curtain when his eyes stopped briefly on mine.

"You too, Kacey. Not that I'm surprised that you're such a good actor. I mean, acting's your specialty, right?"

Nessa frowned. Liv giggled nervously, like it was all a joke. Only I knew it wasn't.

I reached for Quinn's hand again and lifted it above the table. My hand was shaking. "Glad you liked the show, *Skinny Jeans*," I shot back. "But not everything you see onstage is an act." I intertwined my fingers with Quinn's and squeezed. "Of course, you knew that already, since you were spying on us, right?"

"I'm sensing tension," Nessa observed.

Liv smiled helpfully. "Maybe if you did some deep breath—"

"I'm fine," I snapped, squeezing Quinn's hand even

harder. Then I reached for a fork and stabbed at my cup-cake, jamming a way-too-big bite in my mouth.

Molly came back with an extra chair. Her eyes flitted excitedly from Quinn to me. And back to Quinn.

Quinn slipped his arm around my shoulders. My stom-ach tightened and the cupcake lodged in my throat.

"Heads down," Molly hissed suddenly. "Phoebe's com-ing over here."

I swallowed. "Who?" I looked around, desperate to focus on anyone but Zander.

"Kacey!" Paige called, making her way through the crowd. She was wearing one of her campaign buttons. No, two, one on her shirt and one pinned to the strap of her backpack. And instead of her usual head-to-toe black, she was wearing all green. She looked like a tall, skinny leprechaun.

"Don't look!" Molly giggled.

"Great show, guys," Paige said when she reached the table. "Especially you, Kacey."

"Thanks," I grinned. "And did you see the part where—"

Molly kicked me under the table.

"Thanks," I said again, leaning in to Quinn.

Paige didn't seem to notice. "So, I was thinking maybe I could spend the night over at your place tonight, and we could work on the debate?"

Molly shot me a death stare. Nessa sucked in her cheeks and rolled her eyes at me.

"Actually, I was thinking about spending the night over at Nessa's tonight with the girls. But maybe we can hang out next weekend?"

Paige's dark eyebrows sank beneath the tops of her frames. "It's just, next weekend I'm going to my grand-parents', so I wanted to get started sooner. Remember?"

"I know." I sighed, a little annoyed. Couldn't she at least wait until my big night was over? "But—"

"PRESS! PRESS coming through!" Abra Laing bur-rowed through the crowd toward my table. She was hold-ing a Marquette mic and flashing the program from the show like it was a press pass. "KACEY! Can I get a sound bite for the MINUTE?" She sidled up next to my chair, bumping Paige out of the way.

"Hey!" Paige glared at Abra. "Kacey and I were in the *middle* of something."

"Paige! I told you. Another. Time." The second the words left my mouth, I knew I could have said them dif-ferently. My voice sounded harsh, even to me.

The table went silent and Paige stared at me. Then her face seemed to relax, and the weirdest thing happened.

She laughed.

"Sure, Kacey. Another time. Like that's gonna happen. You got what you wanted, right?" Her face hardened again. "So the rest of us don't really matter."

"Right on," Zander said, just loudly enough for everyone to hear.

"Oh, give me a break," I snapped. With Quinn smashed against me on one side, and Paige and Abra crowding me on the other, I could hardly breathe. "Just chill out and back off so I can enjoy the rest of the night, okay?"

An uncomfortable silence settled over the table and everyone shifted in their seats, avoiding one another's gaze.

"You know, I thought you'd changed." A look of disgust settled on Paige's face. "But I guess I was wrong." She spun on her heel and bolted for the door.

"Paige!" Zander shoved past Abra. "Wait up!"

"Zander!" Molly looked horrified. "Hello?"

"Let him go," I spat. Zander followed Paige outside, where she paced back and forth, gesturing angrily. He nodded, clearly agreeing with whatever she was saying about me.

I turned back around, feeling a deep stab of betrayal in my gut. "Ready, Abra." I sniffed and gave my hair a quick shake.

"O-okay," Abra stammered, looking like a deer in headlights. "Uh, stand up and we'll get your table behind you." Abra nodded at the camera guy. A bright white light flooded the space around me as I stood, and the tiny red RECORD light started flashing.

"I'm Abra Laing, AND THIS IS MARQUETTE! IN A MINUTE!" Abra shouted at the camera. "I'm HERE with KACEY SIMON, STAR OF GUYS AND DOLLS! KACEY! TONIGHT! YOU MADE A MAJOR COMEBACK! HOW DO YOU FEEL? IS IT TRUE THAT YOU AND QUINN WILDER ARE TAKING YOUR ROMANCE OFF-STAGE??"

I stared past Abra toward the doors. Now Zander had his arm around Paige, whose face was hidden in his jacket. Was she . . . crying? A lump formed in my throat, and I blinked back tears. I couldn't decide if I wanted to take it all back, or run outside and yell at Paige for making me feel so awful on my big night.

"KACEY?" Abra said again. Her eyes darted nervously from the camera to me. "HOW DO YOU FEEL?"

How did I feel? It was an oddly complicated question. Sugar Daddy was packed wall-to-wall with my friends, and castmates, and teachers, each one of them here to celebrate me. I should have felt alive. But the only thing I felt was empty.

IN THE HARSH LIGHT OF DAY
Sunday, 7:14 A.M.

When I opened my eyes the next morning, diluted gray light was just starting to filter through the windows. My room was still dark, but I could see well enough to make out the puffy paint sign Ella had made me: SIMON SAYS: KACEY ROCKS!

Ella's rising and falling silhouette came into focus; she'd fallen asleep in my bed last night after I got home. Her mouth was slightly parted, and there was a dried smudge of chocolate above her lip. She looked calmer than Molly's hair after a relaxing treatment. Not me. My head throbbed, and my stomach was tied in more knots than one of Liv's hand-crocheted sweaters.

With a sigh, I slipped out of bed as quietly as I could and stuffed my feet in a pair of worn red slippers. Downstairs, Mom had left a note next to the coffeemaker.

got a call to sub for the early morning show. be back by 9. pancake stuff's in the pantry & fridge. make sure ella doesn't eat the batter raw this time. cell's on if you need it.

so proud of you, sweet girl!!!!!

love, mom

p.s.: no cake for breakfast! (b/c i ate it)
p.p.s.: did i mention how proud i am?

I crumpled the note in my hand, stifling the urge to start sobbing into the sink. If Mom knew what I had done to get my part back, or had seen Paige and Zander's faces last night, she'd take it all back.

I put the kettle on for hot chocolate and sat down at the kitchen table to check my cell: 15 NEW MSGS.

MOLLY: U WERE GR8. WASN'T I SUPER CUTE IN Z'S HOODIE? I SLEPT IN IT LAST NITE.

NESSA: SUGAR DADDY L8R? I'M OFFICIALLY ADDICTED. IT'S A PROBLEM.

LIV: NESSA WANTS 2 GO 2 SUGAR DADDY. BUT I'M ON A DETOX. TEAVANA @ 4?

QUINN: WANNA HANG LATER?

MOLLY: WAS THE HOODIE CUTE ENOUGH TO WEAR TO Z'S
BAND'S SHOWCASE NEXT WKND? I NEED WARDROBE HELP!

My head throbbed at the mention of the showcase. I
deleted her text and read the remaining messages. The
texts went on and on, but not a single one was from Zander or Paige. I lifted my laptop screen and logged on to
Paige's website, clicking on her latest blog post.

A BUMP IN THE CAMPAIGN TRAIL

POSTED BY PREZPAIGE | SATURDAY @ 10:47 P.M.

The campaign hit a snag last night, with one of my biggest
so-called supporters (we'll call her Sarah Brown) desert-
ing the cause in favor of her fifteen minutes of fame on the
Marquette Middle stage. But like any good politician, I've
uncovered the truth about this so-called friend.

This presidential hopeful wants to know: What happened
to friendships based on loyalty and trust, instead of popularity?

The campaign must go on. So I'll be heading to Marquette's
TV studio Monday to review the DVD of my latest practice

campaign speech, and shoot a promo to debut during announcements in election week.

And remember, to donate to the campaign, click on the GiveGreene link on the left of the page. You can support a brighter future for Marquette, even if some people won't.

Peace, Love, and Democracy,
Prez Paige

I reread the post once, twice, and three times, my migraine sharpening with every passing second. I had picked my comeback over Paige, even though it was her plan that had gotten me back onstage and back with my friends. I hadn't even thanked her. I'd just cast her aside, exactly like Molly had done the second I'd gotten braces and glasses.

GREENE WITH HONESTY
Monday, 7:11 A.M.

"Bye, Mom!" I yelled as I trampled down the stairs Monday morning. If I was going to intercept Paige before she got to the studio, I had no time for family breakfast. I'd barely had enough time to coordinate my outfit in support of Paige's "Go Greene" campaign. I'd settled on an olive taffeta mini with a black cashmere V-neck, textured tights, and black suede ankle boots.

I grabbed my houndstooth coat and black scarf and headed out the door, armed with fresh determination. I could fix this. I had to.

Next door, Paige was just leaving her house with an armful of green balloons, two backpacks stuffed with rolled-up campaign posters, and her enormous foam display board.

"PAIGE!" I shouted, watching her teeter precariously down the steps. "HOLD ON! I'M COMING TO HELP YOU WITH YOUR STUUUUUFF!"

Paige glared over the top of a giant plastic jar stuffed with green Tootsie Pops.

I sprinted down the steps, shoved through the front gate, and intercepted her in front of the fence. "Hey," I said breathlessly.

"Hey," she said coolly, without breaking her stride.

"Need help?" I offered.

"Not from you."

If she thought she could blow me off that easily, she was wrong. "Are you sure? Because if you need some help with your promo—"

"Seriously, Kacey." Paige snapped. "I *said* I don't need help." As if on cue, her Tootsie Pops jar, foam board, and a handful of buttons from her second backpack tumbled to the ground.

"Great." The word caught in her throat.

I swooped down and scooped up a handful of Tootsie Pops, feeling the sting of her sarcasm.

"Paige." I dumped the candy into the empty plastic jar, and it made a hollow thud. I swallowed. "I'm . . . sorry. But I want to help with the campaign now. Okay? Please." I scrambled around like a total desperado, clawing at every piece of campaign paraphernalia I could get my hands on.

She dropped to her knees and stared directly into my eyes. Her black crocheted cap was crooked, and suddenly I wanted to straighten it. "No," she said simply.

An open pin on the back of one of the campaign buttons stabbed me in the thumb. "But . . . I said I was really sorry." My voice cracked. When people apologized sincerely, you were supposed to accept! Had Paige not gotten the memo?

"I only want loyal, committed people on my campaign. Not people who are so self-absorbed they can't even be trusted to hold up their end of a bargain." She screwed the top on the Tootsie Pops jar and stood.

I pushed myself up, something inside me snapping. What did I have to do to get her to forgive me? Throw a televised campaign rally? Get her airtime on Mom's network? Show up to school in head-to-toe green body paint for the next month?

"I *said* I was sorry. I—"

"*I, I, I.*" Paige snagged the last of her escaped materials and picked up the pace again. I scrambled to keep up. "Is there any other word in your vocabulary? You're so obsessed with yourself, you think everybody else has to be just like you! Do what you'd do, say what you'd say, wear what you'd wear! Well, I've got news for you!" she yelled over her shoulder. "Not everybody wants to be Kacey freaking Simon!"

"PAIGE!" I stood there in the middle of the sidewalk, my hands hanging awkwardly at my sides as Paige stormed down the street, leaving the occasional Tootsie Pop in her wake like she was Gretel. My stomach churned violently, and tears welled in my eyes. I wanted to turn back and take a sick day, but instead I forced myself to finish the trek to the train station.

By the time I made it onto the Armitage platform, Paige was long gone. The only people there were a few students and a messenger wheeling his bike to the edge of the platform. I lined my toes up with the yellow caution stripe and tucked my chin to my chest, not wanting anyone to see my puffy, red-rimmed eyes.

"Helloooo!"

I jumped as Molly's voice sounded next to me. She swung her arm around me. "We've been calling you for like a block!"

"Ohhh my God, it's Kacey Simon!" Liv teased, fanning her face with the edge of her scarf like she might faint. "THE Kacey Simon. Can I have your autograph?" She shoved a half-finished French worksheet in my face.

"Hey, guys," I managed.

"What's wrong with you?" Nessa asked bluntly, adjusting the bejeweled bobby pin in her pixie. "You look awful."

"I'm fine. Just tired," I lied, blinking rapidly.

"Haven't you heard?" Liv tightened her flatironed side pony. "Being a celebrity is sooooo exhausting."

I managed a halfhearted smile.

"Maybe these will make you feel better." Liv reached into the pocket of her vintage trench and pulled out a pair of cat-eye glasses. They were just like the ones Nessa had worn Saturday night, except these had tiny emerald stones embedded in the outer corner. "They go on sale today. *Everybody's* gonna want a pair." She slid them on.

I knew one person who would have wanted them: Paige. They would have been perfect for her campaign speech. "They're gorgeous," I said miserably.

"I bet you have, like, a billion *Simon Says* entries after Saturday night," Molly said as she wound her hair into a loose bun on top of her head. "Those losers are probably lining up at the door to get a piece of you."

"Which losers?" Liv handed her French worksheet to Nessa, who rolled her eyes but immediately started conjugating with a purple pen.

"You know. Other . . . people."

"Let's check!" Before I could stop her, Liv's hand shot into my messenger bag, and reemerged with my phone. She lifted it over her head in victory like it was the Holy Grail, then hacked into my *Simon Says* e-mail. "Ohhhkay. Let's see. First, we have *Jilted Joe.*"

"Laaaame," Molly decided.

"'Dear Kacey, I'm writing because I'm desperate.'"

"Duh." Molly already sounded bored. "Get to the good part."

"Ummm . . . been going out with this girl for a few weeks, really likes her, thinks she's the one . . . but lately she's been hanging out with his best friend . . ."

"Awesome," Molly approved. "Draaaamaaaaaa."

". . . not sure, but thinks she may have more in common with the best friend than him. . . . What should he do?" Liv looked up expectantly. So did the rest of the girls.

I chewed on my lip. Reading these letters used to give me an adrenaline rush, but now I felt more exhausted than if I'd just telecast live for an hour straight. I blinked at my friends. Molly twirled her hair expectantly. Liv leaned closer. Nessa stopped conjugating.

"Umm . . . dear Jilted Joe," I began, knowing they wanted me to break it to the kid that it was too late—he'd lost his crush forever. But as my friends stared at me, waiting, my mind went blank. It sounded like the poor kid really liked this girl and he'd lost her to his best friend. What could possibly be funny about that?

"Uhhh, dear Jilted Joe," Molly jumped in, champing at the bit. "First of all, Simon Says is supposed to be anonymous. So thanks for cluing us in to your identity, moron."

"Joe, there's this great book out there that you should totally pick up." Nessa's voice was smug. "It sounds like it was written just for you. I can't remember the title . . ." She pressed her index finger to her lips, pretending to think. "Oh. Right. I got it."

"SHE'S JUST NOT THAT INTO YOU!!!!!!" Molly, Liv, and Nessa yelled in unison.

While the girls howled with laughter and high-fived one another, I stared numbly down the tracks, praying the train would come immediately and take me away from this platform. Their laughter grated on me. How had I never heard the way we sounded before—the way *I* sounded? We were ruthless, ignoring other people's feelings for the sake of a laugh, or a segment on a stupid middle school news show. No wonder Paige and Zander wanted nothing more to do with me. I wanted nothing more to do with me.

At that moment, the train barreled around the corner, its white headlights as harsh and unforgiving as I'd been to my classmates. In the bright light, I saw myself for what I really was. Not an honest, hard-hitting journalist, but a mean girl who spoke her mind. And hurt everyone she'd ever cared about in the process.

DESPERATE MEASURES
Monday, 7:42 A.M.

"I need airtime." I barged into the television studio at top speed, almost taking out two camera guys hanging by the doors. "Sorry. Airtime. Now." I stalked over to the stage and slung my bag under the news desk with unnecessary force. And just the slightest hint of despair.

Carlos was lounging in his director's chair and flipping through the *Trib*. A glowing Bluetooth flashed in his ear. "No, he didn't. OH NO, HE DIDN'T!"

"CARLOS! YES, HE DID!" I barked, plopping into my rolling chair. "Now get me some airtime. Please!"

"Hold up." He rolled his eyes toward me with an irritated sigh. "Miss Thing has entered the building. I'll have to get you back." He yanked out his Bluetooth. "I was in the middle of breaking a story," he snapped. "And listen.

You may have rocked the house Saturday night? Fabulous cast party hair, by the way?"

"Thanks." I pawed self-consciously at my tangled waves. I'd been in such a hurry to catch Paige that I'd forgotten to brush my hair.

"But you're not on my rundown. And you look terrible today. Your eyes are all red."

"I know, I know," I protested, leaping out of my chair and hurrying around the desk. "But this is *really* important." I stopped just short of calling it a matter of life and death; the turning point in my future at Marquette, in my future as a journalist. My last chance to redeem myself. Even though technically, it was all of those things.

I grabbed his clipboard and did a quick scan. Abra's feature on the play . . . the lunch menu . . . an OpEd on the new art teacher . . .

"Look as hard as you want—you're not on that schedule," Carlos said.

The red digital clock in the back of the studio left me exactly seventy-two seconds to make my case.

"T-turkey hot d-dogs, cole slaw, and apple suss. Sauce." To the left of the anchor desk, a sixth grader shuddered in front of the green screen. "With yogurt berry parfait, a-and a selection of a-ssorted cookies for dessert." He gripped his script in both hands. "T-turkey hot dogs. *Turkey* hot dogs. Turkey *hot* dogs."

"Give me the lunch menu slot," I said forcefully. "I'll throw it in at the end of my segment."

The sixth grader flashed me a grateful glance.

Carlos checked his nail beds, purposely making me squirm.

Fifty seconds.

"Look at him," I argued, my voice strained tighter than the strings on Zander's guitar. "If he turns the same color as the green screen, he'll disappear on camera anyway."

"It's t-true," said Lunch Menu Kid. Then he pressed his first two fingers against his pursed lips like he was going to vomit. "False alarm."

"You know I hate changing my rundown," Carlos reminded me, re-rolling the sleeves on his button-down until they were completely symmetrical. "Unless . . . you had something really juicy."

"Totally," I said. "I was going to break it on air, but I could always stop by the *Gazette* office on my way to homeroom."

"Wait!" Carlos leaned forward in his chair, his eyes flashing with fresh interest. "So we're talking breaking news?"

I nodded. "Breaking news. Swear."

"So spill."

"I will," I said coyly, leaning back in my chair. "In fifteen seconds, when you put me on the air."

Carlos paused for what seemed like an eternity. "Got your script?" he finally asked with a sigh.

"Don't need it. Just need one thing, and I'm all set." I leaned forward in my chair and reached into my messenger bag.

"You're on in three, two—"

Time seemed to slow as I looked directly into the camera lens. Everything around me felt sharp and clear. Except for my stomach, which felt like it had been twisted into a balloon animal. "Morning, Marquette, and welcome to the final edition of *Simon Says*. I'm Kacey Simon, and this will be my last broadcast."

Carlos gasped from the sidelines, but as the words left my mouth, I felt one hundred percent positive they were the right words. It didn't matter what Carlos or anybody else thought. I wondered if this was how Zander felt when he was onstage.

"Marquette, I'd like a few minutes of your time." As I spoke, every muscle in my body unclenched, even the tiny ones in my forehead. It was like all the anxiety, frustration, and confusion of the past week were evaporating and leaving me lighter than Sugar Daddy's low-cal whipped cream. "This week marks our fortieth *Simon Says* episode. Which means I've been broadcasting my views on everything from relationship problems to fashion disasters for the past year."

I glanced at the teleprompter, which had suddenly lit up with the words DON'T DO IT!

Ignoring the urge to roll my eyes at Carlos, I turned back to the camera. "And a good friend of mine pointed out that in the past year, instead of helping people with the segment, I've actually been hurting them." I swallowed, wondering if Paige and Zander were watching. "There's such a thing as being too honest. And I crossed the line between being honest and being brutal a long time ago. Maybe . . . maybe I never really knew where that line was."

My voice grew stronger. "And so I just wanted to say, I'm sorry, Marquette. I'm sorry to everyone who wrote in to the show. I made you feel like it wasn't okay to be you. And Simon Says: That is definitely not okay." The words tumbled out of my mouth with ease, as if they'd been waiting forever for me to say them. "Before we go, I want to thank Paige Greene for being a total inspiration for this broadcast. Paige should be a role model for us all. She's always been herself, even when it hasn't been easy. And that's the mark of a true leader." I flashed my Kacey

Simon Smile. "So go Greene. And vote Paige Greene for eighth-grade student body president. Also, it's turkey hot dog day. So I'd suggest a vending machine run between classes."

My fingers closed around the plastic frames in my lap. "In closing, if I'm asking all of you to be your real selves, that means I have to, too." I unfolded my glasses and slid them on my nose. Over my contacts, the glasses made the entire studio go fuzzy. "I hope I'll be back on the air some-day. But until then . . ." I stared directly into the camera, pretending it was Zander and Paige. "Thith ith KAYTHEE THIMON. Thining off."

THAT'S THE PROBLEM WITH LIVE TELEVISION
Monday, 7:47 A.M.

Eight seconds too late for me to take it all back, the sheer terror settled in.

"Uhhhhh . . ." Camera Guy One stammered, positioning the camera between the news desk and his body. "Good show?"

"Thanks." I slid off my glasses and stared as the red digits on the clock counted down. To what, I wasn't exactly sure. The end of my life at Marquette? Of my career? Of my friendship with Molly and the girls?

I groped under the desk for my messenger bag, my forehead beading with sweat. What had I done? Was this the end of Kacey Simon, on-air talent? Had my sudden burst of conscience ruined everything? Would I now have to spend years slaving away to get my career back? I'd probably have to start at the very bottom, with the lunchroom beat.

In a fog, I stood up and made my way into Silverstein, where I ran smack into Paige.

"Hey." Hallway light reflected off her lenses, making her eyes impossible to see. "So . . . I heard the broadcast."

"Oh. Hey." I rocked back on my heels, my heart humming in my chest. A million questions flew around my brain like flurries in a snow globe. Had she noticed my fashion tribute to her campaign? Would my on-air apology be enough? Or would she ditch me, like I'd ditched her in fifth? Maybe I deserved it.

"That was a really gutsy show. Seriously gutsy."

"Really?" I allowed a tiny bit of hope to creep into my voice.

"Really." Paige shuffled in her scuffed black loafers. After a few seconds, she broke out into a huge, excited grin. "I can't BELIEVE you just did that! You're CRAZY!" She pulled me in for a bony hug.

"Owww. Paige!" Happy tears filled my eyes as I hugged her back. "I can't believe it, either."

And then it hit me. No band, no show, no play . . . what did regular kids do with their mornings and afternoons?

"I guess I have a lot of free time on my hands now." I sniffed and hooked my bag over my shoulder.

"That depends," Paige said, linking her arm through mine and pulling me down the hallway toward homeroom.

"On . . ."

"On whether you agree to be my full-time campaign manager. Think about it." She gestured excitedly with her hands, looking like she was speed-conducting an orchestra. "I need somebody who's not afraid to tell me the truth, even when I don't want to hear it. Somebody who'll be straight with me." She elbowed me in the side. "And you need a hobby."

"Thanks for reminding me." I groaned. *Kacey Simon: Campaign Advisor to the Political Stars.* Actually, it had a ring to it. "So . . . campaign manager. Does that include, like, being your media spokesperson or whatever? Because I think we could get Abra to do a profile on you."

"Yes!" Paige squealed. "Exactly! So are you in?"

"Do you even need to ask?" I elbowed her back.

She shrieked and hugged me all over again. "Awesome. Awesome." She pulled away and straightened her glasses on her nose. "So . . . first things first," she said as we hurried down Silverstein. "My promo. Do you think there's any way your mom would broadcast it during a commercial break? Because that kind of exposure would be pretty much invaluable."

"Paige. It's a middle school election," I reminded her. We rounded the corner and headed for Hemingway. "Let's just stick with Channel M for now, and we can think about other markets later."

"Good call," she decided briskly. "Start small, and conquer."

As we neared Sean's classroom, my stomach felt like I'd just stepped onto a high-speed elevator. Molly, Zander, Nessa, and Liv were loitering outside the door, chatting. Possibly about me.

Paige's eyes fell on the group. "You gonna be okay?" she muttered under her breath.

I nodded. "Think so." But the knot in my gut begged to differ.

"Kacey?" Molly's eyes widened the second she saw me. "Um . . . tell me I didn't just see you give up your show." But instead of saying it in a mean way, she just looked confused.

"Um, yeah." I searched Zander's face for clues. He stared back, unblinking. His eyes were a listless gray. "I did."

"Okay, so question one," Nessa planted her hands on the wide cognac belt cinched around her hips. "Why? And question two, did you actually just apologize to the entire student body on air? You were doing those viewers a favor!"

Paige sighed.

"I just . . ." I caught Zander's eye. He blinked and looked away. "I just need to take a little break from the show, is all."

"Reconnect with your soul." Liv nodded, like she understood. "Oooh! Or you could do that on the air! You could have a segment where you review local spas!"

"Love it," Molly decided. For a brief second, her eyes flicked over to Zander, but he just shrugged. "We could be your research team!"

While the girls pitched different ideas for *Kacey Simon's Spa Hour*, I turned to Zander.

"Hey," I said softly to his blue streak. I'd forgotten just how electric it was.

"Hey." Brief nod. "Good show. That was really cool, what you just did."

"I didn't even realize what I was doing until after the broadcast, and then I got, like, stage fright or something, which never happens, and—" I stopped, realizing I was babbling. "Anyway." I could feel my cheeks starting to burn. "Maybe I could stop by the loft before practice and tell you about it then? Plus I have your Dylan album. . . ." My voice trailed off when I saw the hardened look in his eyes.

"I, uh . . . don't think so." Zander pressed his lips in

a tight line. It was like he was sealing himself off, refusing to let me in. "Maybe you could just give the album to Molly, and I'll get it from her if we hang out again. If she comes to the showcase Friday night."

"Oh," I croaked, my heart sinking to the toes of my boots.

Wait. *If?* "Zander—"

He lifted his palm, cutting me off. "I mean, good show, and everything. Really. But I still can't figure out who the real Kacey Simon is."

"*This* is the real me." I kept my voice level, but inside, I was screaming. How could he not recognize it when the real Kacey was standing right in front of him? When she'd just bared her soul on television? When she'd purposely lisped in public? "Zander, I—"

But he'd already turned his back to me. He slung his arm around Molly in good-bye, then started down the hall to his homeroom. I took a stunned step back as Molly, Nessa, and Liv filed into Sean's classroom.

I felt Paige's hand on my arm. "You okay?"

I glanced at the ceiling and blinked a few times. "Yeah."

"No, you're not," Paige said matter-of-factly. "You totally have a thing for Zander."

I opened my mouth to protest, but she cut me off. "Don't bother. I know how to read my constituents. You like him. And . . ." She paused. "I think he likes you, too."

My head snapped toward her. "Really? No way." I could feel the sweat starting to bead along my neck, and I swiped it away.

She nodded. "Way."

I wanted to believe Paige was telling the truth. I wanted it more than anything. But from the way Zander had just treated me, how could I? A real journalist is objective, and never ignores the facts. But what if I didn't want to be objective when it came to Zander? Maybe I just wanted to be a girl. A girl who was crushing hard on a completely forbidden boy. A girl who couldn't possibly do anything about her crush, since that would ruin her relationship with her newly reinstated best friend.

A girl who was totally, one hundred percent in like. Objectively.

I'M (NOT) WITH THE BAND
Friday, 8:47 P.M.

"Is Z not a jillion times more talented than these guys?" Molly yelled, cutting her eyes at the applause and whistles that had erupted inside the dim theater-turned-café next door to Vinyl Destination. The round black tables between the coffee bar and the stage were all filled. The girls and I were crammed around the table closest to the stage, waiting for Gravity to perform the last remaining set in the Rock Chicago talent showcase.

I nodded, feeling like I'd swallowed a ball of wet papier-mâché. I reminded myself that I had to be here. It would look weird if I bailed. Molly would start to ask questions, and I would *not* want to answer them.

"Is Quinn coming?" Liv asked.

"Oh, I didn't invite him," I said dismissively. I'd been

avoiding Quinn all week, which was pretty easy now that rehearsal was over.

Under the table, Paige squeezed my knee supportively. She'd agreed to come for moral support but swore that if Molly called her Phoebe even once, she was out.

"This has to be so weird for you." Nessa cleaned her cat-eye glasses on her sleeve and slid them on again. She took a long sip of her decaf cappuccino, staring knowingly over her mug like she was reading my every thought.

I shrugged and wiped my sweaty palms on my jeans.

"For real." Liv nodded sympathetically. The applause died down and the band flashed peace signs and ambled off the stage. "I mean, coming to a show after you decided you didn't want to be in the band anymore?"

Next to me, Paige bristled. "Uh, that's not exactly what—"

"She didn't come for Z, duh." Molly cut her off. "She came to support *me*. Because she's an amazing BFF." She grabbed my hand across the table and squeezed.

Paige coughed something I couldn't understand into her teacup.

The gut-wrenching guilt that had been writhing in the pit of my stomach all week was so strong that I barely noticed the sharp metal of Molly's skull ring digging into my skin. How could I sit here and pretend to be supportive when all I could think about was Zander, and proving to him that I'd changed? I'd never felt so fake in my life. Maybe Zander had a right to be confused about the real Kacey Simon. Maybe I didn't know who she was, either.

"And that was Musikal Mutiny, with the first track off their debut album." The lanky emcee behind the mic wore a plaid flannel shirt and black skinny jeans, which reminded me of Zander. Then again, everything these days reminded me of him. "Heads up: After the showcase, the bands will be signing autographs and selling CDs in the lobby out front."

"My BF's famous!" Molly piped up.

"Now for the last band of the night, Gravity. Make some noise, people!"

Molly shrieked as Zander and the guys hustled into the spotlight.

I watched the band settle into their places. Even though our table was just a few feet away, I felt miles from the band, like I'd never been a part of it at all.

Zander settled onto a stool front and center, holding the guitar he'd tried to give me at Millennium Park. He was wearing a brown leather jacket I'd never seen before. I searched for the cuff bracelet, but it must have been hidden beneath his sleeve.

"What is UP, Chicago?" He grinned and adjusted the mic

stand. "We're Gravity, and we're psyched to be here with—" His glance fell on our table, on Molly's beaming, proud face. His eyes shifted to me. He froze for a second, then shook his head violently, like he was trying to rid his brain of any memory of me. "Uh, to be here with you guys."

My fingers curled around my coffee cup. I squeezed so hard, I thought the ceramic might crack.

"We're gonna start you guys off with something a little different. It's an acoustic cover of one of my favorite tunes by a classic band. Hope you like it."

Acoustic cover? The second the house lights darkened, I shifted forward in my seat. I knew instantly what song he was going to play, and he *couldn't* sing it without me. Gravity had never done a cover before, had never even considered it until after I'd borrowed Zander's Fleetwood Mac record. I'd told him I wanted to sing—

My eyes stung as the opening notes of "Go Your Own Way" filled the silent coffee house. Zander's fingers slid expertly around the fret board, coaxing beautiful notes from his guitar. Even the rest of the band seemed mesmerized, hanging on his every note.

He leaned toward the mic and his lips parted.

"*Loving you . . .*" As he sang, Zander let his chin drop to his chest. I bit my lip so hard that I swear I tasted blood. Molly couldn't see me cry.

"*Isn't the right thing to do.*" Suddenly, Zander's voice cracked. His fingers slipped out of position on the fret board, and a lone C note sent a shudder through the crowd. In the back, someone gasped.

"Ohmygod." Molly hissed behind her coffee mug. "*What* is he doing?"

I shook my head, unable to look away from the stage. Zander's eyes were cast downward in humiliation. Each time he tried to pick up the song, it sounded out of key. Wrong. My heart stopped in my chest for a full measure.

"*If I could–*" This time, Zander's voice crack was worse than a sixth-grade boy's, and he was completely off key. Bright red was starting to creep from the collar of his jacket into his cheeks. Behind him, the rest of the band's faces were frozen. Mortified.

"How could he do this? I'm totes humiliated." Molly lifted a café menu and shielded her face. "Kacey. Do something."

"Me?" I choked. I wanted to do something; wanted to prove to Zander once and for all that I was a real friend. That I cared about him. But what could I do? I wasn't even in the band.

Zander coughed something into the mic.

"Kay. Cee." Molly hissed through gritted teeth. "Get up there."

"Get off the stage, dude!" Somebody booed.

I whipped around angrily, but couldn't see anything in the dark. And then suddenly, I was on my feet.

I watched myself climb onto the stage, striding toward the mic. Saw Zander stand, saw his blue streak dip as he nodded. For a full beat, it was just Zander and me, alone on a silent stage. And then everything came screaming back: the restless shuffle of the audience, the bitter, acrid smell of burnt coffee. The piercing heat of the spotlight.

I tilted the mic, and we both leaned in close. So close that our lips were almost touching. But I didn't get the same jittery, lightheaded feeling I'd gotten when I'd been this close to Quinn. Instead, I felt powerful.

"*You can go your own way,*" I belted. My voice echoed over the speakers, filling the coffee house.

Someone whistled, and a few claps sounded from the crowd.

Zander picked up the rhythm on the guitar, his head bobbing hesitantly to the beat.

I caught his eye and nodded. *You can do this.* A tentative smile flickered across his lips.

Behind us, the band launched into a full-scale rock attack, and the audience burst into cheers as we sang together. The Beat was pounding so loudly on the drums,

I could feel my teeth start to chatter. My entire body was soaking in the music.

I let the spotlight wash over me, let the crowd fade away as Zander and I brought the house down. Together.

ENCORE
Friday 9:16 P.M.

The rest of the set slipped by in a perfect, easy blur. We were in sync like we'd never been before, and the band rocked for three more songs, plus two encores. We played like it was just the five of us in Zander's loft, alone and uninhibited. Standing next to him, gripping the mic stand as I sang, it felt like I'd never left.

And then the set was over and the house lights brightened over the audience, snapping me out of my dream and into the real world. The world where Zander was dating my best friend, and didn't want me in the band anymore.

"You, uh . . ." Without looking at me, Zander fiddled with the silver tuning pegs on his guitar while the rest of the band packed up behind us. His blue streak slipped over his eyes, making it impossible for me to read him. "I really—"

"Yeah," I said softly, watching as the audience downed the last of their cappuccinos and herded toward the lobby. "No problem." I wanted to ask him what this meant, if this changed anything between us. If he'd forgiven me. But the words just lay heavy on my tongue, refusing to leave my lips.

"Z." At the foot of the stage, Molly stood with her arms crossed tightly over her ripped Gravity tee. She was giving Zander the same look she'd given me when I'd opened my mouth at rehearsal and my lisp had come out. Pity, with a serious dose of disgust. "What. Just. Happened?"

Zander's head snapped up, and his forehead crinkled with confusion and hurt. "Excuse me?" he said sharply. "You were there. You saw."

"Duh." Molly took a step back, as if Zander had a debilitating disease and was highly contagious. "I'm the one who told Kacey to rescue you. Soooo, you're welcome." She cocked her head to one side, waiting for his gratitude.

"Uh, thanks?" Zander's eyes cut in my direction. They glinted like he was on the verge of laughing.

Molly flushed. "So we're going to get some autographs from some of the other bands," she informed me as if Zander weren't standing right there. "Meet us in the lobby in ten?"

"Yeah. Okay." I tried to send him an apologetic blink, but the light in his expression had faded and he was staring at the stage, tracing a circle in the dust with the toe of his sneaker.

"Perf." Molly whipped her hair over her shoulder and sashayed back to our table. She slipped her black leather jacket off the back of her chair and put it on, dragging the zipper just high enough to hide the Gravity logo on her tee. The other girls gathered their bags and coats.

I coughed. "She's, uh . . ."

Trailing behind the girls, Paige turned and flashed me a quick thumbs-up. I tried to send her a telepathic plea to stay so I wouldn't have to be alone with Zander. Before I could, she hooked her jacket over her shoulder and started toward the lobby.

"Don't worry about Molly. She didn't mean it."

"Course she did." Zander's laugh sounded harsh, tinny. He slumped onto the wooden stool.

"Well, she could have said it another way, at least." Irritation edged my voice. "She didn't have to be so mean."

"Whatever." Zander shrugged. "She's right. I screwed the whole thing up."

"Dude. S'okay." The Beat came up behind us and clapped Zander on the shoulder. "All worked out, thanks to Mainstream." He gave me a playful nudge. "We're gonna go sign some napkins. Meet us out there whenever."

"Yeah." Zander's voice was barely audible over the sound of the guys shuffling off the stage. Once we were alone, I studied his face: the worry lines around his eyes, his tight, pursed lips, the way the color had left his cheeks. I'd never seen him look so depressed. It was like he was letting Molly's words demolish his confidence.

I blinked back tears. Maybe he cared about her more than I thought he did. Maybe I'd been naïve to hope he didn't really like her. To think that he could like me instead.

"Zander." My voice cracked. "Nobody cares that—"

"*I* care!" His voice was so strong that I took a startled step back, almost tripping over a speaker. "Don't you get it? This was supposed to be it, you know? Our big break." He jumped up and raked his hands through his hair. "And I couldn't even hold it together without y—" He stopped himself before he said it. "Whatever. It's done."

"But it's not!" The back of my neck suddenly felt hot. "You were amazing once we got going, like you always are! Are you really too dense to figure that out, or are you just enjoying your little pity party?"

Surprised, Zander opened his mouth, as if to argue. But I wasn't finished.

"So maybe you screwed up a little. But that's not the only reason you're upset." I took a bold step toward him, my voice getting louder.

"It's not?" Zander sounded more confused than angry.

I shook my head. "It's killing you that for once, you actually cared what people thought. So what? *Everybody* cares what people think, at least a little. It just means you're human."

Zander lifted his guitar strap over his head and tucked the instrument into its case. The muscles in his face relaxed, but I still couldn't read his expression.

"Could you say something, please?" I snapped, suddenly feeling drained.

"You're . . . right." He ducked to find my gaze, and held it. We were standing only inches apart. My body temperature went from tropical to subzero and back again. "I mean, I did care what people thought. But mostly I cared"—his eyes flicked away—"what you thought."

"What *I* thought?" My voice came out sounding raspy.

He shrugged. "I guess I didn't want you to see me mess up and think that the band was dying after you left.

Even though . . ." His voice trailed off, and he stuffed his hands in his pockets. "It's just different, is all."

"Oh." I bit my bottom lip, my mind reeling with all the things I wanted to tell him. I was desperate to explain why I'd deserted the band, but telling would be betraying Molly. Blaming her, when really, she hadn't forced me to quit anything. I'd been the one to make the choice. And now I had to accept the consequences.

For the first time all night, Zander cracked a grin. "An entire monologue, and then all I get is 'oh'?" He punched me lightly in the shoulder. "Come on, Simon. Gimme your best shot."

"I—" My eyes found his, and tiny bursts of electricity flooded my body, like a million sixth senses at once. My journalistic instincts were kicking into overdrive, and I knew what I needed to do. I needed to tell the truth, to be completely honest. And I could do that without blaming Molly or making her look bad. "I'm just so sorry about everything, Zander. It was so stupid of me to leave the band, only I didn't think I had a choice." My voice faltered. "And I should have been honest and told you everything, like how the band's the best thing that ever happened to me, even if I didn't know it right away. But I was too scared. And now you hate me, and—"

"Whoa! Hate you?" Zander gripped my arms like he was about to shake me. But instead, he just held me steady. "I never hated you. I was just mad when I thought you were using the band." His grip tightened. "I could never hate you. I just really . . . the band really missed you, or whatever."

"Me, too." A wave of relief washed over me, and suddenly, I was squeezing him. And he was hugging me back. "I'm sorry," I mumbled into the soft leather of his jacket. The zipper was digging into my cheek, but I didn't care. "I totally screwed up."

"Just makes you human," he said into my hair before we pulled away. "This girl told me that once."

"She sounds amazing," I half laughed, half sniffed. Our noses were almost touching. I suddenly felt like I was going to vomit. In the best possible way.

"Yeah. She is." He coughed and released his grip. We both stumbled backward a few steps. "So." He scratched the back of his neck, peering at me from beneath his blue streak. "Since your afternoons are free now, do you maybe wanna . . . I mean, the band's not the same without you, and—"

"Yeah. Yes. Totally." I cut him off before he could finish his thought.

"Rock on." He lifted his fist.

"Rock on." I bumped it lightly, sealing the deal. Zander and I were bandmates again. And deep down, I knew we were becoming something more than friends. I couldn't explain how, exactly, but I just *knew*.

Because even former journalists have a sixth sense.

ACKNOWLEDGMENTS

I feel deeply grateful for the many souls whose support, insight, and care have held me up throughout the writing of this book. To acknowledge a very significant few:

Thank you to the lovely folks at Alloy Entertainment. Les Morgenstein and Josh Bank: Thank you for being brilliant, and for giving me the opportunity to bring this story to life. Sara Shandler: Not so long ago, you read two sample chapters. (And you liked them! You really liked them!) For taking a chance on a new writer, and for your guidance and encouragement along the way, I'm so thankful. Nora Pelizzari: You got this ball rolling, lady. I will never forget that.

To my thoughtful, hilarious, and genius editor, Lanie Davis: Thank you for . . . well, just about everything.

For your wisdom in editing this book. For laughing when you think I'm funny and talking me down when I'm anxious. Most important, thank you for encouraging me to focus on my health when I needed to. You're more than a rockin' LP. You're a dear friend.

And to the masterminds at Poppy: Cindy Eagan and Pam Gruber. You are truly a powerhouse of a team, and your direction and creativity have made this book what it is.

Rebecca Friedman, agent extraordinaire: Thank you for your enthusiasm, your wonderfully critical eye, and your vision. What a beautiful beginning.

Jessica Parrillo: You were an Anam Cara in an unspeakably difficult time. Without you, I could not have finished this book. Connie Staton: You have always been there, and I know you always will be. I love you. Gayle Spears and Georgia Calhoun: You nurtured me inside the classroom and out. You made me a better therapist, which has made me a better writer and, I think, a better human being. Kelly Boswell: Bless you.

And most important, to my family: Mimi, Hugh, and Molly. You are an unfailingly supportive force, standing with me always. I love you.

Thank you.
mh

Turn the page for a sneak peek at
How to Rock Break-Ups and Make-Ups,
the hilarious sequel to
How to Rock Braces and Glasses,
coming in September 2012.

CUE THE NEW TRACK
Monday, 6:58 A.M.

I have a unique talent for remembering the soundtrack to every significant life moment in my twelve and a half years, including epiphanies, crises, and unbeatable hair days.

The morning of my very first *Simon Says* television broadcast for Marquette Middle School's Channel M last September, I blasted Beyoncé's "Diva" on my iPod for the entire El ride to school. Four years ago, when my dad told me he was moving from Chicago to Los Angeles and that it was "best for everyone involved," creepy carnival music whistled from the Ferris wheel at Navy Pier.

And as I waited for my best friend, Molly Knight, at Sugar Daddy this morning, the clink of ceramic mugs and the sleepy *chug, chug, ding!* of the old-fashioned cash register blended together in familiar harmony. Outside, my city was starting to rouse, and pinkish light shone on bleary-eyed passersby. For the rest of Chicago, it was just another Monday morning.

The rest of Chicago had no idea how easy they had it.

I sat on one of the cracked turquoise leather couches at the back of the bakery and willed my knees to stop bouncing. But I was too riled up to sit still. Two weeks ago, after a humiliating tumble at Molly's thirteenth birthday party, I'd gone from

KACEY SIMON, SEVENTH-GRADE JOURNALIST, ADVICE GURU, and MOST POPULAR GIRL BASICALLY EVER

to

KACEY SIMON, LISPING, BRACES-AND-GLASSES-WEARING, FRIENDLESS REJECT.

Luckily, my literal fall from grace was yesterday's headline, and now I was back on top, thanks to some major soul-searching and a genius plan I'd executed with my friend Paige Greene. And after I'd saved my best guy friend (and Molly's boyfriend), Zander Jarvis, during the Rock Chicago showcase last Friday night, Zander had even asked me to rejoin Gravity as lead singer.

Friends? Check. Popularity? Check. Band? Check.

Unquenchable crush on my best friend's boyfriend? *Cough*CHECK*cough*.

The scratchy clang of the bell over the door startled me, sending a wave of scalding liquid over the edge of my cup.

"Oww." I licked my thumb and pressed it into the widening heart-shaped stain on the knee of my new bottle-green jeggings.

"Watch it. I'm def borrowing those." Molly clacked across the faded wood floor in towering platform booties. "If it's okay."

"Of course." I jumped up to hug her. "Whenever you want." I didn't let go right away. Maybe I was holding on too long. But I was so relieved to be friends again, there wasn't enough room in my brain to care.

Mols wriggled away, a mischievous grin playing over her rosy lips. "So?" A few wisps of platinum hair slipped from beneath a cropped hoodie.

"So, sit." I slapped the seat next to me.

"First you have to guess what's different about me."

"Ummm . . ." I reviewed her from head to toe. I'd seen the hoodie before, and the black leather skinnies were a definite rerun. I'd watched her buy the yellow RUCKUS tee at the showcase Friday night. It was a consolation prize for being the girlfriend of the dude who bombed onstage, she'd told me when we got back to my house.

"Kacey! Guess!"

"Did your shirt have that stain on it when you bought it?" The old Kacey would have informed Mols that wearing a (dirty) rival band's T-shirt to school made her a subpar rock 'n' roll girlfriend. The new, slightly-less-honest-but-more-aware-of-people's-feelings Kacey ran her tongue over her braces to give her mouth something else to do.

"Not a stain." Molly perched on the edge of the sofa. Her voice dropped to a whisper, and she leaned close enough for me to catch a whiff of gingerbread body butter. "It's the signature of the lead guy in Ruckus. He's in ninth, and his name is Phoenix. Which is so weird, because you know how my grandparents live close to Phoenix and it's, like, my fave place ever?"

"You said staying in the desert for spring break was like being trapped in a huge litter box." I squinted through a fresh set of contacts at the chicken scratch above her left boob. Why were we talking about some strange kid in ninth when Molly had the coolest, most talented guy in seventh by her side?

"You're not guessing." Impatiently, Mols wound a lock of hair around her index finger and yanked.

"Your hair iiiissss . . ." I bit the inside of my cheek. When I was Channel M's star reporter, I never worried about saying the wrong thing. I missed being a reporter. Or maybe I just missed having a reason to give people the straight story without having to feel bad about it. "... blonder?"

"Wrong!" She smacked an imaginary game-show buzzer on the coffee table, then whipped off her hoodie, revealing an angled, shoulder-length bob.

"You cut it all off!" I squealed. "Ohmygod, it looks so much healthier without those stringy exten—" I gulped. "You look so good!"

"Really? You think so?"

I grinned. "For real! What made you do it?"

"I'm starting fresh," Molly proclaimed.

I adjusted the feathered head wrap holding my long auburn waves in place. The piece was fashioned from a costume mask our friend Liv Parillo's grandmother had worn to a masquerade ball a zillion years ago. It was the latest item in LivItUp, Liv's brand-new line of upscale repurposed accessories. "Starting fresh from what?"

"Well . . ." Molly scanned each of the vintage-school-desks-turned-tables in the tiny bakery. The tip of her nose and her cheeks were tinged with pink, and not from the early-morning chill.

"What? Tell me!" I scooted close enough for our knees to touch.

"I broke up with Z last night."

The words took my breath away. I felt like I was back

in the dunking booth at last year's Channel M fund-raiser, the split second after I hit the icy water.

Okay, so it was my producer, Carlos, who'd actually agreed to the dunking booth. But I *imagined* that it probably felt exactly like this.

Molly blinked. "Hello? Earth to Kacey!"

"Ohmygod!" I coughed, my mind spinning with questions. Why would anyone ever dump Zander? Was he okay? What did this mean for us? *Was* there an "us"? Since Molly had asked me to quit Gravity in the first place, I'd been beyond nervous to tell her that I'd rejoined the band *before* I knew about the split. Did this make my news better, or worse?

"What did he—why did you—are you okay?" I asked.

"Aww, Kace. You're the best. I'm fine." She squeezed my arm reassuringly. "It's like I texted Z last night. We just don't have that much in common, you know?"

I nodded. That much was definitely true.

"Plus, I'm Molly Knight. I can't be the girl who dated that loser who sucked onstage."

"Did you tell him that?"

"I would have, but then this hilarious commercial came on and I forgot. Anyway, you're gonna love Phoenix. We have so much in common!"

"Like what?" I wanted to focus 100 percent on Molly,

but a voice in the back of my head kept ordering me to confess that I'd rejoined Gravity. Now that she'd broken up with Zander, she wouldn't care. Right?

"We're both super mature, and we both love how he's in ninth."

"He sounds great. Really. I'm happy for you." *Tell her.*

"I *knew* you would be. Only there's something I kind of need advice on." Molly tugged at the leather choker around her neck.

"About your new boy? Shoot," I said graciously. Boys were the one and only area where Molly's expertise outshone mine. This had to be killing her.

"Okay." She took a deep breath. "Phoenix likes girls who have a thing. You know, like designing is Liv's thing, and being smart is Nessa's thing. And journalism is your thing."

Used to be my thing.

"But since I quit skating lessons, I don't have a thing anymore." Molly lowered her head. "Do you think I should go back to gymnastics? I'm kind of over tight ponytails and glitter hair spray."

"So's the rest of the world. But not to worry." I borrowed the soothing, low tone that sounded so reassuring when Dr. Phil, our school shrink, used it. "You're good at a ton of other things."

"Like what?" Her white-blond lashes fluttered skeptically.

"Like . . ." I reached for my hot chocolate and took a long sip, thinking hard. "Like you always put together amazing outfits. And out of all the girls I know, you're the best at talking to boys. You don't get nervous or anything."

"I guess."

"Most of all, you're an amazing friend. I was just thinking how glad I am that we're friends again."

"Me, too," she said quickly. "Things weren't the same when we weren't talking. And"—she pulled a brown throw pillow into her lap and squeezed it—"I'm really sorry about how mean I was to you."

"Same." I wanted to hug her again. "Okay. So we've got outfits, boy-talking, and friendship. What else do you like?"

"Parties, for sure. I had a killer time at my b-day party. Everybody did." A horrified look flashed across her face. "Until you bit it, obv."

"Obv." My teeth ached at the memory. "Okay. Parties!" I settled back into the couch cushions and thought for a few seconds. "What if you were a party planner, or something? You could plan special events at Marquette! Like fund-raisers and dances and stuff."

Molly's head snapped toward me. Her delicate features

locked into a deadly serious expression. "Yes. Party planner. *Yes.*"

"Actually, I heard the student council was looking for someone to head the Party Planning Committee for the spring dance. I bet I could get Paige to approve your app by the end of the day!"

Molly's nose scrunched in disapproval. "Paige Greene has to approve me?" She and Paige, my old fifth-grade BFF, got along almost as well as my six-year-old sister, Ella, and I had during her *I know you are, but what am I?* phase.

"Well, she *is* seventh-grade class president. But it's just a formality," I assured her.

She pretended to weigh her option. Singular.

"Okay, I'll do it!" Mols reached over and hugged me.

"Yay! I really think this is a great idea," I said into her shoulder. *You know what else is a great idea? Telling your best friend the truth! Say it! "I. Rejoined. Gravity."* My mouth tasted dry and stale, like I'd been sucking on mothballs.

"Me, too. Thanks, Ka—" Suddenly, Molly jerked away. "Wait. You never said if you thought it was a good idea to break up with Zander." Her eyebrows shot up in panic.

"I—uh—" I hadn't had time to process. For that, I'd need at least a couple of hours alone in my room. And a good, soul-searching-themed playlist. I channeled Dr. Phil again. "Do *you* think it was a good idea to break up with Zander?"

Molly's cornflower-blue eyes flitted anxiously across my face. "I dunno. I guess. I mean, we really didn't have much in common. Plus, I heard he was into some other girl while we were dating."

My blood ran cold. "What? Who?"

"Ridic, right?" Molly half coughed, half laughed. "Z was totally into me when we were dating. *I* was the one who broke up with *him*, remember?" A tiny vein in her forehead throbbed.

"Yeah. I remember." I crossed my arms over my black dolman-sleeve top, suddenly aware of a draft in the bakery. "So, did you hear who it was?"

"Please. If I knew who it was, we wouldn't be having this conversation. I'd be out kicking her a—"

"OHMYGOD. I just had the most amazing idea." I cut her off before she could give me the gory play-by-play. "What if I rejoined Gravity, and then I could get the inside scoop on whether he was into someone else while you guys were together?" I reached for my hot chocolate mug again, afraid to steal a glance at her expression.

"You mean, like, you'd be a spy? Just for me?"

"Mmmm." I chugged the rest of my hot chocolate with

complete disregard for the third-degree throat burns I was inflicting on myself. And the lie I was inflicting on her. But if I'd learned anything in the past few weeks, it was that sometimes the truth wasn't the best option.

"Yes! Do it! That's totally brilliant."

"Mmmmm." I kept my mug between us. "Okay. Great. I'll talk to Zander after school."

Molly fell back into the sofa, a dreamy look on her face. "Perf." Then she sat up again. "But wait. You can't just find out whether he was into some girl *before*. You have to find out if he's into anyone *now*. He can't date anybody for at least a year after me. It's the rule. Girl Code."

Girl Code? "But aren't you and Phoenix—"

"That's different. I was the one who did the breaking up. I'm allowed to date."

"Oh." I squeezed my mug so hard I was sure tiny hairline cracks were forming in the painted ceramic lip. "Okay." The rule was insane. But the look on her face told me she couldn't have been more serious.

"So that's it, then. You'll get the dirt and report back to me. And if *any* girl even *thinks* about liking him—"

I bent over and reached for my messenger bag with numb, trembling fingers.

"—that girl will be in major trouble. She has *no* idea what I can do when I'm pissed," Molly finished.

"Got it," I said weakly.

But Molly was wrong. That girl had a pretty good idea of what Molly Knight was capable of. And that girl wasn't looking for that kind of trouble.

Not again.

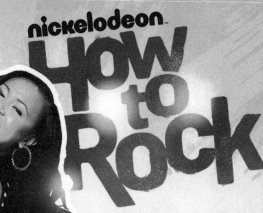

STARRING
CYMPHONIQUE MILLER
AS KACEY SIMON

**Saturdays
8:30pm/7:30c**

Episodes and music

Available on
iTunes

nick.com/HowToRock